# THE SEASON TO BE WARY

# THE SEASON TO BE WARY

Rod Serling

With an Introduction by Mark Olshaker

ROD
SERLING
BOOKS™

ISBN-13: 9781493716999
ISBN-10: 1493716999

*For Sammy Davis, Jr., my friend.*
*He has probably gotten just about everything*
*possible out of life except a book dedicated to him ... until now.*
*—Rod Serling*

# CONTENTS

# THE SEASON TO BE WARY

## INTRODUCTION BY MARK OLSHAKER

I first met my hero Rod Serling when I was a 14-year-old ninth grader, at a speech he gave in Washington, D.C. as president of the National Academy of Television Arts and Sciences. My mother, who was a part-time educational radio producer, wrangled an invitation for me. Rod was amazingly kind and generous to me, then and thereafter, because that night began a cherished friendship that lasted ten years – to the end of his tragically short life.

Now, two questions might arise as you read the preceding statement. The first is, why was a much-lauded celebrity so solicitous of this teenaged admirer to whom he owed nothing? My answer would be: That was the nature of the man.

The second question, following hard upon, would be, what was it about an adult television writer that could so fire the imagination of a junior high school kid? My answer would be: That was also the nature of the man.

Like many millions of others at the time and since, I was enthralled by *The Twilight Zone* and its character-driven morality tales infused with just enough fantasy and science fiction to be intriguing, but never so much that the story didn't seem believable within its own context. What O. Henry did for the short story, Rod did for the 30-minute television drama. All of us have our favorites for which, after all these years, we can still relate in detail the ironic, karma-fulfilling endings. *TZ* turned out to be the perfect intellectual and spiritual prep course for my '60's generation; the generation that grew up idealistic enough to believe that anything was possible and cynical enough to fear that nothing was true. And perhaps most profoundly, these mythic programs and scripts seem just as intriguing, significant and literary to me today as they did when I first encountered them so long ago.

I was also enthralled with the man who introduced each episode and, I learned, conceived the show and wrote most of the scripts. For whatever reason, by my mid-teens, I already knew I wanted to be a writer, and Rod Serling, with his magic voice, personified for me all the possibilities of this noble calling.

*Twilight Zone* led me to every other script of Rod's I could get my hands on: the four teleplays and commentary published in book form as *Patterns*, scripts published in anthologies with other Golden Age immortals like Paddy Chayefsky, Reginald Rose, Gore Vidal, Robert Allen Arthur and Tad Mosel. I devoured the three paperback compilations of the short stories Rod had written from *TZ* scripts.

In my impressionable teens and early twenties, when my professional ambitions were percolating, Serling hooked me on the screen and on the page with his intensity and charisma, his journeys of imagination, his guts and nerve in relentlessly engaging the central moral issues of the day.

The phrase "role model" is overused and undervalued in our culture. But Rod was a role model to me in a very real sense. I tried to write like him and I tried to think like him. If, eventually, I developed my own style and my own way of thinking, it was through the crucible of Rod's values and way of approaching character and subject, as well as morality. Had I idolized and been encouraged by someone else, I might be a different writer today.

*The Season to be Wary* came out from Little, Brown in 1967, composed of three novellas that represented Rod's first published foray into long-form fiction. I was in high school by then and rushed out to buy and read it.

Like *Twilight Zone*, these three stories are taught, character-driven narratives with a deep ethical point of view and a sense of justice that was realized with a strong element of fantasy or sci fi. All three are cautionary tales on the moral hazard of living life without empathy for one's fellow man and woman. And like the *Zone*, they hold up just as well 45 years later as they did the day they were written.

Much of the action and storyline in these novellas is interior, as if Serling, with this new narrative form to work with, is just bursting to try out a trick that wasn't applicable to script or short story. In fact, nearly all of the action is created to maximize the interior monologues and sensations within the heads of the main characters.

What I also noted upon a recent rereading is so many of the themes, techniques and leitmotifs that characterize the Serling oeuvre, including the often baroque style that served his propensity for moral point-making so well. Rod was always trying to get a point across, and his values and character show through in just about everything he did. And for him, that point often came in the distinctive, rhetorically styled speech of condemnation delivered by the character that voices Serling's own principled point of view:

*"What you are, Herr Strobe, is quite another thing from an animal. You are a pervert. You are a butcher of six million people. But you are no human being, either. A human being could not fill so many graves and think of it as an offense that might be apologized for ... What you have done to this earth, Herr Strobe, is not an offense. It is a mortal sin that even God cannot forgive."*

*"Mr. Connacher, count on something, will you? Count on the fact that you'll be answering to God one of these days. The One whose name you conjure up and bandy about with such ease. Because if there is a God, He'll pay you back for what you're doing."*

*"And you, Miss Menlo ... you are sufficiently perceptive, aren't you, to recognize the morality or the lack of it. Tell me, Miss Menlo — Who in the hell gave you the right to make any judgment as to what is moral and what isn't?"*

### The Escape Route

"The Escape Route" deals with a subject that understandably obsessed him throughout his adult life: the Holocaust and the enormity of evil that seemed to subvert all notions of justice, or even punishment and retribution.

He had first essayed the problem in one of the most powerful *Twilight Zone* outings: an episode entitled "Deaths-Head Revisited." Former SS commandant Gunther Lutze returns to the ruins of Dachau to reminisce about the time when held the power of life and death in his hands and could inflict untold suffering at will. In the course of his visit, he comes to realize that the ghosts of the inmates he tortured and killed still inhabit this unholy place. They convene a tribunal in a barracks building to try him for his crimes against mankind, and after finding him guilty, sentence him to permanent insanity, forced to experience the agonies of his victims for all time.

Accepting that crimes this hideous were beyond the bounds of earthly justice, Serling's fierce moralism came up with a punishment that took that justice one step beyond, and in so doing, meted out a satisfyingly appropriate vengeance.

With "The Escape Route," he updates the challenge and moves thousands of miles away from the scene of the crime. Former *Gruppenfuehrer* Joseph Strobe, late of Dachau, is living a miserable little existence in Buenos Aires when he and his fellow Nazi refugees get word that Adolf Eichmann has been captured by the Israelis and brought back to Jerusalem to stand trial before the world. If they got Eichmann, are any of them safe?

In this story, though, there are no concentration camp scenes and only summary evocations of torture and mass murder. The piece is, rather, a psychological study of a guilty and unrepentant man on the run. And again, for crimes so horrific that mere death will not balance them, Serling turns to ingenious fantasy to render supernatural justice.

### Color Scheme

If there was any subject that brought forth more passion from Rod Serling than the moral implications of the Holocaust, it was the civil rights struggle and the basic quest for a society that treated all of its members equally. When his daughter Anne was writing her remarkable memoir, *As I Knew Him: My Dad, Rod Serling*, I introduced her to Rod's Antioch College classmate Monroe "Mike" Newman. As he reminisced, he told us of how even before Rod decided he wanted to be a writer, he vehemently urged all of his friends to patronize only one of the two barbershops near campus because the other one would not cut the hair of African Americans.

When his writing and producing career was in full swing, Serling was among the very first, if not the first, to use black actors in meaningful and sympathetic dramatic roles in series television.

"Color Scheme," the story of what happens when a rabble rousing preacher and hatemonger by the name of King Connacher comes to a small and nasty Mississippi burg on the eve of a civil rights march, is another tale of supernatural scale balancing. Its magical device is one that was used to great comic effect in the classic 1947 Broadway musical *Finian's Rainbow*. But in "Color Scheme," it is utterly grim and serious.

More than anything else, this is a story of transformation. There is the mystical human transformation on which the action and character development hinge. But even more important, he is writing about an entire civilization and way of life that, from one side, at least, was going through a wrenching and very much unwanted transformation. "Color Scheme" was written only a few short years after the marches, sit-ins, bus boycotts, federally forced school integrations and the murderous Mississippi Freedom Summer of 1964. This was still the era of Governors George Wallace, Ross Barnett and Lester Maddox and Police Commissioner Eugene "Bull" Connor, with his attack dogs and fire hoses. Reading the novella, it is critical to remember that when it was originally published, the great civil rights struggle of the 1950's and '60's was still in full action mode, and while the individual victories were encouraging, the ultimate outcome still hung very much in the balance.

*The Season to be Wary* as a whole is dedicated to Rod's close friend Sammy Davis, Jr., a pioneering African American entertainer who was a "triple threat" with his fine singing, dancing and acting. Rod told the story of how Sammy gave him the idea for "Color Scheme" one night over a beer and that, "It stayed with me for five years ... haunting, intrusive and preoccupying. Television wouldn't touch it. I hope I've done it justice – giving birth to Sammy's baby on the following printed pages."

According to Anne Serling, her dad and Davis had been trying to develop a fantasy film for television and it was only when that project fell through that Rod conceived of the book idea.

This point about television afraid to touch the story is highly significant in the understanding of Rod Serling's career and the context in which he wrote, particularly during television's so-called "Golden Age." Sponsors and network standards and practices departments ruled the airwaves in those days and anything the least bit controversial could be subject to the meat cleaver of censorship and/or what Rod used to refer to as "ritual track covering." It is easy to see how a writer like Rod repeatedly chafed himself raw and bloody against the unyielding grindstone of network fear. As he once baldly explained in a speech at the Library of Congress in Washington:

*"Drama on television must walk tiptoe and in agony, lest it offend some cereal buyer from a given state below the Mason-Dixon. Hence, we find a kind of ritual track covering in which we attack quite obliquely the business of minority problems. So instead of a Negro, we give battle against that prejudice visited upon American Indians, or Alaskan Eskimos, or Armenian peasants under the Czar. Now yes, all prejudice is alike down at its very ugly roots, and all prejudice is indeed a universal evil. But you*

*don't conquer intolerance by disguising it, by clothing it in different trap-*
*pings, by slapping at it with a wispy parable."*

On this point, Serling knew whereof he spoke. He had been tremendously moved and horrified by the 1955 torture, murder and martyrdom of 14-year-old Emmett Till by two of the upstanding white citizens of Money, Mississippi, after Till, who had a speech impediment, allegedly whistled at the wife of one of them, who was tending the family grocery store. The two killers, quickly acquitted by an all-white jury, later admitting their actions in a deal with *Look* magazine.

Serling addressed the case directly in a script he wrote for *The United States Steel Hour* entitled "Noon on Doomsday." By the time the producers and CBS executives finished with it, the victim had been transformed into a middle-aged pawnshop owner and the killer, by Serling's own description, "a neurotic malcontent who lashed out at something or someone who might be materially and physically the scapegoat for his own unhappy, purposeless, miserable existence."

Two years later, he tried again to write about the Till case, but this time the closest he could get was a western town of the 1870's.

*"By the time 'A Town Has Turned to Dust' went before the cameras my script had turned to dust ... Emmett Till became a romantic Mexican who loved the storekeeper's wife but 'only with his eyes' ... The lynch victim was called Clemson, but we couldn't use this 'cause South Carolina had an all-white college by that name ... The phrase 'twenty men in hoods' became 'twenty men in homemade masks.' They chopped it up like a roomful of butchers at work on a steer."*

Nazi villains were okay, because we had already reached a consensus about them. But even the hint of a projected Serling script on race would get the White Citizens Councils up in arms and threatening sponsor boycotts of everything from laundry detergent to industrial steel.

This time, in book form, Rod could do what he wanted. There was no more ritual track covering and he could write about white Southern hate and intolerance the way he saw it. And after twice being thwarted in reference to the Till case, he actually incorporated specific details into "Color Scheme."

In a satisfyingly fitting irony occasioned by the story's magical element, the villain gets his rightful due after talking familiarly with a white woman. Again, Serling has ordained justice on its own harsh terms.

### Eyes

"Eyes" has no larger social context on the order of "Escape Route" and "Color Scheme." Instead, it hearkens back to a familiar theme from *Twilight Zone* and Serling's original teleplays – specifically, the venality, cravenness and moral vacuum in the souls of those who live through the manipulation and exploitation of others.

It concerns one Claudia Menlo, an old, shrunken and fabulously wealthy Fifth Avenue heiress who has been denied only two things in life – eyesight and a conscience. And she is perfectly willing to use the lack of the latter to obtain the benefit of the former.

Once again, Serling returns to the milieu and metaphor of boxing; not the glamorous world of million-dollar championship bouts, but the tawdry, pathetic world of used up has-beens and wretched never-will-be's he inhabited so affectingly in "Requiem for a Heavyweight." He returned twice more to this setting of unrealized aspiration and longing in the *Twilight Zone* episodes "The Big Tall Wish" and "Steel" (written by Richard Matheson).

Like Mountain McClintock in "Requiem," ex-boxer Indian Charlie Hatcher in "Eyes" embodies Serling's exploited class, discarded like unwanted toys when they are broken or no longer entertaining, and only returned to when they can be of some additional use to another. The connection between the heiress Menlo and the penniless, brain-addled Hatcher, intermediated by fancy lawyers and doctors, is former fight manager and perpetual bottom-feeder Anthony Petrozella, who "had larceny in him all the way from his crotch to where he parted his hair."

There is no fantasy in this story and the science fiction is kept to a procedurally necessary minimum. The O. Henry-like ending hinges instead on an actual freak occurrence that provides a "realistic" but emotionally satisfying denouement. There are no rewards for the righteous in these far reaches of Serling's moral universe, but Rod – in real life the kindest and most sensitive of men – is rigorous in meting out severe punishments for the wicked.

Though the sales figures for *The Season to be Wary* were disappointing, it remains an important part of Rod Serling's literary legacy for several reasons. First, each of the three novellas is a fine literary work in its own right, entertaining, challenging and thought provoking. And as I realized in comparing the literary sensibilities of my hero-worshipping teenaged self with the somewhat more mature man I became, Serling had a voice and style that could appeal to all ages and a penchant for limning the crucible of moral choice that will always be relevant and meaningful.

Second, the book led to what became Serling's last television series, *Night Gallery*. At about the same time he wrote the novellas, eager to see if this somewhat longer format would work on television, he adapted "The Escape Route" and "Eyes" into scripts, along with another story, a gothic chiller entitled "The Cemetery." He must have realized that "Color Scheme" was still too volatile for television.

Serling submitted a proposal and outline for this anthology movie idea to a number of the major studios. Universal was sufficiently interested to put it into development. Producer William

Sackheim championed the project against so-so executive response and it was green lit for production with an impressive talent roster. "The Cemetery" starred Roddy McDowell and Ossie Davis. "Escape Route" boasted Richard Kiley and Sam Jaffe. "Eyes" starred screen legend Joan Crawford and Tom Bosley. Its direction was assigned to a young man without professional credits who had essentially snuck onto the Universal lot and convinced Sackheim and the head of the television division, Sidney Sheinberg, that he had potential. His name was Steven Spielberg.

*Night Gallery* aired on NBC the evening of Saturday, November 8, 1969, with each of the three mini-movies introduced by Serling in a macabre art gallery setting. The ratings were high and the show was given a regular hour-long time slot. The unique aspect, compared to *Twilight Zone*, is that individual story length within that hour could vary. Though Serling did not produce, did not have the same creative control and ultimately felt the general quality was disappointing, the show ran three seasons and featured some of his own most poignant and affecting work, including "The Messiah on Mott Street" and "They're Tearing Down Tim Riley's Bar."

The third significance of *Season* is that I believe it signaled the planned first step into what would have been a new phase of Rod's career. It is no secret that by the early 1970's, he had grown weary of the battles for quality and integrity on network television, in addition to the grind of churning out material at the pace television demanded. He was looking for more movie assignments and other ways to express himself.

Based on conversations I had with him, I think one of the reasons he took on *Season* was to see how he would do with a narrative form longer than the short story. He had tried it once before, five years earlier, with what he referred to as *A Reading Version of the Dramatic Script* of "Requiem for a Heavyweight" that he published as a Bantam Books paperback. *Seasons* shows a marked progression in style, form and quality over that earlier effort and encouraged him to try actual novel writing. When I visited him at his California home near the end of 1971, he showed me the manuscript of a novelized version of much-lauded *Hallmark Hall of Fame* teleplay, "A Storm in Summer." Though it was never published and I've never seen any official mention of the manuscript, he also told me at the time he had an idea for another novel he wanted to do. Less than a month after my visit he wrote a letter to Anne, who was away at boarding school in New York. In it he mentioned, "the novel I'm finishing now (which I think you'll like)."

It is a tragedy on many levels that Rod didn't live long enough to become the novelist he was certainly capable of being. It would have been a valuable and exciting addition to the sizable legacy he did leave. As it is, all we have of that potential is *The Season to be Wary*, but it stands on its own, and as a tantalizing hint of what might have been.

*Mark Olshaker is a novelist, New York Times best-selling nonfiction author and Emmy Award-winning documentary filmmaker. He is president of the Norman Mailer Society, a member of the board of directors of the Rod Serling Memorial Foundation and the editorial board of Rod Serling Books.*

# THE ESCAPE ROUTE

He lay on the sweat-logged, soggy sheets — his ice-cube-blue eyes, set deep in a bald, bullet head, staring up at the cracked ceiling; his aching middle-aged body pleading for sleep, but his mind a runaway dynamo, racing back and forth across the bombed-out landscape of his life. And it had been a full life, and a rich one! Gruppenfuehrer Joseph Strobe, former deputy assistant commander of Auschwitz. Former confidant of one Heinrich Himmler. Former wearer of black shiny boots, crisply pressed black uniforms; and former frequent maker of love in the back seat of his personal, chauffeur-driven Mercedes-Benz.

It all came back to him then, lying on that sagging, lumpy mattress of a threadbare room, while the traffic noises seeped in through the open window, riding on a soft sigh of wind from the distant Andes. Other noises, too. Distant music from the Teatro Colón, the opera house, a taxi horn and a distant shrill siren, a woman's laugh, a garbled argument. Buenos Aires at night — the torpid, sluggish heat noises of a hot country, of a people who grew bananas and shook castanets and ate garlic. Former Gruppenfuehrer Joseph Strobe found himself probing and digging into old graves of memory that beckoned back to the other time — to the exuberance and energy and vigor of a people, a nation, a purpose. He remembered the cheers. The deafening sounds of voices. The crowd noises. Germany had *been* a crowd. Life had been a rally — a continuous convocation that produced a rolling thunder of guttural screams sweeping across the sky over the vast auditorium of the Berlin Sportpalast, or the massive stadium at Nuremberg. A hundred thousand … two hundred thousand people who would greet the Fuehrer — their mass adulation like a mammoth surf breaking against the sky, echoing back in thundering waves. Oh, God, he missed them — those sounds, those voices. He missed the roaring reverberation of that Third Reich … and he missed standing there on a platform, black uniformed and young, booted and breveted, impervious and indestructible.

But it was all past tense. All former. And his regrets were formless wraiths crawling into his mind, dirtying up the clean order of his memories. For Gruppenfuehrer Strobe's life had not the benefit of the Valkyrian finale. It did not end as it was supposed to have ended — gloriously and cataclysmically in one earth-shattering moment of Goetterdaemmerung. Rather, it had ground to a stop in spasmodic little agonies; it had flaked off in bits and pieces, like the flotsam of a refugee column casting off sad little remnants on a road of defeat. Death had sent out its feelers … its hints … very early in the game. At El Alamein and then at Stalingrad. Sicily and then Salerno. And after that, death became a part of Germany, and a part of a daily process. Some of it showed itself when the patrols of the U.S. 69th met the forward elements of the Russian 58th Guards Division at Torgau on the Elbe. That was on April 25, 1945. It was the next day that Strobe buried his black uniform in a field two miles from Dachau.

Death stage number two took place on the Czechoslovakian border, when he shaved off his small black mustache and obliterated his SS tattoo with acid. An hour before, he had found the bodies of two SS men captured by partisans — they mutilated his SS tattoo with acid. An hour before, he had found torn mouths still open in a protest that they had "simply followed orders."

And death had continued — a long and protracted funeral with no eulogies and no mourners. Strobe had gone to Prague and spent six months there eating garbage in the upstairs room of a bombed-out factory — hiding in a sewer at night. Then he had shipped out as a stoker on a leaky freighter to South America. He had not known the other German crew members, but he had recognized them as blood brothers. They wore dungarees as if they were a uniform. Their backs were ramrod straight, their lips thin and hating, their muscles firm and toned from the calisthenics of killing. In his eyes and theirs, haunting and unaccustomed fears flitted past. But the eyes rarely showed surrender and never showed guilt. The Third Reich had died in a whimpering denial. But a handful of its more elite Boy Scouts remained alive — a few errant wiggling fingers of a corpus delicti, breathing and walking and sighing with a wistful nostalgia for the New Order — now the Old Order ... now the Dead Order.

Strobe had been a year in Brazil working in a steel mill. A month hiding in Caracas. Then five years later, after a dozen name changes, he had found asylum in Buenos Aires, where the track record of the Third Reich and the judgments of Nuremberg seemed of little consequence, and where in the Argentine government itself there seemed to be an informing touch of not a few Nazi values. It was here that he picked up his name again. (To be called Strobe once more was a gesture of a certain defiance; a little like putting on a swastika brassard and saying, "So do something.") He also found a job. The former Mercedes-Benz owner drove a delivery truck in the daytime and drank beer at night and watched the years peel away, dimming the recollection of the past glory.

Until one day it happened. He had heard it on the radio.

Eichmann.

Neutral and quiet and matter of fact — a radio announcer reading the news.

One Adolf Eichmann had been picked up by the Israeli secret service. It was an official announcement from the Israeli government. The prisoner was already at that moment en route to Tel Aviv.

The plane carrying him had left the Buenos Aires aerodrome two hours before. It had not been a pronouncement with rolling drums or significant trumpet blasts. It had been simply a news item and there had followed the soccer scores and the weather report. Adolf Eichmann was en route to Israel for atonement. But Buenos Aires had defeated Caracas five to three. And there had been a fire on the Paseo Colón and a large religious ceremony held in Aconcagua in the Andes. And incidentally ... quite incidentally ... a man whose real name was Adolf Eichmann, who had been tried in absentia, was no longer in absentia.

It had meant little to the castanet players and the banana growers and the garlic eaters. But to Joseph Strobe it had meant much. Someone had torn open the grave and was disinterring the bodies. The flesh had decomposed but not the sloganry that were the epitaphs. "Crimes against humanity." "Six million Jews." "Murder factories." Joseph Strobe, and men like him, had stopped their running and stopped their hiding and stopped the ritual track-covering. From the Caribbean to the Urals they had planted new roots, assumed new identities, manufactured new lives. They had done all this confident that there was a statute of limitations by which even a ten-year horror might be swallowed up to disappear into the gullet of frantic and ever-changing history.

Ghosts had come back to former Gruppenfuehrer Strobe at that moment. They had run past him like a mob on a dark street. They had whispered into his ear. Eichmann. They had taken Eichmann. And Eichmann had hidden, too. And had changed his name. And had married and had a family. Fifteen years had gone by, but the Israelis had simply waited. Watched and waited. A patient breed, the Jew. An incredibly patient breed.

For a week after the announcement of the apprehension of Eichmann, Strobe had clung desperately to the pattern of his living. He had gone to work and come home from work. He had eaten his meals and drunk his beer and had sought out no shadows or new anonymity. And when a certain frightened portion of his mind had sent out impulses of phobia, he had kept up a running monologue: Eichmann, of course. He had been number-two man to Martin Bormann who, in turn, had been at the right arm of the Fuehrer. Certainly, they would take Eichmann. But Strobe? Laugh. Laugh and reject. He had been a lousy Gruppenfuehrer. An unknown. A small potato.

To work and back home again — embracing the normality of his existence ... clutching at it as if by denying this new jeopardy he could prove that it did not exist.

Meals and beer-drinking.

And the running monologue to assuage the apprehensions that squatted like lead-heavy gargoyles deep in his gut: Eat, Strobe — and drink your beer, Strobe — and think of it rationally. There are a hundred men they'd seek out before your name came up. At least a hundred. Bormann. They'd dig tunnels into the earth's crust to get to Bormann. And what about Heinrich Mueller? He was head of the Gestapo, now living in Russia. And what of Dr. Josef Mengele? The good doctor had operated on five thousand human beings — mangling them, scarring them, killing most of them. He was in Paraguay now — not very far away. They would certainly look for Mengele before even thinking of him. There were hundreds of others. Hundreds. Prizes, every one of them.

Back to work and home again.

And the running monologue: Rationally now, Strobe. Rationally and coolly. Who are these shadowed hunters, these omniscient purveyors of belated and perverted justice? A handful of Jews. A dozen ... maybe two dozen Yids from a comic-opera desert country five thousand miles away. Izzy and Abie and Irving and Seymour — probably in leather coats like the Gestapo, and with wide-brimmed hats pulled down over their eyes. Play actors putting on the trappings of their tormentors. Play actors.

*But they had taken Eichmann.*

The continuing monologue: Strobe, old chap — they are Jews. They are the most predictable people on earth. The least subtle. My God, can you fear Jews? Can you fear a breed of sheep? Strobe, old chap — you watched them die. Quiet and unprotesting. Docile and resigned. A hundred an hour. Into the gas vans. Columns of twos. Men and women and children. This way to extermination. This way. And don't jostle there. Keep intervals. The dying must be orderly. It must be according to mathematics. It must be efficient. This way to the showers — by the numbers. And they had died by the numbers. By incredible numbers. In multiples — and multiples of multiples. Thousands and hundreds of thousands. And always unprotesting. Never a voice raised, let alone — an arm. Are these what you fear, Strobe? This species of born victim? Come, Strobe — drink your beer.

*But they had taken Eichmann.*

Strobe rose from the bed — the lumpy, sweat-smelling bed — and walked through the airless room to the dresser. He took a cigarette and lighted it, feeling his undershirt clinging to him as if glued there by some sticky, stinking substance. In the flare of the match he looked at his reflection in the mirror and hated what he saw. The once smooth and unfurrowed face was now lined and creviced — the flesh under the eyes pouched and sagging like purple hammocks left out in the weather. Fifteen years could diminish a man. They could take the youth out of his face and the maleness from his body. But even when the match had gone out, Strobe could still see his eyes staring back at him. He saw something in those eyes that had been born just a week ago. And he recognized it. He had seen it before when it was he who dispensed death with the wave of a riding crop or a nod of the head in a given direction. He had seen the look in other men — the naked animal expression of unutterable fear and languageless agony. Fear that churned and bubbled and built up beyond the point where it could come out of pores or retreat into insanity or lie down in black unconsciousness. He had seen it in a Catholic priest in Auschwitz when they had crucified him on the parade ground. He had seen it on the face of a Jewish dentist from Berlin when they put the syringe of acid into his testicles. He had seen it in a Hungarian gypsy when they had blinded him with needles. The unspeakable terror that looked back at him with his own eyes was familiar. An old acquaintance had come back to visit. It perched there in the glass, unbidden and unwelcome, and reminded Strobe that the order of the universe had been turned upside down. The hunters had become the hunted; the victims were now dispensing the death. It was his certain knowledge of this which made him acknowledge to himself that his nightly monologues were ceremonial rites, venerating a special and personal immunity that he knew had no real existence. The tortured logic, the incessant self-reassuring, the clutching of the slenderest of straws — these were part of the ritual.

But even while standing there, silently acknowledging his fear, Strobe was enough of a pragmatist to know that the acknowledgment was not enough. There was a next step, there was another chapter to follow this one — and this chapter had not yet been written. In his time he had helped empty a world of its illusions, so he knew, again with a silent admission, that simply to hope or pray or wish was an illusory process in itself. Mercy was an illusion. Compassion was another illusion. And salvation and safety were the most tenuous visions of all.

When he walked back over to the bed and looked at the deep, still-wet indentation his heavy body had made, it occurred to him that it looked like a grave. Here lies Joseph Wilhelm Strobe; age, forty-seven; height, five foot nine; cause of death: he had changed from a lion into a fox while some children of Israel had made a transformation from sheep into hounds. He butted the cigarette out in an ashtray and then looked around the sparse, deadly depressing room. No, he could not pray. He knew no language of supplication.

He was an expert on death — both the dealing and the prevention. But in this soon-to-be next chapter of his life, which had begun just hours before, he must find new tools to a new trade. He must become an escaper of traps; he must learn all over again to be a survivor. The only illusion he had ever embraced was the past fifteen years of his existence. This room, the delivery truck, his nightly beer-drinking — all the things his pragmatic soul had accepted as reality — he now knew to be part of the dream. The fifteen years had not been a haven. They had simply been a respite. The reality was outside in the night ... outside in the shadows. The reality had leather coats and a black sedan and a list of names in a notebook.

"The hell with it," Strobe said aloud. "The hell with it." And then a fresh new monologue: So, Strobe? They possibly seek out you. Fine. Excellent. That means you were *someone!* That means you made a mark. You had a niche. You were important. Excellent. So this we have established. Now what do you do? Do you stay in this room and sweat away your flesh and feed on your nerves and pace back and forth like an animal in the zoo? Do you lie down on that stinking mattress and call it a casket? Come, Strobe — come, old chap — head high and shoulders back. Go to the rathskeller, drink some beer, let the kikes know whom they're dealing with. Let them know this is Gruppenfuehrer Strobe, who once carried a riding crop and would point it to the left and then to the right and say that this one dies and this one lives ... and this one dies and this one lives. You, Strobe. You did that. You put death into the sweep of a riding crop. So don't skulk in shadows in a shitty little furnace of a room. Go out and remind the bastards who it was who held the riding crop!

"To hell with it," Strobe said again and again, aloud. He buttoned up his shirt and threw on his coat and went out the door. He would go to Lanser's rathskeller now. There would be friends there. Germans, like himself. There would be ... what would you call it ... a mutuality of interests. And then, smiling grimly — the company of misery. The oneness of fear.

He walked out the front door and lighted another cigarette as he looked across the street at the Palacio del Congreso and its flood-lighted dome and statuary. It made the street bright and reminded him that from now on darkness was an enemy. The shadows were hostile ground. And to be alone — this was a condition that favored the hounds. He started down the sidewalk, filling his lungs with the cooler night air and feeling some of the tension dissipate. But he knew … he knew from this moment on … he was the fox. *He* was the hunted.

Twenty minutes later, he arrived at Lanser's rathskeller — a smoky cellar decorated with Japanese lanterns and filled with guitar music and guttural laughter. Germans, like himself. There was Lanser behind the bar, pouring a beer, laughing with a tall blonde woman sitting by herself at the far end of the bar. Imperishable Lanser with his round, idiotic face, his big blue eyes, and the remnant of blond, wavy hair, now whitened and diminishing. But always with the smile, the grin, the happy look. During the other time, he had been a friend of Koch — a right arm, a handyman. And Koch had had lampshades made out of inmates' skin and given them as a gift to his wife. And it was Koch who had killed all those thousands at Buchenwald. So, Strobe found himself thinking: Pour your beer and smile that Goddamned gargoyle smile of yours, my friend Lanser. You are not out of the woods either. You are not out of the scent of those bloody Jewish hounds.

He had started toward the bar when a voice stopped him.

"Herr Strobe?"

Strobe stopped and looked toward the voice. He recognized him instantly. Gruber. Tall and thin and very Prussian. He had once commanded a division and then had been transferred to the Einsatzkommandos under Ohlendorf. It was Ohlendorf who had masterminded the extermination of the Russian peasantry when they had first invaded the Soviet Union. And Gruber had been high-ranking and very important. Decorated by the Fuehrer, personally. And when the old man rose from the table, it occurred to Strobe that he always stood straight and bowed from the waist, and screwed up one of his eyes as if he were wearing a monocle, and clicked his heels in a military acknowledgment of a decoration just received. Gruber, the Prussian. A silent, taciturn, wary man who fifteen years ago, and also on this very night, made Strobe uncomfortable. It was the same now as then. A disquieting little feeling of inferiority crept into Strobe — the same inferiority all Nazis had felt when in the presence of the old-line staff men with the vons in front of their names and the military genealogies that dated back to Frederick the Great. A gnawing unpleasantness that came with looking into the eyes of a man who knew himself to be superior and better bred, with finer blood and a coat of arms — dusty now and put aside, but still a matter of record.

Strobe automatically put out his hand and Gruber shook it, then motioned for him to sit down. Strobe did so, stiffly, noting subconsciously that Gruber looked particularly old that night, and particularly tired.

"I'm glad you showed up tonight," Gruber said in a soft voice. "I was hoping you would."

He snapped his finger at a passing waiter and pointed to Strobe. A moment later, another waiter brought over a tray with mugs of beer. Gruber took one.

"And some bourbon," Strobe said to the waiter. "Bring the bottle."

As he said it, he looked at Gruber, who smiled at him.

"A night to drink, eh, Herr Strobe?"

The tall, thin man, who had once been a colonel general, leaned forward across the table. "But not a special occasion tonight, is it?"

Strobe made a display of nonchalance with a flamboyant shrug. "What would be so special tonight?"

The old man stared at him steadily. "We fence a little, don't we, Herr Strobe? We engage in a little duel — the two of us."

"I don't know what you're talking about," Strobe muttered.

Gruber smiled. "I'll tell you what I'm talking about."

He lighted a cigarette, then put it into a holder. Again the affectation, Strobe thought. The nonexistent monocle and the cigarette holder and the bowing from the waist — just as if this were a parade ground and Gruber still had a division of troops waiting to be reviewed.

"Herr Strobe," Gruber said very gently. "We all know of what happened to Eichmann. It is also common knowledge that after Eichmann there will be others." He exhaled a thin stream of blue smoke, then wet his lips. "I am on the list, you know, Herr Strobe."

"I didn't know," Strobe said.

"Indeed," Gruber said. "I found out the day before yesterday. I have a brother-in-law who works at the Hotel Plaza del Rey, on the desk. Two men checked in there this past Monday. Swiss passports. But they could be anything. Their names could have been Swiss or possibly German."

Strobe nodded impatiently.

"One of the chambermaids — also German — found a collection of photographs that one of the men had left behind one morning after they went out. My picture was among them."

"That doesn't prove a great deal," Strobe said, without conviction. He was saying the words like sticking his toe in cold water to feel the temperature.

Gruber smiled at him — a patient, condescending smile, as if explaining a lesson to a thick and unimaginative student. "It means," he said softly, "that the two men are, of course, not Swiss. They're very obviously Israeli. They are also here to collect a few of us as they collected Eichmann."

The waiter brought a bottle of bourbon with two glasses. Strobe poured one, then looked expectantly at Gruber, who shook his head with a smiling "no, thank you." Strobe took the shot glass and downed it, then immediately poured another. He looked up to see Gruber staring at him.

"I'd finish the bottle if I were you," Gruber said.

"Oh?" Strobe answered, feeling cold.

"You see, Herr Strobe, my photograph is obviously not being carried around South America because I have a pretty face or because I am being considered for a beauty contest." There was a pause and then his soft voice grew pointed, like a barb. *"Nor is yours."*

Strobe allowed himself the second drink, feeling its heat mix with the cold, and then being defeated by the cold. He felt actually icy now as his hands shook while he poured his third glass. "My picture?" he heard himself saying, forcing an evenness into his tone, trying to smooth the words out like ironing pleats out of trousers; hating the shake and quiver of that icy fear that had taken hold. "My picture?" he repeated.

"Yours," said Gruber. "Your picture and mine and a few others. No one whom the chambermaid could recognize as living here *except* you and me."

He very carefully took the cigarette out of its holder, pinched off the end, then laid both holder and cigarette down on the table alongside of one another.

Meticulous, thought Strobe. So Goddamned meticulous. He lines everything up with such order and such symmetry. Even the words he throws out at you to announce your peril — these, too, are in a straight line — even and symmetrical.

Again Strobe poured himself a drink and this time sipped at it, not meeting the other man's eyes for a moment. Then, in as neutral and noncommittal a tone as he could manage, he spoke as he met the other man's eyes.

"Tell me, Herr Gruber. What do you intend to do about this?"

It was Gruber's turn to shrug. "I have made ... certain arrangements, Herr Strobe. A relative in Uruguay — someone with certain connections. It will involve a passport alteration and some other manipulations, but it goes without saying that I must leave here."

Strobe nodded in agreement.

"And you, Herr Strobe?" Gruber said, still smiling. "What will you do?"

Strobe continued to sip at his bourbon, then put the glass down. "I? I shall ... wait it out, Herr Gruber. Wait a week or two, perhaps."

"A bit of advice," Gruber said, sounding more like the Prussian colonel general. "I wouldn't wait too long. If I were you, I would begin ascertaining any and all available escape routes." The smile became thin and even more Prussian. "There are times when a tactical retreat is a sounder strategy than a prolonged reconnoitering of familiar ground."

Their eyes met again, each man disliking the other — Strobe resenting Gruber's superiority; Gruber offended that this pig-faced man had once outranked him. So much like all of those brown scum. Stupid, bullish, cruel men, who defiled everything traditional, and who, Gruber thought for the thousandth time, took men like himself down in the pit with them — without any code, without any honor, and without a thought of consequence. They were always screaming about the Jews, but it was they who corrupted Germany. It was they who bled it and poisoned it and made it die. Again he stared at Strobe and felt a loathing rise up in him like nausea. Why did the man have to sweat so? He found himself staring, fascinated, at the glistening wet dome and the slitted blue eyes that blinked so incessantly. The naked fat face of the man. The sour smell of his fear. Yes, there was fear there. Behind the thick, stolid flesh — inside the big frame — was a cavity, deep and decaying with the bile of rising panic. Strobe was afraid. And Gruber felt at least a modicum of satisfaction that this was one Nazi he could return the favor to. They had destroyed him. They had cut him to pieces. At least he could scratch back just this once.

"You perspire rather freely, Herr Strobe," Gruber said with a thin, hating smile. "Why do you sweat so? The place is not hot. No one else sweats."

Strobe looked up at the cold, appraising dislike on Gruber's face and his lips trembled. "My sweat bothers you, Herr Gruber? I'm so sorry. I'm truly very sorry. I offer you apologies for my sweat."

Excellent, Gruber thought. He had reached him. But if only there was something more he could do to him. Something to *really* bleed him. Again he looked him up and down, studying his face and hating him with a rich, open, satisfying, cathartic hate. This was what was left of Germany. The good men died but this is what survived in the ashes — this bloated, brooding pigface with the sweating dome and the nervous eyes. But this was enough. This was quite enough. He leaned back in his chair, almost as if in a gesture of dismissal.

"So the information is yours, Herr Strobe. I simply wanted you to know."

Strobe rose to his feet, feeling his legs shaky, his head swimming slightly from the drinks. The white, dignified, thin-lipped face in front of him was slightly out of focus, and Strobe had difficulty putting Gruber's twin mask back into place so that there would be but one face.

"May I say something to you, Herr Gruber?" Strobe said, smiling, and swaying slightly. "You have been most frank and candid with me. May I reciprocate with an equal frankness?" He loved the way he spoke now. It was the liquor freeing him. It did this often. It gave him a new speech pattern, foreign to him but singularly impressive. "May I tell you, Herr Gruber, that in matters of retreat, I yield to your superior knowledge of *that* specific. It has been my experience over the years that in matters of running away — the general staff was most expert ... most ... most consummately expert."

Then it was Strobe's turn to note, with satisfaction, that he had struck home.

Gruber's white face turned a shade more pale. He rose very slowly, his back stiff — ramrod stiff. He wanted to tell Strobe that what he'd just said was a reflection on his honor and the honor of the general staff and that he resented it. But he knew that such language, in a smoky rathskeller in Argentina in the year 1960, was nonsense — garbage. So he simply stared at Strobe, forcing the other man to eventually turn his eyes away, and then he smiled his thin, Prussian smile. "Herr Strobe," he said very softly, "do you know what you look like? May I tell you? You look like a white, quivering pig on its way to the slaughter. A white, quivering, protesting pig."

Strobe felt his insides knot up. He slammed a fist down on the table, upsetting the bottle. "Why you fucking aristocratic monocle-wearer! *You* tell *me* what I look like. You piece of shit, you. You opinionated piece of shit —"

The room gradually became quiet. People turned to stare at Strobe.

"Herr Strobe," Gruber said quietly, "your voice, please. You are being stared at and listened to. Attention is not exactly what you require at this moment."

But Strobe had gone beyond logic or restraint. "You," he screamed out, "tell *me* what it is I require? You? Well, I'll tell you, Mister Aristocrat, Mister General Staff, Mister Highborn Prussian swine — *you* can tell *me* nothing! Understand? From you I need nothing, I require nothing, I ask for nothing. Only that you get the hell out of my sight!"

And as Strobe screamed and pounded and ranted, he was oblivious to everything but the contentment and the satisfaction that came with allowing his mind and mouth to explode, permitting his fear to come out in the form of anger. He did not even feel Lanser's hand pulling nervously on his coat sleeve, or see the warning in his frightened, idiotic smile and his pleading eyes as he whispered repeatedly, "Joseph, Joseph — please. Please Joseph. You're making a scene. Joseph.

Throughout the onslaught, Gruber stood there silently, rigidly, allowing his superiority to stand as an impassive wall against this frothing fury that pounded at him. And when Strobe had run out of words and out of breath, Gruber simply nodded and dropped his head a little — as if waiting another beat for the last fragment of fury to spend itself. Then he looked back into Strobe's eyes.

"Are you quite finished?" Gruber asked quietly.

"I am finished," Strobe said, his voice shaking. "I am finished with you."

"With me?" Gruber said, with a crooked smile. "My dear Herr Strobe — you never had any business with me. Not then ... not now. We are linked together by an accident of nationality — but we are distinctly separate ... and distinctly different."

Strobe sat back down, feeling the liquor, sluggish, heavy and hot, running through him, muddling up his mind now so that his cleverness and his sageness were no longer available.

"May I," Gruber said softly, taking a step toward him, "tell you of the most fundamental difference that there is between us?"

Strobe's head felt too heavy for him. It wobbled from side to side, and a special exertion was needed to make it stop its movement. He blinked his eyes up at Gruber. "You may tell me any Goddamned thing you want," he said.

"The difference," Gruber continued, "is that if they find me, if they take me, and if they string me up someplace in a hot Palestinian sun, I am sufficiently human to regret having my life end. But *this* difference between us, Herr Strobe ... Herr Gruppenfuehrer Strobe. I will die knowing that they are right and I have been wrong. Just that one single variation of view. *That I can tell right from wrong.* And how different that is from you, Herr Strobe, and your breed. Even now, even while you're being hunted down, you still do not know why. You still do not perceive that you are wrong and they are right. And it is this kind of ignorance, Herr Strobe, that lost you the war. It is this kind of ignorance that will eventually take your life."

Then the old man clicked his heels and bowed slightly from the waist. A quick smile toward Lanser, who stood there transfixed, and then he walked very slowly — back straight, head high — to the door and went out.

Strobe felt Lanser's nervous hand patting his back. He twisted in the chair and pushed the hand away. "Herr Lanser," he said thickly, "if you are handling me as a gesture of comfort there is no need. If you are feeling the material of my coat, I'll tell you exactly where I bought it and you can get one for yourself."

Lanser blinked nervously, looked briefly around the room, then leaned over the table, his face close to Strobe's.

"Joseph," he said softly. "No scene, please. Not tonight. Since the Eichmann thing ..." He shook his head and his voice trailed off into nothing. He gave a nervous shrug. "You understand, don't you, Joseph?"

Strobe noted that Lanser's face, too, had a twin mask, and then a second. He focused hard until all three faces joined as one, and then he reached for the bottle, missing it at first, then finding it, and poured himself another drink. He held up the glass.

"To you, my friend, Lanser — prost!" he said. He finished the drink in a gulp and sat there, staring at his hands.

Across the room a bent little man with a black patch over one eye limped slowly toward the rest rooms carrying rolls of paper towels. Strobe saw his reflection in the bar mirror. The little man's name was Zamorski — a feeble-minded Pole with little rivulets of scars that ran in crazy-quilt patterns across his face. The one eye that gaped from the ruined face looked out blandly and cheerfully but with no hint of any kind of understanding.

Strobe stared at the disappearing reflection and again felt the twinge of fear that was part of the night's pattern. Lanser, that stupid, Goddamned idiot — to keep a crazy Polish bastard around the place for people to see and, not improbably, sometimes to hear. He had been a inmate at Buchenwald, picked up across the Polish border in 1939, and Lanser, stupid and unimaginative Lanser, had been his special tutor. It had taken a year for Zamorski's spirit to be pulled taut and then torn apart. Shortly thereafter, his mind had followed. For some incredible reason, he had attached himself to Lanser, following him, groveling like a pet dog, thankful if he were stroked occasionally — more thankful if he were not kicked or beaten. When Lanser had escaped from Germany, he had pointedly taken Zamorski with him. This plodding, mindless, one-eyed ruin was his passport. The Russians never looked for SS men in company with their victims. And to Lanser, because he was a simple man, because he had few dreams and aspired to very little, Zamorski was the reminder of better days. He kept the Pole around just *like* a pet, never wondering — as Zamorski himself appeared not to wonder — what incredible bond of life or death kept the simpleminded tormentor and the mad martyr together. Indeed, it apparently had never registered in the Pole's battered brain that this protector in the white apron, who smiled so continuously and who petted him, had once fed him salt herring for three days, while chaining him, without water, to hot pipes in a furnace room. The look in the one eye that gaped foolishly about him was filled with nothing but admiration for his master. It also seemed never to have occurred to him that even now — twenty years later — the smell of tobacco awoke in him some nightmarish, screaming fear. He had probably forgotten, too, that it was Lanser who'd shoved a burning cigarette in his other eye so many years before during a lazy Saturday afternoon at Dachau when Lanser — simple, unimaginative Lanser — had felt bored.

Strobe shook his head and tried to push the recollection of Gruber out of his mind. The recollection of Gruber and the business of the photographs. He was not surprised. He had expected this. But still, to know for certain … to suddenly get a confirmation of his jeopardy … came with a shock. He felt his nerves taut again and that formless fear crawling through his body. And with it came an anger. That it should be Gruber who made the pronouncement. Gruber, so happy about the damned thing — so pleased to be the chronicler of his doom. That sonuvabitch, Gruber. Strobe let his eyes wander around the room, trying to find a target for his anger. He thought of the Pole, and then of Lanser. He rose from the table and walked slowly toward the bar where Lanser had resumed talking with the blonde.

"Lanser," Strobe said, motioning him to come over.

Lanser warily walked behind the bar to stand opposite him. He had never cared for Strobe — not really. They had mutual friends and other things in common that went deeper than flesh — but there was something imponderable and unfathomable about the man. He was like a walking stick of dynamite — volatile and easily lighted. And in that thick-set frame was power: explosive power; blind, directionless, destructive power. Lanser's foolish smile came on as he took a bottle from behind him and put it in front of Strobe.

"On the house, Joseph. Drink hearty, old friend."

Strobe took the bottle, uncorked it and put it to his lips, drinking fast and deep. He put the bottle down on the bar and wiped his mouth with the back of his hand.

"You know something, Lanser?" Strobe said in his thick, guttural, drunken voice. "You take risks, do you know that? You take bloody risks."

"Risks?" Lanser said, the smile fixed.

"Risks," answered Strobe. "Risks like the Pole."

He nodded toward the rest rooms where Zamorski was just coming out, shuffling past the tables, smiling his sad, unknowing little smile.

"You mean Zamorski?" Lanser sounded surprised. "My little pet, Zamorski?"

Strobe took another drink. "Your little pet, Zamorski," he said. "Your little pet, Zamorski, could put a rope around your neck. You're a stupid shit to keep him around, Lanser."

Lanser gazed with special fondness toward the wreck and laughed softly. In some little compartment of his mind he recalled the hours of fun he'd had with the Pole so many years ago. He half closed his eyes in the warmth of his recollection. God, how that Pole could scream. For hours he could scream. No wonder he had so little voice left now. No wonder so few sounds could come through the toothless mouth.

In the beginning, Lanser had had to learn cruelty. He had been a farm boy in Silesia. He had whipped animals — a balky horse or a snarling dog — but these were acts of anger. The acceptance of the dispassionate torture of human beings had come to him with instruction. He learned the art much as he learned to wear his shiny black uniform with the death's-head insignia with comfort and ease. He had buried his qualms along with his overalls that smelled of cow dung, and had also learned to stifle his own screams when he heard his first victim screaming. Then the process had been easier. He was by nature a toady, a fawner. He looked up to other men. He liked having superiors. And when his dull and unimaginative brain produced a form of torture that made these superior men smile at him and congratulate him, this was fulfillment. He became addicted to praise and had a continuing need of it, which is why Zamorski had been so important to him. And Zamorski had been a marvelous subject. Resilient, available, sometimes screaming but never protesting. To torment the Pole became a daily procedure, like brushing his teeth. All this Lanser recalled as he continued to look at the Pole, feeling as he did some link, some bond, some ligature with another time. In some incredible way, he shared something with that shuffling hulk — and because of it, he felt almost an acme of tenderness. He let his eyes move slowly over the patchwork of scar tissue on Zamorski's face, at the milky nothingness of the right eye and the dumb, neutral deadness of the other — like a hunter appraising his trophies on a mantel. And then, with both compulsion and reluctance, he turned his eyes away and in turn studied the former Gruppenfuehrer. He, like Gruber, saw the glistening wet bald head and the blue eyes that darted left and right and kept blinking. And also, like Gruber, he sensed the fear in the other man. Lanser was disturbed, seeing this fear. Mixed with his disquiet at Strobe was an admiration for the man. Strobe had been a Gruppenfuehrer. A superior. Well above him. He had been a major Nazi, one of the originals. His exploits (mentioned on seventy-six different and separate counts at Nuremberg) were a matter of public knowledge — and to Lanser's mind made him special and very superior. But here Strobe was, standing drunk in his bar, looking fat and old and nervous. The Pole, Lanser decided to himself, could scream — because that's what Poles were for. Untermenschen. Subhumans. Despite everything that had happened, there *was* a proper design to things. Some men were built to scream. Other men had a mission to make them scream. And a Nazi ... for a Nazi to be afraid — to look as Strobe looked — well, it simply wouldn't do. He tried to smile again at Strobe and instinctively wanted to reach out and touch his big arm again, to pet him, to reassure him, to perhaps turn him back into what he had been before. But Strobe barely looked at him. He simply stared at his reflection in the bar mirror.

"Gruber tells me that I look like some pale pig on its way to a slaughter. A pale pig, Lanser. Is that how I strike you? Is that the way I look?"

Lanser swallowed. "No, Joseph," he said placatingly, "you don't look like any such thing. What the hell ... what the hell ... you have nothing to fear. Nothing at all."

Strobe wrenched his eyes away from his reflection and stared at Lanser. First Gruber with his gratuitous advice and now this smirking innkeeper — this grinning horse's ass — with his own unsolicited analysis of the situation. "How is that, Lanser?" he asked. "I have nothing to fear?" He grinned. "You know this for a fact, eh?"

Lanser licked his lips nervously. "I mean, Joseph," he said hesitantly. "I mean ... it doesn't appear to me that ... well ..."

My God, thought Strobe, of the two — the thin-lipped, long-nosed Prussian shit and this peasant ... this sycophant, this dog robber — he could almost prefer the former. He sat down on the stool next to

Lanser. "Lanser, my old friend, whereas I look like a pale pig — shall I tell you what you look like? Shall I tell you what you are? You are a fetcher and a pimp. You're an oversized boot-licker. You were never anything else. And you tell me I have nothing to fear. You're wrong, And if you think that *you* have nothing to fear, you are also wrong. Because you see, Lanser, you have no one left to hide behind. No one — no thing. Koch is dead. Your protector is dead. There are no more errands for you to run, so you are back where you belong — behind a bar with an apron, serving beer and schnitzel. And this, Lanser," he said, pounding his fist on the bar, "is what is right and what is proper. This is what you were built for and born for."

The murmur of voices in the room subsided. People were staring at Strobe again. His voice had carried over the smoke and the noise and pierced through a dozen conversations.

Lanser was pale, but his eyes warned. "Listen to me, Joseph. Please. Listen to me. You are upset, that's all. You're upset. Let us have a chat, you and I. Back there —" He pointed to a curtained partition at the far end of the room. "Go on back, Joseph, and I'll follow you."

Strobe looked across the room and then back to Lanser and nodded. "Why not? We'll talk, you and I, Lanser. Like two old friends and comrades. Correct? Like two old friends and comrades."

Lanser nodded and smiled tentatively. This crazy bastard could tear the place apart if he wanted to. "Of course," he said, trying to sound soothing. "We're two old friends and comrades, and we can have a chat."

Strobe rose and took a step away from the bar. He looked across the room at Zamorski, who was collecting glasses from an empty table. The Pole's stiff, jointless fingers were like those of a child, desperately engaged in some brand-new and complicated game. He turned to see Strobe staring at him, and his battered mouth twisted into what looked like a smile. Then he lowered his good eye, turned away and walked his shuffling, slow gait over to another table. His legs were scar-tissued toothpicks, barely able to sustain him.

Strobe watched him for a moment, then turned back toward Lanser. "That gives you pleasure?"

Lanser, tense, fearful of touching some other raw nerve, forced a smile. "He brings back memories."

"Of this, I have no doubt." Strobe walked the length of the bar and disappeared through the curtained partition. He entered the small, sparse room where Lanser did his bookwork. After a few minutes, Lanser came in. The two men looked at one another — Strobe challenging, Lanser timid and fearfully watchful. Strobe sat down on a threadbare sofa. Lanser leaned against the windowsill and took out a cigarette, avoiding Strobe's eyes as he lighted it.

"So tell me something, Lanser," Strobe said. "I have nothing to fear, is that what you said?"

Lanser made a nervous little movement with his shoulders. "Joseph," he said, "they took Eichmann — this we know. But why should that necessarily affect us?"

Strobe leaned forward on the sofa. "Why should it affect us? That was the question, wasn't it?" He shook his head back and forth. "Where in Christ's name did you spend the war, Lanser? Or me? Or Gruber? Or any of the others? Were we postmen someplace in Bavaria, delivering letters? Or were we street-cleaners in Vienna?" His big fleshy fingers gripped together. "They know where we are. They start with Eichmann. They don't finish with Eichmann." He felt the fear rising up in him again. "Let me tell you something, Lanser. I may well be a pale pig on the way to a slaughter. But I'm not the only pig — and there will be more than one slaughter."

Lanser walked in jerky, nervous steps over to a chair and sat down. "Joseph, my friend," he said, his voice shaking, "what did you expect? Really — what did you expect? That the rest of the world was like Zamorski?" He pointed his cigarette toward the curtain, and then shook his head. "Mindless and half blind? Do you think our living here is a secret? Think about this, Joseph," he said, gesturing with his cigarette, "think about it clearly. It doesn't take a secret service to come up with this information. We live here and people know we live here. Do you remember Richter? He was at Treblinka. A hundred witnesses identified his picture at Nuremberg. They had him on every count in the book. Well, let me tell you something — he kept a picture of the Fuehrer on his living room wall, two blocks from here. He kept it hanging there until he died last year."

Strobe's voice cut into the other man. "Would he keep it there tonight?" he asked. "Would he keep it there now after what happened to Eichmann?"

Lanser shook his head. He tried to keep his voice gentle and soothing. "Eichmann. You keep talking about Eichmann. Joseph, Eichmann was Eichmann. He was top echelon. He was like Bormann. Or Himmler. Or the others. He was the cream." He butted out his cigarette and rose from the chair. He was uncomfortable with Strobe. He was always uncomfortable with him. "Do you know something, Joseph?" He tried to smile. He tried to keep his voice light. "Perhaps you have … delusions of significance." He forced a laugh. "Understand? Delusions." He made a gesture with a thumb and forefinger. "We — you and I — were small potatoes. Small potatoes, Joseph. We were minor bureaucrats."

Strobe heard the words and kept staring at Lanser's mouth. How often had he heard those words. How often had he said them to himself. Always the same. The ritual of fifteen years ago. What do they call it? A syndrome. That's what this was. A syndrome. The small potato syndrome. Me? You'd take me? My dear American colonel from the judge advocate's office, my illustrious Soviet commissar sitting on the tribunal, my patient and compassionate Frenchman — Briton, Pole — all of you … you'd take me? I am one of the small potatoes. Really the small potatoes. An insignificant dot way down in the lower echelon. A nothing, really. A clump of earth. And they were all alike. Lanser, himself, all of them. Insignificance had been the order of the era. Self-deprecation was the only guarantee of survival.

"Small potatoes, Lanser?" he said. "Minor bureaucrats?" His voice was soft. He shook his head. "That's not what they called us at Nuremberg. That's not what they called you *or* me. You were Koch's right arm. Six witnesses said so at the trial. And I was mentioned dozens of times. Dozens of times, Lanser."

"But Koch is dead," Lanser said in a mournful little voice. "He is dead and Nuremberg was fourteen years ago." And then suddenly an anger built up in him. This bullnecked man, spreading his fear around, wrecking his own peace of mind, tearing into his composure. His voice rose and became shrill. "What are you, Joseph, anyway? Some kind of grave digger? Some kind of shroud cleaner? You burrow under tombstones like a maggot. And when you unearth some decomposed bone, you carry it, screaming, into public places." He felt shock at what he had said and the way he had said it, and almost immediately tried to retreat. Again the forced smile, again the soothing tone. "Joseph ... Joseph, old friend ... listen to me. This is how it's done. This is the way to get a rope around your neck. You keep carrying this Eichmann thing around town, yelling about it at the top of your lungs and sweating from it — this is how you shine a spotlight on yourself. This is how you get noticed." He took a few steps over toward Strobe, holding out his hands as if begging for something. "Joseph ... Joseph," he said, "do me a favor. Go home now. Go home and rest. Get a night's sleep. Maybe take a vacation for a week or two. Understand? Get this thing out of your mind. Perhaps ... perhaps you'd best not come back here for a while. It might be ... it might be safer."

Strobe rose from the sofa. "Safer," he repeated. "Neither of us has anything to fear ... but by my staying away from here, it'll be safer. You think like a fucking peasant. You have the logic of a man who shovels horse shit for a living. You won't admit to any fears of your own, but you'll pass a few judgments on mine, won't you? I ruin the business, is that it, Lanser? I give the place a bad name?"

"Joseph," Lanser said breathlessly, "Joseph, old friend — believe me —"

25

"No, no, no," Strobe interrupted him. "Believe *me*, Lanser. Believe me when I tell you that these are not ghosts that I run from. And they are not ghosts who'll be chasing you, either."

"You don't understand," Lanser almost whined.

Strobe's big head went back and forth. "I understand," he said hoarsely. "I understand more than you know. I understand, for example, that you will keep your Pole around here. You'll clutch at your little pleasures, and you'll feel relieved when I walk out of here — me and my ghosts." He took a step over toward Lanser. "But one morning, Lanser. One morning, when you wake up you may see these ghosts hovering over your head. And then, my old friend, you may do a bit of sweating yourself — a little belated perspiration." He reached into his pocket and took out a pack of cigarettes, lighting one. He met Lanser's look — a look that carried with it both fear of himself and fascination. "What is it?" he said softly. "What disturbs you now?"

"I don't know," Lanser said. "It's just that ... I've never seen you frightened before. I've never seen you look this way."

The cigarette bobbed in Strobe's mouth. "I've never felt this way before. But it could be worse, old friend, old comrade — it could be much worse." He dragged deeply on the cigarette. "I could be Eichmann," he said softly. "I could be flying to Israel now." There was a pause. "And you could, too."

Lanser's smile never quite made it. His lips twisted ever so slightly, then he closed his eyes, turned and walked out of the room.

Strobe remained there motionless for a moment, his big shoulders bent. He took the cigarette out of his mouth and looked at its wet tip. He closed his eyes for another moment. "We made a mistake," he said aloud to the threadbare sofa. "We made a terrible mistake," he said to the chair Lanser had sat in. "We didn't kill them all," he said to the empty room.

By two-thirty in the morning, whiskey had done all it could do for Strobe. It had slowed down his panic, made the wheezing bellow of a

bad tuba sound like the Berlin Philharmonic, and for at least an hour
had obliterated from his consciousness the name of Eichmann, the
name of Gruber, his photograph in the hands of nameless men. He
kept nodding and smiling and keeping time with the bald, drunken
tuba player who finally passed out right on the stage and slept there
for several minutes before Lanser directed that he be pulled off. At
one point Strobe had even taken a fancy to the long-legged blonde
at the bar and decided that she reminded him of one Ilse Hilger, a
former frequent passenger in the back sat of his Mercedes-Benz long
ago. He had beckoned to her across the room and bought her a drink
after she'd sat down. But by then Strobe's whiskied fantasies were on
the way out. The blonde, so enticing from the perspective of thirty
feet and two bottles of Calvert, turned out to be an aging Cinderella
whose magic midnight had passed years before. Close up she was a
tired walker of many streets with a backside paying the price of a
thousand bar stools and a thousand mattresses and a social circle of
men like Strobe who borrowed her for some drunken and impas-
sioned moments until she discovered, too late, that her own capacity
for passion was as extinct as her virginity. For just a soft and gentle
moment Strobe had appealed to her. He had called her "Liebchen"
and stroked her cheek, and from her own drunkenness there arose a
dream. But it had lasted all too briefly. The thick-chested, bald man
had turned morose, knocked over her glass and finally pushed her
away. She had gone back to the bar and finally left with a sailor who
would make fumbling love to her in an alley with all the finesse of a
tomcat, but at least briefly and for pay.

Strobe slept at the table, and it was hours later when he awoke
and stared across the now empty room toward the bar. Lanser had
disappeared. He looked at his watch. It was past six. He looked
across toward the front windows. Outside, the dawn was a sick, gray
pallor of a dying night and a fragile, newborn morning. The place
smelled of whiskey and smoke and aged urine. Strobe pushed his
chair back and rose to his feet. His head felt like an overheated block

of concrete, and he had to fight down nausea and dizziness as he moved toward the bar. And as he walked, it all came back. His fears were like some kind of cancer deep inside of him that woke when he did. Endless and unchanging, they followed him everywhere. And as he walked, stiffly and painfully, through the gray gloom of the dirty little room — he wanted to cry. He was on a treadmill, moving from one quaking anxiety to another. And there was no hope. There was no relief. There was no end to it.

But escape was an instinct with him now. Even as the despair washed over him, another portion of his mind was already dictating what the next steps were. The lessons of fifteen years were most explicit. The hunted man had to live his life in little fragmentary blocks of temporary safety. Clumps of seaweed to be clutched at while drowning — but nonetheless clutched at. Plans to be made. Good only for the next few minutes. But this was how survival was measured — only in minutes. The lessons, and the memories of them, stirred inside him. It had been that way once before. The planning. The escape route. Where to go and how to get there. What hours and what hiding places. Back door or roof or basement or attic. At this moment it was all he could think and all he could remember. At this moment, it had never been any other way.

He looked at himself in the bar mirror and saw an imitation Strobe — an inferior model from a copying machine that had turned out an old man with haunted eyes. Then he realized that the lights had been turned out and it was only the dawn outside that illuminated the room. The place had obviously been closed for hours and Lanser — that sonuvabitch, Lanser — had not awakened him to send him home or even to any kind of safety. He had allowed him to sleep there at the table, naked and vulnerable, like just any drunk. Zamorski he treated better than that. Even Zamorski. Zamorski was probably sleeping comfortably in bed someplace. Zamorski he had let go home. That Goddamned Lanser with his insane perversions, his very special sentiments that came out of a mental asylum.

Zamorski, the Pole. And he was resting comfortably somewhere. While he, Strobe, might spend the last day of his life staring at himself in a dirty bar mirror, trying to piece together the murky imperfection of what he saw with the young and indestructible conqueror of the other time.

That Goddamned Lanser!

That stupid and obsequious peasant shithead who allowed his guilt to walk around the bar and pick up glasses in his claws, and dirty towels of the men's room, and imitate a man.

That Goddamned Lanser who had to take his trophies with him — even on an exodus.

And then, walking around to the other side of the bar, he saw Lanser.

Lanser smiled at him.

A half-moon smile, but a very red moon.

The smile was not formed with lips.

Strobe was being grinned at from Lanser's throat.

A slit in the jugular, like a second mouth.

Lanser lay on his back, arms at his sides. Very peaceful. No protest in the open eyes. Perplexity. Very surprised at the whole thing. On this Monday evening in Buenos Aires, in his very own bar, and on his own private and personal time, Herr Lanser had had his throat cut.

The unprotesting eyes looked up with more repose than Strobe had ever seen in them. And in some subconscious portion of his mind he wondered that he himself felt no shock at this grinning and sudden death.

"So, Lanser, old comrade," Strobe said in a mild, conversational voice to the quiet man at his feet. "Small potatoes or big potatoes — what difference? The pig dies the same as a lion when the throat is cut." He continued to stare down at the silent man and to himself said, "And the same with the German. You put a blade to the windpipe — he'll bleed just like the Jew."

He remained there for a long and silent moment, just staring and thinking. And from some indistinct place in his memory something else came back to him. "Hath not a Jew hands, organs, dimensions? If you poison us, do we not die? And if you wrong us, shall we not revenge?"

Strobe suddenly felt looked at. He turned very slowly. Across the room, near the curtained partition, stood Zamorski. And almost nothing had changed. The scar tissue who walked almost upright. The ravaged face. The one eye that had assimilated more hell and horror in an hour than most men could witness in a lifetime — it still looked out with no particular emotion.

But the Pole's right hand, with the bent and misshapen fingers — the Pole's right hand was ever so slightly stained with red.

Then Strobe knew. He understood. The Pole had certain attributes. He had certain strengths. On some levels he was almost human.

For one thing, he had incredible patience. He could wait quietly for over twenty years.

And the stiff, jointless fingers — broken so many times — would never strum a harp or caress a woman or paint a pastoral scene of the willowed banks of the Vistula.

But they could hold a knife.

It may have been a moment later ... or an hour. Strobe knew only that he had raced out of the bar, propelled more by shock than fear. That Zamorski could have killed. A mindless animal or a dog or a crocodile —— it made just as much sense. To find, suddenly, a logic and a point of view and a capacity for revenge in this hulk ... this wreck ... this broken thing who could not even speak. And he had killed with his logic. And God knows how many years it had been locked inside. Waiting. Simply waiting. It was as if in one night ... one solitary night ... all the order of the universe — as Strobe knew it — had been turned upside down. Jews collected Nazis. And Zamorskis killed Lansers.

Strobe thought of this as he hid in the shadow of a building, looking out at the empty streets. Even then, his habit patterns were more persistent and encroaching than his shock. His manual of survival, written in sweat and sleeplessness and tension, warned him that a man was particularly vulnerable in the still, unpeopled streets of the early dawn. This was not the time for an escape. A black rabbit in the snow. So Strobe walked — in an almost tiptoed agony, his back to the stores — staying in shadows, watching as the glow of the sun touched the grayness and dispelled it. Then there were the early-morning sounds of garbage cans and traffic. Shopkeepers appeared, awnings were let down, the city stirred and came to life. Strobe could then become invisible. He forced himself to walk in a measured, slow pace down the Avenida de Mayo. His legs ached, his tongue was like some sour, foreign object shoved into his mouth — swelling and choking. The hot concrete inside of his head bubbled in the morning sun and pain beat a snare drum across his chest. But he did not dare stop. He continued to walk, playing the role of the early-morning stroller, past the Plaza de Mayo, crossing the Avenida Rivadavia, until he reached the soft and comforting green of the Parque del Retiro, where white-coated cleaning men stabbed fluttering pieces of paper and barely looked at him. He sat on a bench and stared across at the cathedral, where giant bells chimed out over the murmur of morning voices and morning sounds and beckoned the believers to early Mass. He watched as the lines of black-mantillaed women walked slowly up the stone steps toward the high oaken doors of the church.

Sitting there on the bench, he felt the pain subside. His breath came back to him. His breathing, like the wheeze of a ruptured concertina, carried with it its own special pain — but this time, bearable.

He looked across at the church again and listened as the bells gradually diminished. God was across the street. Strobe had to smile. God was across the street. But what could he request of Him?

Very little, he knew. Very little. He had nailed too many Christs onto crosses, fifteen years before, to seek or expect respite, let alone salvation, from inside a church.

He let his body sag. He was so desperately tired. But he knew other things, too. Even as the hot sun pierced the leaves of the trees above him, he felt the ice-cold understanding of what had happened. What had triggered Zamorski. He could remember a decade and a half before when the inmates of Dachau had heard the rolling thunder of the American artillery — the look they got when they stared at the SS. The hidden and secret smiles on the ravaged faces. Just as Zamorski had looked at *him* hours before. The night was ending. God was reentering the world. And so the tormented had stared at them with understanding eyes and laughed their secret, silent laughter. It was this way with Zamorski. As of the moment they had taken Eichmann — the gods began to topple.

Strobe rammed his fingernails into his palm and drew blood. He knew what he should have done. He should have taken his bare hands — his still powerful hands — and wrapped them around the scrawny Polish throat to demonstrate the final lesson. No matter the hour and no matter the year — there was still an order to things. There were those built to give pain and those to receive it. But he, Strobe, had forgotten. He had stared at the Pole — stared at him in shock and fright — stared at him in panic and disbelief. And then he had run. Supermen, he thought, smiling grimly. The myth of the master race. One god was manacled to some Jews on a plane. Another lay on a dirty bar floor with his throat cut. And yet another ran down the streets of Buenos Aires on a hot May morning listening to church bells and wondering about God.

Strobe rose from the bench and again moved toward the sidewalk that circled the church. He was rational now, with the logic of all hunted animals. The ordered instinct of the prey. What next? Maybe a small hotel near the river alongside of the federal district. One of those little and nameless hotels that stood in a row. Hole in there and wait. Find the time, the hour, the place, the avenue of escape. But no, it occurred to him quickly as an afterthought, not that. If he headed in that direction and he were being watched, they would know approximately where he was going. Back to his room. That's where he must go.

He moved down the street, feeling the sun baking into him, wondering what he looked like as he smelled the sour smell of whiskey and sweat all over him. On the corner in front of the art museum he paused briefly.

And then he saw the black sedan parked across the street. The driver and a companion alongside. Not looking at him. Nothing like that. Dark and indistinct faces. But Strobe's instincts froze him with a warning. He looked at the car briefly and then started up the long concrete steps toward the entrance of the art museum.

The door was locked. There was a sign reading OPEN AT NINE. He checked his watch. Eighty-thirty. Too early. Thirty minutes too early. Fifteen years too late. Over his shoulder he saw the black sedan still parked there, the two men looking at him. No subterfuge now, they were looking at him. They were staring at him. Strobe walked down the steps very slowly, very carefully, as if descending a ladder from a big target. Again he sought the crowd. To stay with people — that was the prime requisite. He moved down the sidewalk to an outdoor café and sat down at one of the tables.

A waitress, young but with circles under her eyes, moved tiredly toward him and threw down a menu.

"Coffee," he barked. "Black."

"Coffee," the waitress repeated, like some kind of automaton. She disappeared into the café and came back a moment later with hot coffee.

Strobe sipped at it, turning his head every now and then to look toward the black sedan. He saw a policeman approach the car. There was a pantomime of conversation, then the car pulled away. Strobe watched it cross the intersection and move down the next block. He checked his watch again. Five minutes had passed. Time was on its hands and knees, crawling in slow motion.

He remained at the table for the bulk of the half hour, starting every time a car drove by, jerking his head to see if it were the one. But the black sedan did not return. He did not see it again until he had left the table and was starting back on the sidewalk, when once again, just as he was passing the museum, it pulled around the corner of his side of the street. Again he ran up the steps of the big gray building and this time he pushed his way through the revolving doors inside.

He stopped near the information desk alongside of a Bernini statue and took a handkerchief out of his hip pocket to wipe his perspiring face. His mind galloped and charged. What to do next? He put the handkerchief back into his hip pocket and stood there motionlessly. This was respite — but not salvation. He was safe — but for how long?

The receptionist, an angular woman with hair severely pulled back into a shapeless bun, looked inquiringly at him. Strobe forced himself to smile, then turned to survey the Bernini statue. He cocked his head in the manner of a practiced and thoughtful connoisseur, pursed his lips and whistled softly as he walked past her toward a gallery of oils off to his right. He moved into the long rectangular cavern flanked by swatches of color — sunsets and reclining nudes and landscapes and still lifes and ...

He stopped short. He was four feet away from a large canvas. A woman, obviously an American tourist, going by him clucked disapprovingly at it and whispered some negatives to her male companion, who nodded in turn, agreeing with her. They were looking at the same canvas as Strobe — a mountained lake scene with a man fishing from a rowboat. The sky was a soft azure blue, the rock walls purple and spiraling, the lake reflecting them a dark purple. The face of the fisherman was indistinct and in a quarter profile, turned away from the brush as he might turn from a camera lens.

"Like a rather bad postcard," Strobe heard the woman say to her companion. "Will you look at the colors? I mean, really! Have you ever seen anything quite like it — outside of a drugstore rack, that is?"

"Sign painters," the man responded with a regal lift of the eyebrow. "Poster dabblers," he added, his voice like that of a jurist dismissing a petty case of thievery. "Why is it that the bad painter will always and invariably attempt to improve on God and nature?"

Their voices drifted off down the long room while Strobe stood there looking at the boat and the mountain lake and the outline of the fisherman. The fisherman with the broad shoulders … the heavily muscled back … the bald head visible underneath a slouched cap.

The fisherman.

Contented and tranquil — unassaulted by any force or entity or opponent.

He sat there, relaxed, with his back against one of the gunwales, his fishing rod limp over the side, the purple water lapping gently against the hull. There was a warm sun touching him, soothing him. There was a breeze — yes, a breeze — that rippled the water. And it was all captured on canvas. All of it captured. All of it painted into changelessness.

And the fisherman. It was unmistakable. *The fisherman was him — Strobe. He* was in the rowboat. *He* was on the mountain lake.

He felt a tremor run through him. Shock. Surprise. A wonder that galvanized and stunned. It was as if he had suddenly walked into a revelation. But even as he stood there in the aftermath of this revelation, Strobe felt something else akin to neither shock *nor* surprise. It was as if he were a man ending his search and finding, without ever having doubted that he would find; feeling a quiet gladness and knowing with certainty that a man could hunger only so long. Then there must be — there had to be — some kind of forgiving God. But part of the revelation was the change in Strobe's hunger.

He had goose-stepped half of his life along with a generation of other men, marching toward what they all believed was immortality. But their flags had withered away; their leather boots had rotted — along with a million men who had worn them.

This was part of Strobe's certainty as he stood staring raptly at the painting. He had been hungering for the wrong things. He had spent the second half of his life trying to regain pages of a calendar. But now he knew. Time was irretrievable. Time died just as men did. And he could no longer goose-step as in the past any more than he could furtively slink as he had been doing in the present. If there was, indeed, an escape for him there it was. In a painting. Existing — an arm's length away. Beckoning. Inviting. Calling out to him in a language of serenity and peace. A condition he had never known — but now craved like an addict.

*I am in the picture. I am. I believe. I am because I believe. I am in a rowboat. I feel the sun. I feel the wind. I am on the lake. If I reach down, I'll feel the wetness of it. If I put my head up, I'll smell the moss and the pines, the damp earth and the wind.*

And then it happened. The floor bobbed underneath him. A to and fro motion. Like a little boat gently prodded by an errant wind. He opened his eyes. The sun warmed him. The purple mountains loomed over him — protecting. He saw his fishing rod. An oarlock. He felt the gunwale against his back. And he smelled the scent of lichen and moss and distant green earth. And he felt peace. Some mystic surgery had removed his cancer and left him clean — unassailed. His body and mind — burned out and scourged by endless running ... endless jeopardy and endless pain — were soothed, eased, lulled, given respite, given salvation.

*I want nothing more. I ask for nothing more. Only to be frozen into this timeless canvas. You, there, God. You invisible thing reputed to be forgiving and compassionate. I ask little. Just leave me this painted sun. Leave me this painted lake; leave me this Canaan ... this promised place ... this Eden made of oil and varnish. I cannot leave it. I cannot ....*

But the lake disappeared. The rolling boat turned into a concrete floor. The mountains dissolved into a gallery of paintings. The gentle, wafting breeze was a woman's voice — nasal and harsh.

"Look at this one. Will you look at this one?"

Strobe was back in the museum. He wanted to scream at the woman to shut her mouth. To stop destroying his idyll. Please ... please ... give him back his respite ... his peace. But the forgiving God had turned His back on Strobe, much as He had turned His back on Strobe's victims of long ago. Reality had returned. And there was the pain again. The fear. The tension was like an anchor hooked into his flesh, dragging him down.

He turned toward the woman's voice and to the painting across from him — the object of her attention.

"Unforgivable," the woman snorted. "Where in the name of God has taste gone?" Her voice was a portrait of disapproval, as seen through a lorgnette — superior and final.

Strobe looked at the other painting. It showed a man hanging from a wooden cross in a concentration-camp prison yard. A swastika was flying on one of the background buildings. The prisoner's face was caught in a shaft of pale sunlight — his agony etched deep into dark lines. The eyes reflected the endless Gethsemane.

Strobe looked at it with no feeling. He was unmoved. It was as if he were a surgeon examining blood. Blood carried with it no horror. It was part of his profession. It was an abstract by-product of his labors. To kill Jews, to string them up, to render them pain — these were natural acts, neutral, and could imply no judgment. Like swatting flies, or grinding a heel on a bug, or tacking a butterfly to a board. And flies and bugs and butterflies could never be perceived by Strobe to be "victims." So, looking briefly at the picture, he felt only a passing boredom. The surging rage that rose up in him had no connection with the painting of a twentieth-century minor Christ. It was directed at the American tourist whose voice had intruded upon his dream and had kidnapped him back into reality.

He glared at her as she and the man continued down the corridor, dismissing the paintings one after the other, and dismissing Strobe with a single perfunctory glance as they walked away.

Strobe, left alone, turned his eyes back toward "his" painting. He moved closer to it and reached out and touched it, closing his eyes, concentrating. But this time nothing happened. The canvas was hard to the touch. The rippling waters were nothing but purple paint. The azure sky was a rough, uneven pigment. The fisherman was just an outlined form made of oil, but not flesh. There was no heartbeat. There was no life.

He heard a warning cough from a guard who had just entered the room, and dropped his hand quickly, shoving it into his pocket. He turned away, averting the guard's stern look, and forced himself into an unhurried pace, letting his eyes wander past the portraits, looking at them with feigned interest. But not really seeing them. Already he had turned back into a tired automaton; he was like a computer thrown together with bones and nerve endings, programed and calibrated to perform only one function — to seek out danger, to recognize jeopardy, to stay alive. He knew only the facts related to survival. There was a car outside with two men in it. They had his photograph and his name on a list. There was a Pole named Zamorski. There was someone named Eichmann flying at thirty thousand feet, heading for a gallows where he would die just inches off the ground. The facts — and with them, the names and faces — were a clangorous bell that clapped back and forth inside of his mind. Nothing had changed. It was all as it was before.

He spent a fitful, nervous hour wandering through the various galleries. Past a Hals, a Vermeer and a Picasso. He pondered with a great show of interest next to a Klee and forced himself to look somehow charmed by a collection of Impressionists. He wandered past statuary and some mobiles and some meaningless abstract drivel of someone like Jackson Pollock. But none of it made any sense to him. For no matter where he walked and no matter where he aimed his eyes, he was conscious of only one thing. He had been the victim of a monstrous practical joke. He had been led by some gentle, helpful hands through a portal into heaven, only to be pulled back down into hell.

Just before leaving the museum he cast one last look into the gallery where it had begun. The view of the mountain lake was obstructed by a hanging mobile. Only one man was in the room. This was an elderly Jew staring at the concentration-camp picture and softly crying.

"Alter Jude — old Jew." Strobe thought the words. "Don't stand there wetting yourself with tears and searching for God. God is the wishful thought conjured up by dying men, naked and defenseless and in desperation, calling to a benefactor who does not exist. He is a product of pain, and only that."

This is what Strobe thought as he walked through the lobby of the building and out into the street. He paused briefly, looking to left and right.

The car was gone. In its place was a sign announcing that there was fifteen minutes parking only. Standing there in the hot sun, Strobe had an almost irresistible urge to laugh. Vengeance is mine, saith the Lord and the avenging angels ... so long as the wrath takes no longer than fifteen minutes, or at least can be handled without double parking.

Strobe felt giddy, lightheaded — and, he knew, fairly close to some kind of crackup. He had taken all he could take for a protracted period of hours. There was a point reached where mind and body had to rebel. He took to the sidewalks, re-crossed the Plaza de Mayo, walked past the cathedral and once again into the Parque del Retiro, and finally stopped at a public phone booth at the far end of the narrow avenue of the Calle Florida. There were friends he could call. For money, or for hiding places, or for advice. The first number was busy. That was Bock's. He was a respected stockbroker now who had once been with the SS. But Bock was busy buying and selling his municipal bonds. Then he phoned Diestl. Diestl owned a grocery store on the other side of the city. He had many children and many bedrooms. But Diestl was not in, so said his wife. And who was calling? A friend, Strobe told her, and then he hung up. Names and faces made brief appearances on the stage of his brain — and were perfunctorily dismissed. Lanser — the obvious one — this one would be loaning no more money to anyone. And Gruber — that Prussian sonuvabitch. With his connections, his manipulations. He was the most obvious — and by far the most able to help. But the least accessible. Especially after the scene of the previous night. No, he could seek no help from Gruber. He was certain of that. But of other things — of his plans, of whatever might be the modus operandi of his survival — these he was not sure of at all.

He left the phone booth and started once again to walk past the row of shops with the crowds of people filling up the avenue. Somehow and sometime he would have to get help from the outside. He knew this. This part of the plan carried with it the only simplicity that he knew. But for the moment, he would go back to his room. That covered the next sixty minutes. And this was how he must parcel out his life from then on — in little slabs of minutes.

As he walked, he let his mind wander again. Already that brief feeling of peace — so elusive, so ephemeral — was nothing but a vague memory. It was this hot sun that had reality. It was the long expansive street where any moment the black car might appear — this was what had substance.

He paused for a moment underneath the awning of the florist shop. His mind was full of gears and wheels, turning and meshing. Hiding place. Route to a hiding place. Escape. But where would he go? Where *could* he go? It was like 1945 all over again. It was like the Czech border and the Prague factory and all the other way stations of so long ago. The heat was almost unbearable. The sun, a shaft of furnace air that followed him even in the shade. But he forced his mind to function and knew then that his room was so obvious as to be *not* obvious. That's where he'd go for the time being. His room. That stifling, airless little cubicle that for the next sixty minutes at least would be his fortress. He wondered then, looking beyond the dark shade of the awning into the white sunlight, whether or not the black car was still out there somewhere. There were many cars and many people. The pursuers sought invisibility in crowds just like the pursued. And perhaps the driver and the other occupant were on the sidewalk already, following him. Perhaps across the street, under another awning. Perhaps inside of one of the stores, peering at him through the glass — watching him, studying him, surveying him and his movements. Or at the outdoor café. Maybe they were drinking coffee ... and just waiting. But he had no choice at this moment. Stay with the crowds. Stay with them until he could find his hiding place.

He joined a group of shoppers and walked with them for three blocks until a jitney pulled up to its stop on the corner. He waited until the last moment, then hurriedly jumped on. He rode the jitney to the midsection of the city, a quarter of a mile from his hotel, and then he got off and walked again, his eyes twisting and revolving, his mind like a thin string of wire, pulsating as it sought out danger.

Then he was in his room. He closed the door and locked it, then bolted the night latch. Fatigue was a dead weight attached to him — a part of him. He lay down on his bed. The room was as usual — hot, dark and close, smelling of him and strong laundry soap and some neutral mustiness, defying origin, that enveloped the tiny space. But it was familiar. The heat and the smells — they belonged to him.

And then he was on his back on wet sheets, staring up at the cracked ceiling. It was as if the bulk of his life was an uncomfortable horizontal perusal of ceilings and walls: a lifetime of itchy, sodden moments flowing slowly into other itchy, sodden moments.

He must sleep now, he decided. There would be more running. The escape had not really even begun. But for the time being — there must be sleep. He closed his eyes and lapsed into what passed for rest. Sporadic, fitful dozing, full of spasmodic dreams — each, in turn, featuring a brief walk-on of a person from his past. Lanser was there for a moment with his smiling red throat. And the milky-eyed Zamorski, of course. Staring at him as if American artillery could be heard just over the hill, coming to his defense. And inexplicably there was the face of the Hungarian gypsy he had once interrogated at Number 8 Prinz Albrechtstrasse, when they had brought him in. For some reason his sleeping mind remembered this incident clearly. It had been a long interrogation, ending with needles thrust into the gypsy's eyes, and he could remember the gypsy staring up at him through the red fog — through the maimed and useless orbs — as if he still retained some kind of sight. And the gypsy had cursed him. He could even remember the words. "My pain is brief," the gypsy had said, "but yours, Gruppenfuehrer — yours will last for an eternity. I will that to you. I leave it to you as a legacy. Pain — eternal pain." There were the gypsy's face and the sound of his voice parading across Strobe's unconscious mind. Other names, other faces. A dog he had once owned that he had named Blondi, just as the Fuehrer had named his Alsatian bitch. And the dog's bark. It came back to him. And the officer's club at the SS barracks near Duesseldorf where he had sung so many songs and pounded his tankard on the table. Pounded it and pounded it.

In his dreams he stopped the pounding, but it continued. More pounding — loud and persistent. And he awoke. There was someone at the door. It was the landlady's voice, petulant and irritated.

"Mr. Strobe?"

He bolted upright in bed.

"Mr. Strobe," the landlady's voice whined at him through the door, "you're wanted on the telephone."

Strobe grunted a muffled "thank you" and got out of bed. He waited until he heard the landlady's footsteps disappearing down the hall, then he carefully unlocked the door and unlatched the bolt.

He took a step out into the corridor, looking to left and right, then walked toward the phone on the wall near the landing, with the receiver hanging down limply like a broken arm. And then it suddenly hit him. Who knew he was there? Who had followed him? His palms were wet as he picked up the receiver and put it to his ear. No sound. No distant breathing from the other end. He cleared his phlegmy, constricted throat and heard himself say, "Hello." There was no answer at the other end — just silence. "Hello," he said again, louder. "Who's there?"

Still no answer.

Strobe felt the sweat on his face. "This is Schultz," he said, idiotically. "This is Herr Schultz speaking. Whom did you wish to speak to?" And as he said it, he knew it *was* idiotic. It was dull and lame and pointless. The time for subterfuge was long past. Whoever had called on the phone knew who he was and where he was. But there was still no answer. And then there was a click at the other end.

"Hello?" Strobe said. "Hello?" He pushed the phone cradle up and down. "Hello?" he kept saying persistently — but the line was dead.

Strobe slowly replaced the receiver. He looked down the flight of steps, wondering if he should ask the landlady if the person had left a name. No, he decided, best not. He turned and walked down the hall and back into his room. He locked the door again and rebolted the night latch, then stood there trying to breathe the hot, still air. Small lapping waves of pain swept across his chest. And he knew why. His fears now once again had a form. Almost everything else could have been explained away. Even the men in the car. They could even have been brush salesmen from Brazil. Or a couple of American tourists waiting for their wives. But this. A phone call to him. This was explicit and pinpointed his jeopardy. Like his photograph in the hotel room. Someone knew where he was. Someone *had* been following him. He *was* under surveillance. And, of course, it had to be Israeli. It had to be.

Once again he went over to the bed and sat down, slowly massaging his chest.

Odd, the thought came to him. Very odd. To be pursued by Jews. And to be so frightened that his heart was trying to pound its way out of his body. Once again, the monologue: Strobe, old chap — what can they do to you? Think of the worst now. Think of the absolute worst. They could apprehend you. They could spirit you away in a car, and then to the aerodrome and then to Israel and then what? Think of the worst now, Strobe. The worst. A trial, of course. Certainly, there must be a trial. A bookish Biblical breed like the Jews would insist on a ritual of law and order, a set of statutes, legal precedents and official charges and prescribed punishments. But Strobe, old chap — what of the punishments? What would they do to you? Again, the worst. Kill you. Hang you. And what of that? Thirty seconds — forty at the most — of strangulation. Of screaming silently for air. Less than a minute of agony. Strobe, you remember, of course, don't you? You've seen men die. You've seen them die for two, three, six hours. You've seen strangulations performed by experts that would take an afternoon. So think rationally now. What is the worst?

This time, burying his face into the pillow, he forced his eyes closed. There was a moment ... just a single moment ... when he remembered the picture in the art museum. The fisherman in the rowboat on the mountain lake. A brief insanity, he thought. A delusion generated by his fear. The absolute bottom level in the pit of his desperation.

But the scene.

A lake.

The boat.

The peace.

*Old Jews and old Gruppenfuehrers — take note. Ask nothing of God and expect nothing in return. The best that can be hoped for is insanity. The ultimate in man's condition is madness. This must be his salvation.*

The pain subsided in his chest, and his eyes remained closed of their own volition. But his fear stayed with him, perched on the end of the bed, resting with him on the pillow, blooming deep inside of his head like a poison plant. But now he had to sleep. Both body and mind had taken all they could for that one moment. He had to sleep.

A few minutes later he floated in the black design of things, mercifully unaware of Poles, Hungarian gypsies, barking dogs and the unbearable pain of living.

Some sleepless sentry post inside of his mind near the border of his wakefulness gave him warning. A quiet sound outside of his room, but he heard it immediately and was awake in an instant, muscles and nerves taut, heart pounding. He rose quietly from the bed and walked across the room toward the door. He heard the sound again — the scrape of a foot across a thin carpet, then the squeak of a shoe, then the scrape again — this time louder, closer to the door.

Strobe flattened himself against the wall, conscious suddenly of the smallness of the room, its one window three flights up with neither ledge nor fire escape. He had already checked that. A shabby and mean little trap with an antiquated night latch standing between him and whatever nightmare was in the corridor.

The shuffling sound came to an end with one more scrape across the carpet, then a muffled sound against the door. Not a fist — more like the palm of a hand.

Strobe stopped breathing. He heard the sound again. "Who is it?" he whispered. "Who's out there?"

There was a silence from the other side of the door, then a voice in return. "Herr Strobe? Open the door, Herr Strobe."

The voice was a low whistle, like a broken flute. Strobe needed no clues as to identity, but they were there for him. The shuffling drag of a crippled foot; the voice sepulchral and rusty from disuse; the muffled scratch on the door that could only come from a hand broken and rebroken.

Strobe undid the night latch and slowly opened the door.

Zamorski stood there in the corridor. Still he looked no different. His one eye gazed blandly at Strobe. Neither angry nor accusing. If anything, suggestive of an apology. The corners of his thin, bloodless mouth arced upwards. Like a smile. Almost a smile. But not quite a smile.

"Herr Strobe," he said, in his thin, reedy voice. "I followed you, Herr Strobe."

Strobe backed into his room and the cadaver followed him in.

"I followed you," he repeated. "I found out where you went."

Strobe stared at him, fascinated. The perverse, unwilling — and yet compulsive — interest of the man who buys a ticket to a freak show.

"What do you want, Zamorski?" he asked. "What are you doing here?"

"I followed you."

"So you said. You followed me. You followed me and you found me. So here we are, Zamorski. So you have business to transact with me? You have something to tell me ... or something to do to me? Get it over with."

"Herr Lanser is dead."

"Of this I am aware. I saw Herr Lanser. I saw his throat."

"You saw his blood on my hand. I killed him, you know. I cut his throat."

It was remarkable, thought Strobe. Quite remarkable. The ghost was so conversational. And so rational. So matter of fact. So dispassionate about things. He had slit Lanser's jugular and here they discussed it back and forth like a couple of old cronies talking of some mutual friend with a sore throat.

"What is that to me?" Strobe asked him. "I wasn't planning to make an issue of it. You've done away with him in your own way — that was your business. That was not my business."

The apparition stared at him. "Wouldn't you ... wouldn't you like to know why?"

Incredible, Strobe thought. Absolutely incredible. Now there came the logic of the thing. The explanation. A ghost with his dialectics.

Zamorski didn't wait for a reply. He moved closer to the bed. "He did all this to me," he said, turning his broken fingers toward himself. "My bones, my body, my face, my eyes. He did all this to me. He did it with whips and with chains and with branding irons. He did it with racks and pincers and nails and thumbscrews. He did it with screwdrivers and lighted cigarettes."

Incredible, thought Strobe. The Pole has made an inventory of his torment. He has remembered everything. Total recall. And Lanser had called him "mindless."

"So what do you want me to do about it, Zamorski? I never touched you. I did nothing to you. And Herr Lanser has been paid back for whatever he's done. You saw to that."

"But have you, Herr Strobe?" The one eye suddenly lighted up. "Have you paid?" He laughed aloud — a cacophony of sound that was startling in its suddenness and loudness. "Gruppenfuehrer Strobe," the Pole said, raising a withered right arm, "do you know how long I've waited for this? Do you know? I have waited a dozen lifetimes. And would you like to know something else? A really incredible thing. But there have been moments when I felt sorry for Herr Lanser. I felt sorry for him because he had no idea what he was doing. He was insane, like the rest of you. And I felt sorry for him. This is astounding, nicht wahr? That the corpse can feel sorry for the grave digger? That even after all of this, there is still something human left inside me that makes me feel for another man?"

Strobe's mouth felt dry. He felt like a prisoner in the dock. The courtroom was this dark, airless little cell; and the prosecutor was this wraith — this specter, this chimera — who lived when he should have died; who killed when he himself was the victim of murder; who stalked and accused when all the logic and reason on earth dictated that it should be the other way around. Strobe stared at the apparition and then struck out at him, conscious even as he did so that he felt no anger, even when the flat of his hand touched the face. And he felt no satisfaction at all when the Pole doubled up like a bent willow and landed on the floor.

Zamorski lay there for a moment, then slowly rose to his hands and knees and stared up at Strobe. There was no anger in return in the look. To receive pain by blow, whip, branding iron, anything — this was his way of life.

"Zamorski," Strobe said softly, "I can't let you live. You know this, don't you?"

Zamorski nodded. "Of course. Of course," he said, matter-of-factly. "But I must tell you something, Herr Strobe. I pass this onto you now as a lesson. Something you have never learned. You cannot create life by killing. I know that now myself, because tonight I killed and I created nothing."

The Pole, scrabbling, pushing, hanging onto things, got back to his feet and stood there. "So I have paid, Herr Strobe."

The small and tenuous voice seemed to come from a tunnel a hundred miles away. "I, Zamorski, the Pole, have paid by learning the lesson. But I put the question to you. Have *you* paid? Have you paid for all your sins against God? Have you paid for your whips and your gas ovens and your murder camps? I, Zamorski, the Pole — with no bones left and no flesh left and no hope left — I put the question to you, Herr Strobe ... have you paid?"

It seemed the most natural thing in the world for Strobe to do precisely what he did do — reach out and take the thin, pipe-like neck into his hands. He pulled the Pole close to him and very slowly began to squeeze, gradually increasing the pressure with all the strength he had. And while he did so, he had a thought. In all the fifteen years of hell, in all the sleepless nightmares, in all the ravaging fear — this was a fresh incubus. This was the flesh and blood victim come back to haunt. This grotesque somnambulist, who persisted in walking and breathing and talking when long ago he should have relinquished himself to worms, followed him and took away his sleep and would try to reveal his whereabouts. As his fingers tightened around Zamorski' throat, it occurred to him that there would be an irony to this particular death. Zamorski, the Pole, would have to suffer himself to die … only because of his persistence about naming his murderers.

The one eye looked straight into Strobe's face as his breath was slowly shut off. No anger, even now. The same resignation. The dispassionate acceptance of death was identical to his lifelong acceptance of agony. But before his breathing stopped and the one eye closed, he dredged down into the furnace of his life and conjured up one last spark.

"Herr Strobe," he said, as death overtook him. "Herr Strobe — still you lose. You always lose."

Then the breathing stopped. The frail thing that had been Zamorski, the Pole, collapsed under Strobe's grip — a docile and weightless corpse. The bag of parchment skin and toothpick bones slumped to the floor leaving behind only an aged agony in the echo of a voice.

Strobe lighted a cigarette and sat on the bed, staring down at the corpse. Not remorse, he decided — that was not what he felt. Just some vague stirring of regret that it had happened so quietly and so inconsequentially. The Zamorskis of this earth were slowly, piecemeal, destroying him. And when he strangled one of them in his bare hands, it should have been more poetic and more emotional and an incident of some note. As it was, it was almost as if it had never happened. Only the thin, crumpled figure on the floor reminded him of the act. And even this, Strobe felt, was quite unfair. He would still suffer his nightmares. Somehow, Strobe thought, disjointedly, there must be a clue to all of this. It lay somewhere in the fact that the Pole could die with such calmness and self-possession, while he himself would go back to fighting death — joyless and sick with fear, desperate to prolong something that had no value and had run out of meaning. I clutch at life, Strobe thought. I clutch at it because it is all I know and all I have. I have nothing else. I am a forty-seven-year-old expatriate from a dead country, a lost era, a departed time. I have some shirts and some pants and a bed to sleep in, when I can sleep. But I have nothing else. I have not a Goddamned thing else.

He looked down at the dead Pole. Incredible, he thought. Simply incredible. That lump on the floor. That unknown and unmourned collection of scarred skin. He is richer than I. He is happier than I. God alone knows … some God … whatever … that death is the cheapest thing. It is life that costs.

Strobe closed his eyes and sat motionlessly on the bed. This was his insanity. Not that he imagined himself to be transformed into portraits on gallery walls. But that after life had beaten him and torn him to pieces and burned him out and left him rootless and without a single dream — that he should still hunger for life.

He opened his eyes and stared up at the ceiling. There it was, slowly taking form; flowing gradually into the proper lines and the proper colors. A rowboat, a mountain lake, the smell of moss and damp earth and distant flowers. He rose from the bed.

"I don't care," he said to the dead Pole, "if I am simply going mad and that none of it exists. I tell you, I don't care. It is all I have left. It is simply all I have left."

He walked out of the room, down the corridor and the stairs and outside into the street.

Layers of pink and gold stretched across the sky as the day surrendered to twilight. That a whole day had passed was something that Strobe was only dimly aware of. The two violent deaths with the magic interval of the art museum had robbed him of the perspective of time. He studied the sidewalk in both directions, noting that already shops were closing, traffic had slowed down, the city had entered the quiet interval between day's end and the noisy neoned play period that marked the night.

Strobe walked down the sidewalk to the corner and waited for a bus. He had no plan left. Instinct — some kind of reflexive sixth sense — told him to stay on the move, but it was a move with no particular direction and no particular destination.

He took a half-empty bus back toward the center of the city. He got off on the corner of one of the countless little side streets full of nondescript bars blaring out nondescript guitar music and flamenco and a repetitive beat of a tango. He went into the first bar he saw and sat down on a stool. He ordered a double bourbon from a dour, silent bartender — and when it came, cupped the glass in his hand as if it were hot coffee. He sipped at it — long, luxurious slurps — while the bartender stared at him, unsmiling. He felt the liquid hot in his throat and then hot in his innards. He had had no food for over twenty hours, and after the first drink he could feel the enveloping glow of alcohol begin to push away the tensions. He ordered another double and this one he threw down in a gulp and then savored the gradual dulling of sight and sounds. Already he was beginning not to give a damn that Zamorski was dead in his room and that at this moment he was nothing but a cork bobbing in the sea of the city with literally no place to go. He smiled at the bartender and tapped his finger on the bar for another drink. It was poured and handed to him, and the room, to Strobe, was beginning to look cozy and comfortable. Stronger, more lasting and persistent than any whiskey was a little nugget of knowledge inside of his brain that told him that this was ersatz. This diminishing of tension was the counterfeit contentment of the middle stage of a drunk. But his mind was too worn and frazzled from the collective shocks of the day to really care much. He smiled again at the bartender, feeling a rising compulsion to talk — to be friendly, to make comment on things.

"You have a nice place here," he said, thickly, with his accent. "A very nice place. I like small and intimate bars."

The bartender nodded, not giving a good Goddamn what kind of bar this German preferred.

"You should have music though," Strobe said, with mild reprobation.

The bartender nodded again, winding up his classification of the heavy-set man in front of him. He knew the type. It was a familiar breed of compulsive drinker who would spend at least two hours trying to escape into a bottle and getting very profound in the process. If you ignored them they sometimes shut up. He turned his back and busied himself, drying some glasses. But Strobe's voice followed him.

"A friend of mine had a bar near the Palacio del Congreso. He had a tuba player who played every evening. He himself played the bass. The customers would join in the singing."

The bartender, his back to Strobe, nodded a terse, short nod.

"His name was Lanser. Not much of a man, really. A countryman of mine. That much he was. But a wheedler. A fawner with certain delusions. That was his trouble. He had delusions."

The bartender looked up at Strobe's reflection in the bar mirror. This one would go on for quite some time. He was sure of this. Why the hell did the mouths always come in here?

Strobe smiled at him. "I myself," he continued, portentously, "have no delusions. None. I know what the world is." The liquor bubbled inside of him, loosening his restraint. "The world is actually a cesspool. It is a septic tank. Were you aware of that? And we humans are very small turds floating along in it with the singular destiny of being dissolved. That, my friend, is what the world is and what we are."

The bartender nodded again in agreement with this talkative plumbing expert. The world was, indeed, a septic tank and a cesspool, if that's what the man wanted. Or it was an Elysian fields. The customer was always right. Particularly, he decided, when the customer had already had eight shots of bourbon and had red-rimmed, brooding eyes and a look on his face that could mean trouble.

Strobe turned in his stool to survey the room. The faces of the people kept slipping in and out of focus, detaching themselves into twins. Strobe had to squint to make each face become one again. He catalogued the faces, searching for eyes that might be interested and sympathetic. Find someone, perhaps, who would understand. He wanted to talk about the picture in the art museum and what had happened that afternoon. And how desperately, and with a sick ache, he craved to relive the experience. If he could just find someone to talk to — to discuss things with. The Jews, for example. They could talk about what had been done to them ... and why it was so necessary that it had been done. But then, even better, some new thing emerged, shining, in Strobe's mind. A woman. That's what he would like now. A woman. Some fat and buxom body that he could burrow against. Some thickly built, fleshy form with giant breasts and meaty thighs. A tub of a woman that he could put his fingers against to touch and feel and pinch and squeeze and hurt. Hurt. This is what he wanted. It was a part of his passion, and always had been. Though he had never allowed himself to think of it that way, pain and passion had always been intertwined in all of the endless hours on back seats and barrack mattresses and everywhere else where he had taken a woman. His language of love had been a woman's scream. He could not kiss without biting. He could not caress without tearing. He could find no fulfillment unless it came with the giving of pain. But he could explain this, too, if he could find someone to talk to.

He left the bar stool and moved his heavy bulk across the room, stumbling against a chair, knocking a glass off a table. One couple looked up, startled, whispered something and then turned away. The bartender kept staring at him, his long, sallow face grim. That Goddamned drunken Heinie would start something, sure as hell. One hand slid under the bar to a blackjack hidden behind some bottles.

Strobe paused in the center of the room and blinked his eyes, staring, listening, hungering for things, hungering to be a part of the conversations, hungering to be one of them, hungering to live.

Yes, that was it — to live. He had to live. As Zamorski had had to live. Suffering all the torments of hell on earth, he had yet had to live, if only for his revenge. And he, Strobe, had to live, as well. Because life was all there was. It was precious and irreplaceable, and its value was infinite. *He must live!* His drunken, haggard eyes swept across the room as people stopped their conversation to look at him.

"I must tell you all something," he said, thickly. "I must tell you all that life is the thing. Living is the thing. Existing. Being — that is all that counts." The tears rolled down his face. "I ... I, Strobe, must live. I must be." Then, blindly, he stumbled across the room and out the door, leaving behind a collective murmur of surprise ... of questions that followed him into the night.

To clutch at seaweed as it floated by; or at thin, fragile straws; or at a frail, errant hope — this was the night for clutching. So Strobe went to Herr Gruber's apartment. To hell with pride. To hell with worrying about a feast of humble pie. To hell with everything except survival. He remembered, from a long time before, some-one pointing out Gruber's apartment to him. Very fancy. Very posh. Herr Gruber was an expatriate of some means. A doorman out front. A carpeted lobby.

Strobe went there ready to rip open the front doors with his bare hands; ready to strangle the doorman or kill the elevator operator or climb up the side of the building — whatever was needed to see Gruber. Whatever was required to tell him that he must have a passport, he must have money, he must use Gruber's connections. To clutch. That was the order of the night. To clutch at all things — at everything — so that he would live and see the morning and the other mornings.

As he expected, there was an argument with the doorman. No, the Grubers were not seeing anyone. No, he would not phone up to the Gruber apartment. No, it was a waste of his time. But Strobe had simply pushed him out of the way and gotten into the self-service elevator and taken the ride up. He did not hear the doorman shouting after him, screaming at him that the Grubers were only seeing relatives and personal friends. That something had happened. Strobe heard none of it. He got off on the third floor where he had heard Gruber's apartment was. He walked down the carpeted corridor, arrived at the properly numbered door and pounded on it. After a moment the door opened. A woman dressed in black. Gruber's Brazilian wife. He had heard of her, too. White-blond hair, an aristocratic face — stern, forbidding, but beautiful nonetheless. Strobe felt his impetus slipping, but desperation drove him on.

"Frau Gruber?" he said, with a bow. "Frau Gruber, I am a friend of your husband's. It is imperative that I see him." He stepped inside, putting a foot against the door. "Please. Please allow me to talk to him. It will only take a moment."

The woman stared at him noncommittally. "And you are —?"

"Strobe." He supplied her with the information. "Joseph Strobe. I was with ... the German Army." He tacked this on — false credentials like a door pass, manufactured just for the moment. "The German Army," he repeated. "Your husband knows me very well." He watched the woman as she looked him up and down. An odd one, he thought. She was not afraid. He knew what he must look like — sweating and smelling and wild — but yet, she was not afraid.

"Herr Strobe?" she asked softly. "When did you last see my husand?"

"Yesterday evening," Strobe said hurriedly. "We had a chat together at Lanser's rathskeller. We had ... a long chat." He wet his lips, his eyes furtively looking around and beyond her, hoping Gruber was there and would come out. "As a matter of fact ..." He tried to sound boyish and pleasant and to laugh. "... we had a few words together. That is ... that is the point of the call. I felt I should apologize. We are both under a strain." His eyes searched her face. Did she know? Was she aware of what was happening to him and to Gruber? Did she know of the black sedans and the photographs and the rest of it? He wanted to ask her directly, but her coolness, her self-assurance, the way she looked at him — it kept him off balance. It made him afraid to ask. "Is he in?" Strobe asked. "May I see him?" Again he noticed that the woman was studying him. A careful, probing look. What in Christ's name did she want of him? Why couldn't she answer his simple questions? Was Gruber in or was he out? Was he receiving or was he packing his bag inside of his bedroom? Why, in Christ's name, couldn't she just tell him? "Is he in, Frau Gruber?" His voice took on a grating, jagged edge as more of his desperation forced itself into his tone. "It's really quite imperative that I see him."

"Herr Strobe," the woman said to him, "when he came home yesterday evening, he told me of his conversation with you. He told me much of you."

Strobe felt sudden surprise. "He spoke of me?" he asked. "Of me? Strobe?"

"Joseph Strobe, and you had something to do with Auschwitz. You were a good Nazi, my husband said. An exceptionally good Nazi."

Strobe tried to read something into the woman's words, into her inflection. A good Nazi. But was she saying that as a judgment or as a passing commentary or as an accusation? The woman was inexplicable. She was opaque glass — impossible to see through. Impossible to analyze.

Strobe felt nerves on top of nerves, new fear enveloping his constant and familiar fear. "I ... I served with the SS," he said.

"So my husband said. Tell me, Herr Strobe. Were you as successful at your job as my husband mentioned? He led me to believe that you were quite an important man."

Ah, thought Strobe — one of us. No question about it. One of us. A clearheaded woman. A wise woman. He felt the aged pride come back to him like a mantle draped over his shoulders. He smiled. He made his voice sound important. "I was a Gruppenfuehrer, Frau Gruber."

"So?" she said to him, softly. "And you killed many people?"

It seemed to Strobe that she was smiling at him. Fine. Excellent. She wanted to hear. So he would tell her. "Many?" he asked her. "Many people?" And then it came out of him — a pouring, unchecked torrent of pride, flooding over the ramparts of years of restraint and fear. "You might say, Frau Gruber, that I had a hand in the destruction of a sizable number of enemies of the state. Consider, if you will, please, that there were many men under me. But by my orders ... by my direct orders, I would imagine that several thousand were put into ovens. At least that many." He felt his hands shake as he spoke and looked down at them. He tried to stop the shaking, but it was impossible. This, however, was no movement of fear. This was the pride again. The excitement that came with the pride. Because he could remember other hands. Clawing, grasping hands — pleading, begging hands. Torn and broken hands. The memory filled him with warmth and, again, pride. Pride. They had shaken the earth — he and the others. That part of history was no myth. They had collected one half of the world and put barbed wire around it. "I am pleased, Frau Gruber," he said, thickly, feeling the liquor again. "I am most pleased that you understand. There are many who don't."

"Jews," she supplied.

He looked at her suddenly. "Why, yes," he agreed. "Jews."

"They're after my husband — these Jews."

So she did know. Well and good. Better that way. "Yes," he said, sympathetically, "they're after your husband and after me. But I can assure you, Frau Gruber ... I can assure you that your husband and I are made of the same stuff. We don't roll over and die just because a handful of Jews decide to throw a net over us. Not your husband and I. We are not that kind of man."

It was then that he saw the look on her face. A subtle change — an almost imperceptible alteration. The change, in itself, revealed nothing. But still ... there was a change.

"Herr Strobe," she said, after a moment's pause, "I don't know really what kind of man *you* are, but I know my husband, or at least … I knew him. He would never permit himself to be taken by Jews. That kind of irony he couldn't live with. He was the kind of man, you see, Herr Strobe, who would pick his own way to die." There was a moment's silence. "My husband hanged himself last night. In the basement of this building. He paid the price, Herr Strobe — but he preferred his own form of currency."

Her lips trembled. There was grief there in the face — an unutterable, unspeakable grief — but Strobe could not grasp what she was saying. There was, he decided, a joke going on. A joke that eluded him. The woman was obviously not speaking literally. This was that meat-cleaver, heavy wit, so very Prussian, that her husband had probably taught her.

"Frau Gruber," he said. "Frau Gruber, I'm afraid I don't understand —"

"Don't you?" she asked him. "Are you stupid, Herr Strobe? It's really quite simple. My husband came home last night from the rathskeller. We talked for an hour or so, then he left the house — supposedly to take a walk. I never saw him again … alive."

Strobe exhaled, but breath was all that could come out. Not words. Not language.

"But you should feel complimented, Herr Strobe. His last thoughts were of you."

"Of me?" Strobe said dumbly. "Of me?"

"Of you," she answered. "He said that when he looked at you it was as if he were looking at a machine that he had built; that he had designed and planned and created. He said that there were normally decent Germans who had created a monster. But that the real crime came in that the monster was not created in their image … but the other way around. It was the monster who usurped and corrupted until it reached a point where Germany became a nation of monsters."

She closed her eyes. Strobe saw the tears on her face. He stared at her. So much death, he thought. So much death over a period of a few hours. Lanser. Gruber. The Pole. And each with a confessional. A few bon mots to salvage the soul. To justify. To excuse. To expiate.

"My God, Frau Gruber," he whispered, "I didn't know. I simply didn't know." Then, with his stomach feeling ice cold, while the rest of him burned in fire, he shook his head back and forth. "What shall I do?" he asked her. "What shall I do? I thought he might help me. He had connections, he said. He had friends or relatives or someone who could change his passport. I came here tonight to beg him ... to plead with him ... to help me."

He noticed then that the woman had stopped crying. She was staring at him again, and her mouth looked crooked, and she had grown very pale.

"Herr Strobe," she said, her voice soft, "he has already helped you. Though you may not understand it, he has shown you the way. He has demonstrated to you that there is a moment when life simply runs out."

"No!" Strobe roared at her. "There is no such point. No one ... no one willingly takes on death. That's crazy. That's insane. You must clutch at life. You must take it to you. You must hold onto it — covet it, protect it. It is all there is." He stood there, shaking, sweating, his eyes pleading for understanding.

"I see," the woman said, almost in a whisper. "It is life that is so sweet, life that is so precious."

"Exactly," he said to her. "Exactly that."

"Then tell me, Herr Strobe. As to the Jews and all the others whose lives you took. What about them? What about their lives?"

Strobe wanted to claw at his head to let his thoughts out. Phrases stuck together. Ideas seemed glued to the inside of him. "The Jews? The others? But you don't understand. You simply don't understand. They had no right to survive. And there was no alternative.

We had no other choice. It was either them or us. You understand that, don't you? Them or us."

The woman nodded. "Them or us," she repeated. "Why, it's arithmetical, isn't it, Herr Strobe? It's an equation of a sort, isn't it? Them or us."

"That's it," Strobe said, eagerly. "That's what it comes down to."

"What a pity," the woman said. "What a pity my husband never understood this. It was his feeling, Herr Strobe, that he had run out on his faith. That he had betrayed it."

"Faith!" Strobe clutched at the word and shouted it aloud. "Faith, indeed. That's what I'm talking about, Frau Gruber. I'm *talking* about faith. We had a faith, you see. It is what we believed in. Germany was a faith. The Fuehrer was a faith. Our destiny was a faith."

"I see," she whispered to him. "Why, Herr Strobe, you've done yourself an injustice. You should have explained that to me. You should have explained it to my husband, too. Why, you've not credited yourself properly. You've been misjudged. You had no particular passion for killing, did you? That's obvious now. Killing was ... well, it was a faith, wasn't it? A religion. And the crematoriums — they were shrines, weren't they? And the gas ovens — temples of worship. And the slaughter of children — this was just some kind of ceremonial, wasn't it? A sacrament. And here all along I thought your kind dealt in butchery. Nothing of the sort, Herr Strobe. A religion. A faith. That's what it was."

Why, Strobe realized suddenly — this woman hates me. She despises me. See how she backs away from me — how she inches off, as if recoiling. Actually recoiling. "I've ... I've said the wrong things to you, Frau Gruber," he said. "You mourn your husband and here I come into your home when you would rather be alone." It was not really what he wanted to say, but at the moment he did not know *what* to say. He only knew he couldn't let this woman escape. Somehow, some way, he had to capture her goodwill, appeal to her, make her sympathize with him. "You see, Frau Gruber ... your husband ... your husband needed understanding. One reaches ... for understanding."

"Is that what you're looking for?" The woman's voice sounded suddenly harsh. "Understanding?"

"Something of the sort," Strobe said, feeling the awful urge to cry. "I've been hunted like an animal. At this moment ... I swear to you ... like your husband, I am being hunted just like an animal." He blinked back his tears. "But I am not an animal. *I am no animal!*"

Frau Gruber was silent for a long moment, then she walked closer to him, her eyes never leaving him. "Of course, you're no animal, Herr Strobe," she said. "An animal takes no joy in killing. Nor does it ever feel the urgent necessity to explain its killing. If you were an animal, Herr Strobe, I might offer you the understanding you seek."

With the sudden selective clarity of alcohol, Strobe saw her lips twitch and heard her voice for the first time sound high and unsteady — almost uncontrolled.

"What you are, Herr Strobe, is quite another thing from an animal. You are a pervert. You are a butcher of six million people. But you are no human being, either. A human being could not fill so many graves and think of it as an offense that might be apologized for. Like a belch after a meal, or picking one's nose at the opera. What you have done to this earth, Herr Strobe, is not an offense. It is a mortal sin that even God cannot forgive. But that you walk the streets — and others like you — this is a sin I attribute to God. Something that I can't forgive Him for."

Strobe kept shaking his head back and forth, mentally putting up his hands, trying to ward her off, trying to shut out her words, "Frau Gruber," he said, "please ... please —"

She was so close to him now, less than a hand's length away, that their faces were almost touching. An insane woman. Really. An insane woman.

"Herr Strobe," she whispered at him. "Do you want to hear a really monstrous thing? Do you want to know how sick with guilt this poor dead husband of mine really was? He married a Jewess. He actually married a Jewess. This corrupt, strutting Prussian who was dying of sadness and dying of regrets and dying from all the guilt that choked him. But even more monstrous, Herr Strobe — even more unbearable ..." Her voice trailed off into what sounded like a sob. "... I loved him." Speech came back to her. "A Jewess loved him. God help me. God forgive me. I loved him."

Not real, Strobe thought. Not real at all. This was fantasy. Mere fantasy. She's just saying these things. She's still trying to confuse me.

"Now leave me, Herr Strobe." Her voice was suddenly ice cold. "I have much mourning ahead of me. I have to mourn my husband's death and also his life. I have to mourn his guilt ... in addition to my own." Her eyes had closed. Now she opened them and stared at him. "But this ... this one last thing, Herr Strobe."

She advanced on him and Strobe backed against the wall, stumbling over his feet, looking at this white, stricken face that exuded such hate.

"Before you leave, Herr Strobe," she said, following him, "before you leave ... this little sign of an affection that you seem so to crave. This little gesture of love. A kiss for you, Herr Strobe. May it be the first of many."

The flat of her hand smashed against his cheek. The nails left a gouged furrow as the hand went past him, and then he found himself out in the corridor, the door slammed in his face, the echo of it reverberating through the corridor. Automatically he turned and walked toward the elevator, and automatically — unthinking, unseeing — he pushed the button, and with his mind still numb, he found himself down on the sidewalk. Again, his lungs, like bellows, wheezed and sent out streams of sporadic pain. Cars went back and forth. Any moment ... any moment one of them might stop. He ran down the sidewalk,, thinking of the woman, seeing the look of ice-cold rage, stronger than her mourning, deeper than her grief.

*This was the crime of the Jew. That they could still show fury. That they could be trampled into the earth, their flesh burned away. That they could leave nothing behind but gold fillings and the smell of smoke. But somehow ... some way ... they survived. They always survived. They came at you in the dead of night, or enticed you in their apartments, chaperoned by the ghosts of dead Aryan husbands. Zamorski, Strobe wanted to scream up into the night sky. Zamorski, he wanted to say, you were wrong. I have paid. I am paying now. You people are still collecting the debt of fifteen years. You are tearing chunks out of my body. And chunks out of my brain. Zamorski — in the name of the Jew, Christ — close the ledger book. Close it, please. You have been paid in full.*

Nightmare. Walking and running and hiding. A newscast from a radio in an open window. The body of Vladislau Zamorski — no known address — found strangled in a hotel room. Police seek link with previous night's murder of saloon owner, Karl Lanser. And there was a picture of Zamorski on a television set in an appliance-store window. Zamorski, as seen in the frozen white light of a coroner's flashbulb. At last the world had taken note of Zamorski, the Pole. It had found out his first name and acknowledged it on television. It had given him a shot of formaldehyde without charge, and an accommodation on a slab, along with a case number in a police file. And wheels had been set in motion to find out who it was that had choked the life out of him. The sad and ugly little irony of Zamorski, the Pole, who had had to die to achieve an identity and a first name and someone to care. During his wretched and tortured life, no one had even said a prayer for him. And there he was in the unkind flash of a camera bulb, laying claim in death to the single legacy he had been denied in life — the simple acknowledgment that he was a human being.

More nightmare. Strobe, running and running and running, and seeing the face of Zamorski reflected in every store window. A dark and one-eyed Caliban; a Polish Cyclops. And even as he ran, Strobe saw the new irony. Now he was running from the police. There were new hunters. Every prowl car that drove by might suddenly stop and a spotlight whirl toward him. Seek him out in the darkness. Pinion him in a stab of light. A new crime to pay for. One man. One lousy Pole. Added to the list — the ten-thousand-name list. Put it on top of the mountainous pile of names — the funeral pyre built so long ago. And maybe this one name — maybe this one thin, bloodless skeleton would make the column topple; would bring the whole structure crashing down. More sidewalks. More blocks. More shadowed buildings. The black sedan, not visible now — but someplace. And still the running. Avert the faces of other people. His own face might be known by now. Hide. Hide first in a park by a bench. No good there. Police patrol the parks hourly. Movie house. Possibility. Thrown away. Too public. Might be seen in the lobby. Bus. Take a bus. No good, either. Getting late. Not many people riding. Easily picked out. *There is the seaweed floating by. There is the slender straw. This way to salvation. Use this exit out of hell. And Strobe knew. The art museum. The picture, with him in the rowboat. The eternity of peace. Immortality in a rowboat on a mountain lake. I, Joseph Strobe, do hereby resign from the human race, effective immediately. I resign from my running in shadows. I resign from lying on my mattress and painting nightmares on the ceiling. I resign from Gruber's guilt and Lanser's blood-spattered naïveté, and I resign from the Lord's vengeance.*

But another act of the nightmare. Two blocks from the art museum, he saw the black sedan again. Its lights were on. It was moving slowly down the street toward him, and then it pulled up to a curb and stopped. Two men got out from the front seat and started to walk toward him. Not Brazilian brush salesmen. Not American tourists waiting for their wives. Not policemen, either. Two men in dark suits. One walked toward him on the sidewalk. The other crossed the street diagonally, then stood waiting on the opposite curb. There was something in his hand. It glinted in the street light. More Jews with teeth. And with a capacity for fury. And with memories.

Strobe turned and ran. He could hear the footsteps of the men behind him keeping pace. He turned the corner, hesitating for a moment, then started down a side street. The footsteps were getting closer. Into the back parking lot of a building. A truck was just moving away from a loading platform. He stumbled, fell — unconscious of pain or of the fact that he could barely breathe or that his body was a gushing fountain of sweat and filth. He was momentarily hidden by the departing truck and used that moment to fling himself onto the loading platform and through an open door into the building. Up metal stairs to a second floor. He heard the voices of the two men down below. There were footsteps across the macadam of the parking lot. One man was going around to the front. There were other footsteps starting up the metal stairs behind him. Second-floor fire door locked. He pulled and pushed, strained, pounded with his fists. The footsteps were almost to him. Up another flight, his legs like concrete, no longer flesh and blood but more like extensions of himself that went through the motions of obeying him. Street level. Third floor. This door open. He pushed his way through and entered a total darkness.

But now he knew where he was.

The art museum.

A miracle, like the Red Sea opening. He had made it.

There were the dim outlines of paintings on the walls. There were shadowy statues in the corners. He ran down the middle of the room toward another distant door, hearing the one behind him open as his pursuer joined him in the darkness. His head brushed something that swung away from him. He remembered. The mobile. He was in the room! He was in the very room! He stumbled and reached out to hold himself from falling. One hand grazed a statue. His head hit the metal pedestal and even the pain seemed unrelated to him. The footsteps of the man ran past him, then stopped, then started running again — first to one side, then the other — to a far corner, then a near one.

The footsteps continued, first loud, then softer — nearer, then farther away, playing hide and seek with him in the darkness. But it was only a question of time. He knew he could neither fight nor defend himself. He had run out of strength. He was the animal at the end of the hunt — surrounded, enclosed, exhausted, and soon to be caged.

But this could not be the end. He willed that it would not be the end. Some intuitive, blind and impulsive thing inside of him guided him and strengthened him. And for a reason.

As the footsteps moved back and forth, getting closer, Strobe looked across from his shadowed lair to the indistinct frame of a picture across the room.

Fisherman. Boat. Mountain lake. Peace.

*I have nothing left. I am emptied. I am some stale breath left over from a death rattle. I have known hell. Whatever I owed, I paid. Please ... please ... let me have my peace now. Let me back into the picture.*

He closed his eyes and, while the footsteps grew closer and the figure of the man became discernible, hovering over him, staring down at him, he forced himself through some mystic resolve — some incredible will born of the last shred of desperation's strength — to disappear from the room and from the earth. He moved quietly and unobserved into a painting.

The assistant curator looked sleepily at his watch, then toward the night watchman, who sucked noisily on an unlighted pipe.

"It's two o'clock in the morning," the assistant curator said, irritably. He gazed down the length of paintings, took a few steps off to one side to look behind a pillar toward some statuary, then returned to stand near the night watchman.

"There were noises," the night watchman said defensively. "I heard them very plainly. Footsteps, men running up and down the back stairs —"

The assistant curator rubbed his beard stubble and nodded sleepily and with bored eyes. "I'm not saying you didn't hear voices, Pablo," he said for the fifth or sixth time that night. "I'm simply saying that whoever was here is no longer here. And whoever was here did no damage."

The night watchman pointed toward the base of one of the statues. "What about the blood on the floor?"

The assistant curator shrugged. "Whoever was here tripped and fell." He pointed to the statue. "Bumped his head." He shrugged again, then took a slow walk over to the light switch panel near the main entrance of the room. He flicked off the lights.

The night watchman's flashlight threw out a pale yellow ray that played over the various pictures. He walked toward the assistant curator, switching off the flashlight, and then abruptly turned it on again to let the light play against the far wall.

"What's the matter?" the assistant curator asked. "Still hearing noises?"

"Didn't you hear that one?"

The assistant curator listened. There had been a noise. Nothing distinct. A very distant cry — the cry of an animal or the cry of someone in terrible pain. He frowned and flicked on the light switch again to look down the expanse of the room. He listened again. There was no further sound. He turned to the night watchman. "Dog or something. Must have been run over."

The night watchman nodded but was unconvinced. "I've been hearing it for the last hour. A cry of some kind."

The assistant curator nodded absentmindedly, then looked toward a blank space on the wall. He pointed to it. "What happened to the concentration-camp thing? Was that one of those sent out tonight?"

The night watchman shook his head. "No. We just moved it over there." He pointed across the room to the far wall. "*The Fisherman* is on loanout. The director told me to put the concentration-camp thing in its place."

The assistant curator looked toward the painting of the man, arms outstretched on the cross. Hateful-looking thing. He'd never liked it. But it was odd about the picture. Much of its detail seemed to become evident only after one observed it for a period of time. For example, he thought, walking over toward the painting — he had never noticed the face of the victim on the canvas or the fact that he was a heavy-set porcine man with a naked skull and blue eyes. Yes, you could actually see the blue eyes — open wide, with such a look of agony and such a look of terror, frozen there in paint — but incredibly alive looking. He shuddered and almost winced as he turned away from the painting. Really an ugly thing. A disturbing thing. Why, in God's name, did some artists persist in dredging up aged horrors like that? He motioned to the night watchman ahead of him and flicked off the light switch. As the two men left the room, each one thought he heard — but neither mentioned — the persistent, thin cry that arose from the darkened room behind them.

The assistant curator went home.

The night watchman brewed himself a hot cup of coffee.

And two Israelis drove slowly through the dark streets back to their hotel, neither of them speaking, but one of them thinking over and over again, "A man just can't disappear. He simply just can't disappear."

And former Gruppenfuehrer Strobe hung on a cross, screaming — constantly screaming — perpetually screaming. And he would never again stop.

# COLOR SCHEME

*Color Scheme* was Sammy Davis, Jr's original idea. He told it to me one night over a beer It stayed with me for five years ... haunting, intrusive and preoccupying. Television wouldn't touch it. I hope I've done it justice — giving birth to Sammy's baby on the following printed pages.

...

On the morning of the pilgrimage, the crusaders arrived in a 1935 Dodge pickup with its transmission packed with sawdust, a similiar-vintage Ford sedan with no muffler, a half a dozen buckboards, and the rest on foot. They came in quiet, straggly little groups — all seventy-eight of them, not counting the children — and stood there in the "churchyard," waiting for Gabriel or Christ or whoever to bugle them into the Promised Land. The "church" was a weatherbeaten oversized shack with an unpainted hand-sawed wooden cross perched atop one of its slumping gables. It had once been a pool hall — before that, a saloon, and before that, variously, a schoolhouse, a bus station and, during a less devout period, a one-dollar whorehouse known as the Mid-Mississippi Social Club.

There was a sign underneath the cross which read, THE FIRST BAPTIST CHURCH OF CHASEVILLE. But even the sign could not detract from the ugly image of the house, squatting there like an aged courtesan doing belated penance for its gallons of rotgut whiskey, its million hours of snooker, and every act of illicit love bought and paid for in one of its dusty little cubicles. The cross, of course, was His symbol. But it looked like some foreign object mustered out of the dust as a forlorn reminder that God was not dead, He was simply hiding someplace in the State of Mississippi. Sitting tilt in the hot early morning sun, it seemed not to have been raised aloft in a fervor of piety, but, rather, to have been nailed there as a last-minute crucifixion. Still it was part of the day's pilgrimage.

The crusaders each carried a placard or a sign or an American flag while they stood there, silent and motionless. WE SHALL OVERCOME, the signs read. FREEDOM AND JUSTICE FOR ALL — that was the message on the placards. LOVE THY NEIGHBOR — ever so neatly printed and emphasizing the nonviolent character of the morning's crusade. It was noticed by the white Unitarian minister out of Chicago, Illinois, as well as by a cameraman looking through a telescopic lens on an NBC mobile tape truck across the way, that the signs were not held aloft or flaunted or waved or brandished. They were clutched close to the bodies in unyielding black fists, suggestive of the secret wonder that these people felt at what they were doing. That morning they were going to go marching — all seventy-eight of them. They were going to go marching. And in Chaseville, Mississippi — for seventy-eight black-skinned believers — that was one hell of a march!

Oven-hot, dusty air swirled across the tracks in miniature whirlpools with thin little wails of sound. For a moment it was the only sound, until a voice came back at them from the "Promised Land" — a line of cars a thousand yards beyond them, across the tracks. It was a loudspeaker attached to a black car from the sheriff's department, and the voice that came out of it rode the waves of the early morning heat with a deafening electronic blast. The rebuttal from Canaan. A pale prophet with a badge talking into a microphone and announcing that there was no Messiah and this was not Judgment Day. This was the State of Mississippi, and any gathering, assembly or march was illegal and would be punishable by imprisonment.

"Now you nigras," the sheriff's voice blared out, "we don't want no trouble here, and if you all had sense, you'd go back to your houses and you wouldn't let no troublemakers come down here and make you do somethin' you're gonna be sorry for. Now you all listen to them agitators and you're gonna wind up in jail. That is, if you're lucky. I'm gonna tell you somethin' right now — if you come marchin' across these tracks, I ain't guaranteein' protection that'll get you *into* a jail. There's a lot of townsfolk over here who may get to you before I do. So I'm tellin' you — stay on that side of the tracks, and that way there won't *be* no trouble!"

Then the pale prophet surveyed the line of equally pale archangels — those deputies of the Lord — and he saw how they held tight to their shotguns and bicycle chains and cattle prods. He knew their tensions — because they were his. And he knew the reasons. The enemy wasn't just that black handful across the tracks, carrying placards and hopped up on "love" and "brotherhood." This was just an advance guard brimming over with sugary bullshit that dictated that they turn their cheeks. But beyond that handful of seventy-eight black lovers were seventy-eight thousand — and beyond them, more than ten million — spread across the South. This was no handful. This was a black mass who on some given morning might grow immune to the needle of brotherly love. And when *that* mass took a march it would require more than a line of deputies and a loudspeaker. This is what the sheriff thought as he looked toward the tracks. If he could nip a black flower in the bud before it grew into a vine — before it spread out and smothered them. But careful of the roots. Careful of destroying the plant. It would not be sap that flowed across the land. He knew this with a sick and frightening certainty.

The black crusaders clutched their placards and signs and flags tighter and felt a chill from the voice. They would not retreat — they *could* not retreat — but an age-old fear sent a ripple of wavering through their resolve. A two-hundred-year habit pattern could not be dispelled in a morning. Pride and dignity and a sense of their own worth — this was brand-new. This was only three summers' old. It had started when they saw the first pictures of the black sea of faces marching down Pennsylvania Avenue. And then had come the deadly earnest young college students who had been with them the previous summer, telling them how to register and vote. They had felt an incredible stirring inside them and this was not to be denied by a loudspeaker. But they were still back-country Mississippi niggers. And a gut-deep awareness of their blackness came back to them when the sheriff's voice boomed across the dust-filled summer air in a fuzzy and indistinct anger. Clutching their flags and placards and signs, they still felt the sick impulses of the other time. White men. Silver badge. Sovereignty, like some divine right, hovered there in the hot stillness of the morning — implacable and insurmountable. Authority with a Sam Browne belt and a low-slung holster and the gray hawk-eyes underneath the broad-brimmed Stetson. March right up to the Capitol steps — hallelujah. Tell the President of the U.S. that the black citizen is ready and is knockin' and is askin' for what is his. Hallelujah. And hear what Dr. King is sayin' for us. Hallelujah. We got leaders now. We got men up front in suits and shoes and sayin' the words. Praise be God Almighty! The words! Like notes on a trumpet. Like the clarion call of angels. The black man had a voice now.

But in the heat of the Mississippi morning, the notes of the trumpet seemed to fade. The voice of the pale prophet with the hawk-eyes was immediate and had substance and solidity. It chipped at their dream. It brought back a remembrance of fear. Prayers and hopes and visions — they were good to contemplate. But across the tracks were a row of cars and a line of deputies with shotguns, bicycle chains and cattle prods.

With the instinct of a thousand years, they moved closer to one another and felt their mouths go dry. March, man, march. Carry them banners. Shout out them slogans. But, Jesus — look at them deputies. Look at that row of khaki. Look at them big-snouted riot guns. It ain't Pennsylvania Avenue no more. And who suddenly had hidden all the Glory? It's a county seat in a red-neck slice of the Mississippi map; it's a hot sonuvabitch of a July mornin'. And we is seventy-eight black people all filled up with slogans tellin' everybody to love, love, love. And across the tracks there stands Mister Charlie with the twitchy, anxious finger and with the ice-cold fierceness in his eyes. And he ain't about to love, love, love. Freedom, hallelujah! Votes — praise be to God. And to be equal — and treated as humans — Great Day in the Morning! You gonna vote, man. You gonna be equal. You gonna send your chilluns to da school. *But how you gonna do it if you dead?*

*The white Unitarian minister out of Chicago, Illinois, is committed to Good Works. He had met his God at the Meadville Theological School and had decided then that God was fallible and needed help. This is why he is in Mississippi. Because of principles. Principles. Man is essentially decent and fine and honorable. So he makes his short and earnest little speech. He puts the placards and signs into the hands of his black brothers and he tells them to march, unafraid. But then he looks across the tracks at his white brothers and feels the cold wind of doubt. Two and a half blocks away from where he lives in Chicago, Illinois, black men like this had marched, and those essentially decent and fine and honorable white men had brandished swastikas and thrown bricks and laughed when a nun bled all over her bib and fell to the pavement, because she had joined the march. St. George — you Goddamned stupid bastard. There was a dragon in Illinois. What the hell are you doing down here in Mississippi, trying to slay it?*

*So the white Unitarian minister, committed to Good Works, feels a fear of his own. He wants the comfort of an abstract commitment to decency. He doesn't want to walk into the muzzles of riot guns. He's not built for this. But it's too late. Too late in the morning. Too late in the history of man — to back away. He has helped to recruit the Army. And nobody resigns. Nobody.*

The Mayor of Chaseville arrived on the scene in a Legionnaire's cap. He would have preferred a red sash and a dangling sword, because in three terms as mayor, he had long since tired of the small take, the few and predictable prerogatives and the titular dullness of running a provincial little red-neck burg full of cronies and relatives and behind suckers — a town that really ran itself. He put his profile to the cameras as he got out of the car with the flashing red light and the siren and started walking toward the sheriff. He was an aging tiger on the scent and on the prowl and wishing to God he could turn that grubby little town into a decent-sized battlefield and give those Yankee grabbers behind their television cameras something to really shoot that would make news.

He approached the sheriff and beckoned to him. The sheriff simply nodded, looking at him bored and a little pityingly — as a Regular Army man surveys a civilian. Finally it was the mayor who had to walk over to the sheriff. He looked up and down the line of deputies — importantly, strategically — then cleared his throat.

"Jim," he whispered in a voice that could be overheard fifty yards away, "if any of them coons come at you with razors or anythin' else — you know what to do."

The hawk-eyes looked gimlet-gray; the voice was cold. "Throw grenades?" he asked quietly.

"You know what I mean. If they come at you, you gotta duty to perform."

And you, the sheriff thought, have a few duties of your own — like putting a clamp on this town and getting people off the streets and maybe coming out with a proclamation or two to add a few feet to the fuse so this fucking little hamlet doesn't blow itself to hell before lunchtime. This, instead of parading around like some Goddamned monkey in a comic hat looking like a majordomo fresh out of a nut factory.

"I count almost a hundred of 'em, Mister Mayor. Now if a hundred townspeople decide to lay into a hundred of them coons — we may need a little help."

"Help — like what?"

"Help like maybe a call to the governor for the National Guard."

"Shee-yet," drawled the mayor. "You mean to say you can't handle a hundred niggers?" He tapped the sheriff's badge with a forefinger. "You got that and twelve deputy stars to go with it. What the hell else do you need?"

I need, thought the sheriff with the hawk-eyes, one town official — just one — who doesn't look like W. C. Fields, who doesn't have delusions of being Napoleon, and who doesn't scrounge around like an overage fire eater looking for an insurrection the way most men pant after a broad.

"What about them guys on the cameras, Mayor?" he asked. "If there's trouble, they're gonna catch every foot of it. It ain't gonna look too good."

The mayor made an exaggerated pretense of suddenly being aware of the cameras. He looked up at them briefly, then shrugged as he turned back toward the sheriff. "If them niggers get wild," he said, "them cameras are gonna take pictures of it. That ain't no skin off our asses. We got law and order to consider." He nodded toward the tracks. "We told 'em they ain't allowed to march and if they go ahead and march — then that's just too Goddamned bad!" He patted the thick right arm of the sheriff and winked at him. "Just hang in there, sheriff," he said. "Hang in there tough." Then he went down the line, slapping the backs and shaking the hands of the deputies and murmuring a fight talk.

A reporter from one of the wire services stopped him on the way back to his car, and he could be seen walking, waving his arms, holding up a clenched fist, pointing toward the tracks, and loving every tense minute of it.

The sheriff watched him for a while and then shook his head. Jesus, he thought. Why was it so common a thing to find a man in authority whose mouth and ego were Size Extra Large while his brain and his peter were built for a midget? Hang in there tough, my ass, he thought. God help him if those niggers *were* armed and came across those tracks in anger. That fat slob in the American Legion cap would be halfway to Baton Rouge on the fly right after the first volley. He watched the car pull away, the red light flashing, the siren wailing, and the Legionnaire's cap visible in the back window, tight and ludicrous on the bald dome. Tiger. Lion man. Nail eater, full of piss and vinegar.

The sheriff spat into the dust and turned to look back toward the tracks. Of the two, he thought — the garbage-brained phony with the yen for battle and the skinny little nigger minister who was supposed to lead the march — he perversely and unbidden preferred the nigger. It took two good-sized hanging objects from the groin to do what this nigger was going to do that morning. He sure as hell wouldn't want to trade places with him. Or with any of the others. "Freedom now," one of the signs read. Freedom, my ass, thought the sheriff. Now they're free. They're free to take in laundry and do odd jobs and get tanked up on a Saturday night and take a razor to any black buddy alongside. That's the freedom they're built for. What the hell else do they want? He shook his head, uncomprehending. Niggers. Who could understand niggers?

He went back to the microphone, pushed the switch and started to talk again. "Why don't you people go on home?" he said, hearing his voice blaring out above him. "Go on home and forget all about this here nonsense. Go on home and be safe and comfortable and have yourselves a cold beer. This ain't no mornin' to march. This ain't no mornin' to get your heads split open, neither!"

*The little Negro pastor in the shiny suit, ironed a thousand times until it looked now like a black mirror, leads his flock in a whispered prayer and then asks for a moment of silence. His clerical collar is not designed for the Mississippi summer and he feels the sweat collecting underneath his chin. Out of the corner of his eye he sees the white Unitarian minister from Chicago, Illinois, whose head is down and who is praying. Cool white cat. He don't sweat. But then again — the cool white cat has only a short walk to make that morning. The seventy-eight black people, the pastor knows, have to make a pilgrimage — a trek across an abyss. And the first step is a billion miles long — five centuries deep — one hundred generations wide. The appalling distance, longer than miles, wider and deeper than years, between the African jungle and the dusty town square of a little county seat in the Mississippi delta.*

*His step, too, he thinks. And he tries to recapture the pride in the dream that had been surging and flowing in him and electrifying him. But all he can think at this moment is that he is a fraud. He has spent his adult life excoriating the Devil with hellfire and brimstone and damnation sermons. But this is the most dubious of battles. The Devil is a myth that hangs by its thumbs inside the Good Book, dangling there like a punching bag, turning its cheek back and forth, weak and supine; a defenseless straw man built to be destroyed over and over. But not real. Just part of a religious pageant played out each Sunday morning.*

*But the little Negro pastor, when he looks across the tracks, knows that there are other devils and this is the major part of his fraud. He has preached nonviolence. Always nonviolence. Nonviolence and love. Patience and forbearance. "If your neighbor wronged you, forgive him at once. For thou shalt love thy neighbor as thyself. Would you vengefully punish your one hand for having hurt the other?" He had preached this. He had believed it. But does he believe it now? It is the question he asks himself while he looks at the riot guns, the bicycle chains and the cattle prods that wait for them on the other side of the tracks.*

*But it's time now. A thousand years leading up to one morning. And now it is time. He raises his head and lets his eyes scan the bowed black heads in front of him.*

*"All right, brothers and sisters," he says softly. "We is gonna march now. We is gonna march to the town square."*

*He takes a step down from the sagging porch. A long step. A step of infinite distance. And he is followed.*

The sheriff stepped out in front of his car, his thumbs in his gun belt, and called out to the minister who was less than a hundred feet away. "That'll do it, Reverend. Just stay right there. And tell your people to stay there, too. That's as far as you go."

But the skinny little minister kept on walking directly toward him, and the people behind followed. The deputies edged back nervously, eyeing the sheriff, waiting and wondering. Now? Fire now? Or just wade in with the chains? Or what?

The sheriff stood there, torn. Instinct battled logic; a natural dislike for things black, nurtured over the years, engaged in a death grip with an awareness that it would not end here, no matter what they did. This would just be the first skirmish — the first bloodletting. Then his eyes met the little black minister's, and then their brains met, and their mutual knowledge became interlocked.

White man with the badge, the Negro minister's eyes said. Time to step aside. Time to step aside and let some peaceful men march by. 'Cause if you bloody us now, we're gonna come back by the millions. White sheriff — you know this is true. You gotta bend, man. You gotta sway with the wind. You gotta give an inch.

Black man, the sheriff's eyes said, a year ago ... a week ago ... I could've put a string across this track and handed you each a machete — and you still wouldn't of cut it. Tell me something, black man ... tell me what's happened? Tell me what's different now? Tell me why ... explain it to me ... why, on this given morning, I have to step aside?

The sheriff turned to the deputy on his right. "Let 'em through," he said.

The deputy blinked at him. "Let 'em through?" he repeated.

"I said, let 'em through," the sheriff barked out. "Let 'em through and walk alongside with 'em. If they stay in a straight line and don't touch nothin', they can walk around the square and then back here."

The deputy nodded, dumbfounded. "Sheriff says to let 'em through," he called out to the men on either side.

The line of deputies gave way and the seventy-eight black men and women filed through in between the cars and headed down the dusty road toward the main street of the town and the square beyond.

The white Unitarian minister jogged up the line until he was walking alongside the Negro pastor. "Reverend," he said, half out of breath, "does it appear to you that the first honors go to us?"

The Negro minister turned to look at the white Unitarian from Chicago, Illinois, and smiled. "Brother, we gotta town full of white people we gotta get through yet. And then a long black night to follow. And then a thousand towns and a thousand nights. But you're right. The *first* honors ..." He looked down the line of black men and women, carrying placards and signs and flags held very high. And then he smiled again. "... they go to us." Then he looked straight ahead toward the low-slung buildings that surrounded the square and shimmered in the heat; toward the white faces that sprang up on either side of the road, staring at them. He felt a rumbling, thunderous joy build up inside of him, and a thanksgiving beyond any language. "Brothers and sisters," he shouted. "Brothers and sisters — when the Israelites went toward the Red Sea, they sang — they sang. Leave us sing, too. Leave us sing it out loud and clear. Leave us put some music into the air." The crusaders sang "We Shall Overcome," and followed it with hymns and spirituals and marching songs.

The white people of Chaseville stood on the sidewalks and gaped, too bewildered to feel any fury; too stunned to raise an arm or a fist or a club. They simply stood there and watched in silence. Always insulated, always parochial and circumscribed. It was their very provincialism that lent them comfort. Their universe was the length of a barn-dance floor and most of their traveling had been on front-porch gliders. But at this moment they felt only bewilderment. This was *their* town. It was their street. It was their square. They were churchgoers and contributors to charity, and parents of children. They paid taxes and stopped at red lights and owned

Bibles. But there they stood on the hot sidewalks — the Daughters of the Confederacy, the members of the First Methodist Church, the school board commissioners, the shopkeepers and house owners and soil tillers — blue denim and pinafores and wide Stetson hats. They had always been a social unit, knitted together — indivisible and unshakable — fiercely loyal to one another. But here was something that shook them ... some new element that never had had to be reckoned with before. They looked toward the street and saw familiar black faces going by. There was Buford, who did odd jobs and shuffled and rolled his eyes and grinned. And Buford was marching with his back straight and his head high, carrying a placard. There was Odessa, who washed their clothes — and there she walked with her husband, looking straight ahead, grim and determined. There was Mordecai, who cut their lawns — and he carried an American flag. All those familiar faces were suddenly unfamiliar. They were unsmiling. They didn't look carefree and mindless. They carried their signs and placards with a dignity that was really quite incredible. In the space of just a few hours, something had happened to order and tradition and propriety. The blacks — *their* blacks — had suddenly ceased to be a labor pool or a collection of shanties across the tracks or a happy dark woman who did their laundry. They had become a force. They were a power. They were a nameless threat. This is why the white people of Chaseville stood on the sidewalks so quietly and so without passion. They could deal with an insurrection of slaves. At the moment, they could not cope with the slaves becoming civilized.

The marchers sang as they walked around the square, and the white people noted that it was the little colored minister who led them in the singing. Gawd in heaven, look at him. Will you look at him? Skinny little black bastard, not five foot five. Not a hundred and thirty pounds. And he's leading them. A scrawny little black rooster making like Moses. And a line of once quiet and diffident black people who had tipped hats and said "sir," and had never made any trouble — they were marching. They were actually march-ing. The black meek trying to inherit the white earth. Doomed, of course. So foreign to the God-designed pattern of things that it could never happen. But listening to the clear, high-pitched voice of the little minister riding above the other voices showed you how one fragile little Pied Piper in a black shiny suit could be a magnet to some ignorant, fear-ridden, purposeless people. Something *had* been lost that morning. Something irrevocable and irreplaceable. The comfortable niche whereby the whites played house with the blacks, with the former always being the mama and the papa — this game would never be played again. All because a bunch of dark-skinned baboons had found a figure to rally around. And as they watched him leading his little band around the square and heading back toward the tracks, they wondered if *they* had such a person to rally around. Wallace was in Alabama. Thurmond was in South Carolina. Maddox was in Atlanta. But who would speak for them in Chaseville, Mississippi? Where was *their* voice?

The mayor rested a meaty elbow against the aged roll-top desk and glared across the room at the sheriff and at the town clerk who was his brother-in-law, and his voice sputtered out in a helpless, fruit-less, inarticulate rage.

"You know what we looked like, don't you? You know, do you, sheriff?"

The sheriff leaned against the windowsill, feeling the after-noon heat heavy against his back, oozing in from the outside. He remained silent.

"We looked like some pissy-assed, weak old ladies just standin' there and gawkin' and not doin' a Goddamned thing."

" 'Pears to me," the brother-in-law started to say, "that we should'a done somethin' —"

"Somethin'," the mayor shouted. "Thass right! We should'a done somethin'. When that coon minister took one step beyond the tracks we should'a stuck a pole up his ass and raised 'im to the top of the court house. We wouldn't have no more marchin' after that. And that is for Goddamned sure!"

The sheriff gazed steadily into the mottled red face of the chief executive and wondered how this tub of quivering fat flesh, without muscles and without sense, could generate so much anger.

"What about it, Sheriff?" the mayor screamed at him. "You ready for another Goddamned march in the mornin'? And the next mornin'? And the one after that? 'Cause you're sure as hell gonna have to line up them deputies seven days a week from now on. Them coons got away with it this mornin'. They walked right on through us, and they seen how it was done. And from now on, they're gonna do it regular. You bet your ass, they're gonna do it regular."

The sheriff shifted his weight against the windowsill and stretched out his long legs. "You wanna know somethin', Mayor!" he said quietly. "Them niggers are gonna march right on through the summer, and it don't make no difference whether you mow 'em down with machine guns or give 'em free beer on the corner — they're gonna march. Now you gotta call it, one way or the other. You can turn this town into a fuckin' battlefield and fill up the hospitals and then wake up one mornin' to find a thousand federal marshals sittin' here in your office, tellin' you how to run your railroad. Or, you got an alternative."

"Which is what?" the mayor asked him, his jowls quivering, feeling the excitement drain away and the visions of himself commanding his Army drift back into limbo, replaced by the hot, dull sameness of what it had always been.

"Let 'em march," the sheriff said, moving away from the windowsill. "Let 'em march till their black feet rot off. Let 'em sing and wave them Goddamned banners and by winter-time, they'll forget what they was marchin' for and everythin' else. Why do you s'pose they had television cameras set up by the tracks? 'Cause they figgered we had a stick of dynamite down here ready to go off. And that's what them niggers *want*. They want that dynamite to go off. They want federal marshals down here. The hairier it gets, the better it is for them. My advice to you, Mayor, is just to sit there and breathe through your nose and let 'em march."

"Ah'm mayor of this town —" the mayor started to announce in ringing, pre-election-day tones.

"You sure as hell are," said the sheriff, "but you ain't gonna have much town left to be mayor of if you start givin' any orders to tear into a little band of niggers and start somethin' rollin' here that you ain't gonna be able to stop."

The mayor rose from behind his rolltop desk and walked over to the window. He looked at the statue of the Confederate soldier across the street in the little park. "Funny Goddamned thing," he said in a quieter voice. "One skinny-assed-nigger preacher — he says 'shee-yet' — and a hundred coons squat for 'im." There was a silence. The mayor turned to look across the room toward the far wall.

My God, thought the sheriff — he's thinking. The slob is actually thinking.

"You know what we need around here?" the mayor said. "We need a preacher of our own. We need somebody to give *us* the words."

He walked slowly back to this desk and sat down, running his finger across the corrugated rolltop like beating a snare drum.

"You know who I wish to hell we could get here?" he announced. "Connacher. King Connacher. Let that boy open his mouth for an hour or so and you wouldn't find no niggers marchin' here. Not ever again."

The sheriff turned and looked out of the window. Torn little pieces of handbills that the marchers had passed out drifted across the yellowed grass around the Confederate statue. He thought about King Connacher. If King Connacher came into Chaseville, that town square might be littered with something more than handbills. King Connacher was a walking, talking Gatling gun who could turn a group into a mob, a town into a fortress, and any given summer afternoon into a blood-bath. The sheriff turned and walked toward the mayor's desk, unpinning his badge as he walked. He threw it down on the top of the desk, where it made a thin, tinny, clinking sound in the stillness of the room. The mayor looked up at him, questioningly.

"What the hell's that s'posed to mean?" he asked.

"It's not *s'posed* to mean — it *means!*" the sheriff replied. "If you get a prick like King Connacher into this town, you better make him sheriff. There'll be an openin'."

The mayor picked up the badge, studied it for a moment, then threw it back down on top of the desk. "We've already tried it your way, Jim. Let's try it my way now. I don't want us to lie down for any more niggers. That's my point."

The sheriff shook his head back and forth. "Mayor," he said softly, "a lot of people are gonna do a lot of lyin' down if you bring in some loudmouthed sonuvabitch, screamin' for murder. They're gonna lie down face first. Blacks *and* whites. That's *my* point." He turned and walked across the room toward the door.

"You're gonna be one sorry sonuvabitch, Sheriff," the mayor said to him, warningly.

The sheriff turned at the door to look at the vapid, fat face with the close-set, piggish little eyes. He smiled and shook his head again. "Mister Mayor? *Shee-yet!*" Then he opened the door and walked out.

The white Cad convertible with the beige leather interior pulled off the highway just before the turnoff to the field down below where they would hold the meeting. The driver got out from behind the wheel, and strutted over to the shoulder of the road and looked down.

King Connacher always strutted. He always walked as if he carried a baton, and his little bandy legs took short, driving, stiff-legged steps — supporting the swaggering upper torso, the barrel-chested, broad-shouldered part of him built like a section-gang riveter.

He took a long and warming swig from a flask and looked down at the field, where a large bonfire had already been lighted. A group of men were building the speaker's platform while others tacked bunting and flags on its railings. The canvas and paper whipped around in the hot Mississippi summer night breeze and provided a sharp flapping obbligato to the voice murmurs that rose up and caressed King Connacher's happy ears. He saw his poster being unloaded from a half-ton truck. Fifty times his real size. A giant portrait of King Connacher unfurled to the wind, then nailed onto poles and lighted by two spotlights. King Connacher in his white seersucker suit, a gnarled fist stretched out, teeth bared. And the real King Connacher, looking less than angry and almost smaller than life, stood on the side of the road and took another drink from his flask. He let his eyes move across the field to the parking area that was being roped off. Room for five hundred cars. That's what they'd told him. That's what it looked like. Five hundred cars, average four people to a car. You get two thousand people that way. That's what they were expecting for the night's performance.

King took another swig from the flask and smiled happily. He could remember three years ago — even two years ago — when if he could scrounge up a half a hundred red-necks, that was a night's work and it took doing. But not any more. When they knew King Connacher was driving into a town, they went to work for him. They drummed up the trade and rented the hall and usually begged him to stay for an extra night.

Like a cocky Golden Glove fighter, King took his strutting, preening walk back to the white Cad and threw the flask through the open window onto the front seat. He reached inside and touched the leather and loved the feel of it and the smell of it. Class, brother, class! None of the plastic vinyl crap for him. That was for Chevys and Ramblers and six-cylinder Fords. And under the dash was the hi-fi cartridge-loading tape machine and an FM radio, and in the back was a telephone and a special walnut table — and the whole

Goddamned thing was powered by buttons: windows, vents — the works. You pushed the buttons and things happened.

He stood there for a moment caressing the leather and thinking about the other times and the other conveyances of not so long ago. He had been an apprentice to it all then. He would ride all night on some crummy milk wagon, twelve-stop bus, sweating his ass off in the summer, freezing to death in the winter, and getting off at his stop looking and smelling like a tramp. Those were the days when he built his own speaker's platform and usually it was a wooden box set up in front of the Confederate statue in the town's square. Those were the scrounging days and the grubbing days with the miserable nickle-and-diming of the local sheriff or the ranking Baptist minister or whatever town father ruled the roost of that particular county seat. He had the right goods. He'd known it even then. He'd shout and pound his fist and talk about the niggers and the Commies and the Yankee do-gooders and the kissie boys up in Washington and how the South was the last remaining fortress — the lone bastion of decent white rule. He had an instinct for this product of his and an instinct for the right words, and his delivery of those words was faultless. But he had put the product in the wrong package. He had worn Levi's and blue denim shirts and had had a beard stubble. When the handful of red-necks would gather to listen to him, he'd played it at eye level. His pitch in those days was that he was one of them. He had scrabbled out of the same red clay soil. He had walked, sweating, behind the same kind of mule. "Look at me, brothers — look at me. Look *at* me. Don't look behind, brothers. Don't look over my shoulder. Don't look left or right. Look *at* me. Man, you're lookin' in a mirror. Don't you realize that? You're lookin' right into a mirror. I'm one of you. I *am* you. I ain't a fancy-talkin' congressman and I ain't a high-pocketed, syrup-smooth lawyer. I'm you, brothers — I'm you." And the red-necks would smile comfortably and nod and bid him welcome. They'd share a jug with him and pat him on the back and they would tell him "how all-fired Goddamned good he spoke the words." But after the pitch — after the bonfire died down, after the jug got passed — these creatures — built in his image — would go back to their farms, wallets intact in hip pockets, calloused fingers playing with the same coins in the same threadbare pockets, parting with nothing but their goodwill. And King Connacher would climb on the bus again with a full gut and an empty coin sack and head for the next shabby town where there'd be other red-necks and other jugs and more pats on the back.

King was never able to pinpoint the moment — the very moment — of his enlightenment. But it had come to him one time. You could not move people or twist them or set them up by posing in their image. You didn't soften them up by pointing to the sweat under your armpit and calling it a fraternal bond. Fifty years ago that kind of bullshit won you an election for a nine-hundred-dollar-a-year job as town clerk. And sometimes it might even take you higher, like a Huey Long. But there were more colleges around now. The brains were bigger, the tastes more sophisticated. When you built a base you had to put it on stilts. It had to rest well above the red clay soil. And when you spoke, you stood on that platform and you looked down. And that's what King Connacher had been doing for the past couple of years — standing on platforms and looking down and making people look up.

As he slid back behind the wheel of the white Cad and started that sweet molasses engine that hummed music back to him, he knew he had it made. He was right for the time and right for the place. He was a roaring little evangelist on spindly legs who could wheedle and con and stultify just by a tone or an inflection. He played people like stringed instruments, plucking at this chord or that — always knowing the right note and the right melody. He could turn a good-natured carnival crowd into a screaming mob. He could play on the nerve strings like a harp and unearth hatreds that would come out as a symphony of violence that a regiment of the National Guard couldn't control.

He checked his watch — a "Rolex Oyster Perpetual." Three hundred bucks, with a gold case and a gold mesh band with his initials in old English script. Solid and heavy on his wrist. Rich-looking and obvious. Connacher liked it that way. Then he pulled out onto the highway, U-turned and headed back toward town. He could take an hour nap at his motel and get back there right after the crowd had assembled. He took another swallow from the flask. The old "honey medicine." It sweetened the voice and bolstered up the old tonsils. And though he would never admit it, it blunted the nerves. When he faced an audience, the first few seconds were the bad ones. Sweaty palms and fluttering heart. Just a few seconds was all. But they were there every night and in every place and they had to be hurdled, and the whiskey helped.

Connacher turned on the car radio as he drove — very loud; he hummed along with a hillbilly quartet and felt at peace. Little phrases he would use that night went through his mind — and while he sang, he nodded as one turned up that was particularly effective and pleased him. If given men were graced with particular elements, he was in his right now.

King Connacher on a warm summer night in Mississippi just before he stuck his usual needle in the usual mob — a spinal tap administered with the fast, glib tongue and the fast, glib mind — producing a toxin that bubbled and boiled over the Bunsen burner that was the South, circa the 1960's.

An hour later, Connacher was lying on his bed in the best room of the Chaseville Motel. He lolled around in a pleasant half-sleep, one portion of his mind attuned to the time so that he'd be up and ready for the night's proceedings. There was a knock on the door and he bolted upright in bed.

"Yeah," he called.

A voice answered him. "Mr. Connacher? Wonder if I might speak to you for a moment?"

Connacher rose from the bed, checked his watch, then looked toward the door. "About what?" he asked. "I'm gettin' ready for the meetin' tonight."

The voice was neutrally apologetic. "Won't take but a moment."

Connacher walked to the door, unlocked it, pulled it open. There was a tall man standing there — white-haired, square good features, bushy white eyebrows. The sport coat was an expensive linen. Connacher read him immediately. Thin-lipped, Southern aristocracy. Out of a big plantation house — or at least his forebears were. Class and good blood, both carried well. Maybe a little deference should be shown here, a little quiet respect — more than usual.

"Yes?" Connacher said quietly. "How can I help you?"

The old man returned Connacher's appraising look. "My name is Blake," he said. "I publish and edit and single-handedly write the local newspaper here. The *Chaseville Gazette*. I was rather hoping that you might give me a rather short interview. I won't take up too much of your time."

Connacher took a step back into the room and made a gesture for the old man to enter. Blake did so, his eyes never leaving Connacher's face. He moved over to a chair and very naturally sat down in it. On top, Connacher thought — the old man was always on top. Cold, appraising eyes that seemed to bore into him. Connacher checked his watch again.

"I've only got a few minutes, Mr. Blake. Do you want to ask your questions now?" Then his smile — the big smile — the winning one. "You could come to the thing tonight and I reckon you'd get most of your questions answered out there. I don't hide my philosophies under a bushel."

The old man didn't smile. He just nodded slightly. "I know all about your 'philosophies,' Mr. Connacher. Your fame precedes you, sir." His voice had a soft Southern drawl to it — just a tinge of the superiority of the landed gentry. The old man *felt* superior and Connacher could see that. It irritated him.

"I'm waitin', Mr. Blake."

"So's the town," Blake answered softly. "Oh, they've been waiting better than a couple of weeks, Mr. Connacher, for your much heralded arrival. You talked to our mayor, did you not?"

Connacher nodded, wondering how much time he'd have to spend on this one. A four-page weekly gazette that announced bingo games and church socials. He was long out of *that* league. "I'm waitin' for the questions," he said coolly.

"What do you get paid, Mr. Connacher," Blake asked him directly, "for these 'services' of yours? Take pretty good, is it?"

Connacher pulled out a pack of cigarettes and lighted one. He felt his irritation increasing. "A percentage of the collection, Mr. Blake," he said, while he thought, what the hell business is it of yours? "I don't s'pose you got anythin' against my expenses bein' paid, do you? I got a peculiar constitution, Mr. Blake. If I don't eat — I get the rickets."

The old man leaned forward in his chair, unsmiling. "We've managed very well here, Mr. Connacher, meeting the exigencies of the times without violence. Without trouble. Your stock in trade *is* trouble, Mr. Connacher. I was just wondering what it brought on the open market."

Connacher didn't flinch. He met the older man's eyes. "For the whites to stay in control, Mr. Blake — that must be worth somethin'. A dollar a head — two dollars a head. I'd say there was some value to our keepin' the niggers out of our bedrooms." His eyes narrowed. "Your paper take a position on that kind of thing? You got a point of view?"

The old man smiled for the first time. "Oh, I've got a point of view," he answered. "I've got a very explicit point of view. You see, Mr. Connacher, the people suffer me because of my longevity and my antiquity and the fact that I come from a long line of illustrious Southerners who have made their home here. They don't like me much, but as I say — they suffer me because I'm one of them."

So what the hell do you want from me? Connacher thought. You wanna compare family trees or have a little prayer service, or what the hell kind of Goddamned interview is this? "Mr. Blake," he said aloud, "the following has been established. I come to places, invited, to speak a Southern philosophy. The philosophy of the white man. It happens to be my business."

The smile persisted on Blake's face and he half closed his eyes. Connacher thought for a moment he would laugh.

"Your business," Blake said finally. "I'd call that partial description, Mr. Connacher. That so-called 'Southern philosophy' — that's part of your business. And making yourself heard, *that's* part of your business. And part of your business is obviously turning patent crap into some kind of marching and rallying music. That's the part of your business that sticks in my craw. I know your track record, Mr. Connacher. You come into towns like this with that 'Southern philosophy' and you do everything but blow a bugle and muster the people into a commando regiment. You rile them and needle them and heat them up and do everything but put torches in their hands. I was just wondering, Mr. Connacher, if it ever occurred to you what happens to a mob after you turn them on, then leave them."

Connacher felt more at home at this moment. This was the enemy. He could always cope with an enemy. Just as he functioned most smoothly with the other extreme — the fawners, the supplicants, the True Believers — like the fat mayor of this town who had asked him to come in the first place. But with both ends of the spectrum, Connacher was at his best.

"Mr. Blake," he said, very evenly. "What side are you on anyway? Are you for the niggers or are you for the whites? Seems to me a most simple equation. That's the question I always ask of my audiences. The question generally impresses 'em."

The old man's smile faded. There was frank, cold dislike in his eyes. "Mr. Connacher — I'm seventy-six years old. Nothing you say impresses me. And you don't impress me."

Connacher turned on a smile of his own. "Why, I'm not tryin' to impress you, Mr. Blake. I imagine bein' seventy-six years old, you're a little set in your ways. But I must admit to bein' a little surprised that a man your age hasn't acquired a little wisdom along the line. You run the town newspaper, you say, so you must be an educated man. But you sure as hell don't talk like an educated man. You talk like some kind of hybrid nigger-lover. Yankee-sympathizer Hebrew. You ain't been to Moscow recently, have you?"

The old man closed his eyes and his mouth puckered up. Was he crying or laughing? Then he opened his eyes and he chuckled aloud.

"I say somethin' funny, did I?" Connacher asked him.

The old man shook his head. "Why, no, Mr. Connacher — you didn't say anything funny. But you disappoint me a little bit. I've been led to believe that you turn quite a phrase. The talk was that you were one enterprising little bastard with a gift of gab; you were some shrewd little article that did a powerful job of selling. But here I am talking to you, Mr. Connacher, and you don't even know how to keep an argument going. You back up and shift around and reach down into that bag of yours and you come up with the usual crap about Jews and Communists and nigger-lovers. You won't even stick to a point. You won't rebut me with any kind of logic."

"The interview's over, Mr. Blake," Connacher said, his voice ice cold.

The old man rose slowly from the chair. "It is, indeed, Mr. Connacher. It is, indeed. I guess I haven't been altogether fair. I wanted to meet you, and not just because of an interview. I wanted to meet you and I wanted to leave you with a little message of my own. The message is, Mr. Connacher, that there are a handful of ignorant men around here who look upon you as some kind of a savior. That's because in the country of the blind, the one-eyed man is King. No pun intended, Mr. Connacher. But I put this to you, Mr. Connacher

— as one of the small and indistinct voices of reason that persists around here. Voices you probably won't hear tonight over the crowd noises. I believe you're a dangerous, menacing man whose mission in life is to stir up trouble. Bad trouble, Mr. Connacher. Irreparable trouble. And I look for the day when your breed becomes extinct. I don't know what the other social strata will look like. I don't know whether there'll be segregated schools or mixed swimming holes or black and white barbecues. But at least there'll be no more King Connachers. And this will put us as close to millennium as we'll ever get."

The old man started to walk toward the door. Connacher took a step over to him, reached out, touched his arm, then grabbed him and pulled the old man toward him, having to look up into the grim, set, thin-lipped face, because the old man towered over him.

"Mr. Blake," he said, in a cold fury, "let me ask you one question. Would you want your daughter to marry a nigger? That's what it boils down to."

Blake stared down at him; his voice was very low. "That's always the last dead cat that you pull out of the bag, isn't it, Mr. Connacher? When all else fails — logic, reason, restraint, intelligence, honor — that's what's left. 'Would you want your daughter to marry a nigger?' Well, I'll tell you something, Mr. Connacher, by way of a response. *I'd rather she marry a nigger — than King Connacher!* I presume that answers your question, sir."

The old man very deliberately reached out and removed Connacher's hand from his arm as if brushing off a clump of earth, then he turned and walked out of the room.

At nine o'clock that night, humid and sultry, an aged cornfield was turned into the Hollywood Bowl — a graduated hillside grandstand filling up with two thousand men and women. The high school band belted John Philip Sousa with verve, if not in unison. The mayor, wearing his American Legion cap, gave a brief peptalk prelude through an overloud microphone. His voice was an unintelligible, echoing, raucous fuzz — but the crowd applauded because it was in a mood to applaud. The applause turned into a roar as a white Cadillac came down the hill, and the roar become thunder when the driver got out and — engulfed by town officials, two state troopers and some trooping kids who followed at his heels — King Connacher walked toward the platform.

The high school music teacher, sweating and half faint under his too-tight, high-buttoned uniform, pounded his baton on the back of a chair and the band made a frontal assault on "Dixie." The hillside turned into a moving, wiggling mass as people stood up and waved and shouted when the spotlight picked up King Connacher at the foot of the platform. He smiled and waved back all the way up the steps, then shook hands with the mayor, who put a beefy arm around him and held out his free hand for silence.

"Folks — could I have your attention, please? Could you give me your attention? Could we have a little quiet, please?"

The cheering gradually died away. "Dixie" retreated with a rear guard trumpet and saxophone continuing on to a dissonant blaring halt in the middle of a stanza. Then there *was* silence as the mayor beamed into the thousands of shining eyes set deep against the dark silhouette of familiar faces, fused and blurred into a faceless strangeness.

"My friends," the mayor called out, "he's here now. The true voice of the South. The man you been waitin' to hear. We've had some funny goin's on in this town of late. We've seen niggers walkin' down our streets. We've seen white men pushed aside. Well, here's the man who don't ever get pushed aside, and who's devoted his life to seein' that none of us gets pushed aside. Ladies and gentlemen — Mr. King Connacher!"

Bugles, fanfare, cheers, screams, waving hats, shrieks from women — and the crowd looked up with one face and one set of eyes and one mind to hear the words that they themselves could only think, or blurt out in aged and colorless clichés, or feel way down deep with an unspoken fear. King Connacher would give them the words. He'd say them the way they should be spoken and the way they wanted to hear them. It took four minutes for the noise to abate. King Connacher stood there during those four minutes in front of the microphone, letting his eyes move slowly back and forth. He wore a quiet smile. But then he let it die away and it was time for the grim look. Twelve seconds of silence — he slowly counted in his mind before he leaned across, pulling the microphone to him. Then the first shaft — a thin piercing arrow to stick them to their seats and make them look up and listen.

"It's hot in Mississippi tonight, my friends. It's real downright hot. The good Lord is tendin' to the furnace south of the Mason-Dixon, and he's got a flame roarin'. The coals are stoked — the dampers wide open — and that fire is burnin' bright and hot. But don't be ashamed of your sweat. Don't be ashamed of any itch you got. Don't be afraid of that liquid comin' out of your flesh. You know what it is? It's the righteous wrath of a good people tired of bein' stomped on — dead sick of havin' their freedom torn at and ripped and forced into the dust and trampled."

They looked at him in awe. There was a mass movement of nods. There was a vast collective sea of open mouths. In the single sweep of a minute hand, King Connacher had laid them out on his palm — docile and respectful — and from this moment on he could squeeze them in his fist, make them cry or laugh or march as a body on Fort Sumter. They were his creatures now. He had them. And he knew he had them. He looked up, satisfied, into the dark sky, waited for five seconds, then, almost as in an afterthought — as if suddenly remembering they were there — he looked straight at them again.

"Ever get a feelin' you been someplace before? Ever get a feelin' you been on the same road — marched to the same music, felt the same pain?" He nodded. "Friends ... you been there before. You been at Bull Run. You been at Chickamauga. Your faces were scorched and blistered by the flames at Atlanta. You died in agony a thousand times while Sherman drove you down to the sea. You felt your souls ache when carpetbag niggers pushed you off sidewalks. Man oh man — we all been there before. We're still there. We're still doin' our dyin' and feelin' our aches and gettin' pushed off the sidewalk."

There was a murmur that rose from the crowd. He was right. God, he was right. How suddenly bright and clear it was. They listened to him, scarcely breathing now. Each one was a gray-uniformed, incredibly brave Confederate hero, gaunt and hungry but never daunted, like Robert E. Lee when he rode quietly from the house at Appomattox, bare-headed and grief-stricken. And they were there — his Army, turned back but never beaten — the proud, tired remnant of the South. Invaded, raped and violated by the Communists and the Jews and the nigger lovers who profited by war. And there was Robert E. Lee standing in front of them now in his white seersucker suit with the gold thing that flashed on his wrist as he held his right fist high above him.

"I weep, my friends — do you know that? I weep at what has been done to us and what is bein' done to us. I weep for the ravished ghosts of our people who were our forebears. And my tears are shed with as much sadness and in as much profusion for those of us who still live under the heel of the Northern rapist who still ... believe me ... who still will find not one moment's peace of soul until he filthies our streets and our homes and our schools with the bile and the acid and the poison of his philosophy." (This phrase he'd thought of driving back to the motel.) His voice rose. The arrow was implanted — now throw the grenade. "Make no mistake. When they say civil rights, they really mean uncivil wrongs." (A phrase he'd used in Selma, Alabama, that they'd quoted in a newspaper headline.) "They want to taint our blood. They want us to offer our daughters. They want us off the sidewalk. And once this is done, here comes the black mob. Here they come, my friends — get ready for the parade. The big bucks with the yellow spats and the frizzle-haired sluts with the monkey lips. There's old Martin Luther Coon leadin' the march. He shall overcome. Oh, yessiree. Oh, hallelujah.

He shall overcome. Overcome us. Overcome every white man and woman and child in the South. Overcome our beliefs. Overcome our sense of decency. Overcome our honor. Overcome our morality. Overcome — or *try* to overcome — the one thing that keeps the baboons in the cages and the people on the streets. The God-acknowledged truth of all times — that the white man is better than the black man. He shall forever be better than the black man. Dead, rotting, molding in the grave — he is still better than the livin' black man."

He suddenly ripped open his coat and then his shirt front. The gesture was quick and arresting. There was a gasp in the crowd.

"Let 'em strip off my skin. Let 'em gouge out my flesh, pierce my eyes, roast me on a spit, flog my back to the bones, cut out my tongue. I'll still say it, friends. I'll say it because it is the truth. *The white man is better than the black man!* And when you leave here tonight — let the black man know it. Let 'im know it with your voices. Let 'im know it with your right hands. Let 'im know it with any weapon at hand. This is not just a call to arms. *It is a sacred duty!*"

The grenade exploded. The shrapnel hit them all. They rose as one, screaming that he was right; acknowledging that The Truth had just arrived in Mississippi. And they kept screaming for whole minutes while King Connacher stood there, his head down, in a silent, humble acknowledgment of his own. He, King Connacher, was the new voice of the old South. He was five foot six and forty-four years old. His father had been a tubercular sharecropper who spent his days trying to coax cotton out of the used-up and tired-out earth and at night would sit in the corner of his shack coughing up his bloody lungs into a handkerchief. His mother had been a screaming Holy Roller fanatic whose passion was God's word, Jesus meek and mild, and the blood of the lamb. That this cadaver, this long-dying corpse with the blood-flecked lips, could mate with a mad woman with wild staring eyes, and produce children, was inconceivable. But they did mate and they did produce children. Eight boys and four girls — twelve walking rib cages. Scurvied, belly-bloated, gaunt little things who died off — one a year — until only three were left. King Connacher was one of the survivors. He'd stopped his spasmodic schooling in the sixth grade because he had already acquired the basic wisdom it took to know that knowledge could not be eaten or used to stifle hunger pangs or accepted in a bank as currency to buy seed. At age twelve his body gave him puberty — his hunger gave him strength. Vaguely, subconsciously, he knew that he was sired by a beaten old man who was begotten by another beaten old man and yet another before him. Their ignorance was self-replenishing and self-perpetuating; their poverty was a legacy passed down with each generation. So King Connacher had left home before he shaved. He rode rails, did odd jobs, worked in road gangs and served time learning the one thing the sharecropper's son was never taught in school — survival. He had never read a book all the way through — but every spoken word was filed inside of his brain until he could say it himself. He knew nothing of poetry or art — but he assimilated other people's reactions and made them his own. He was shallow and fraudulent and believed in not very much, but he was also a shrewd, resilient, wiry little bastard who could take punishment and learn from it. This was what started him making speeches to little handfuls of shabby people. He knew their hunger because he had emerged from it. He understood their poverty because he had slept with it. And because their ignorance was his, he knew that all men had to compensate for their stupidity with something else. Anger was cheap; its seed could be planted shallow. And a crop of rich and burgeoning hatred was just the thing for inferior men looking for something lower than they were. It mattered not at all to King Connacher — it never even occurred to him — that he was a destructive force, carrying with him a plague. The white Cad had beige leather, and the wristwatch was made of gold and shone on his wrist, and a scrawny, perpetually hungry piece of little white trash had grown into a giant. This was what mattered. Nothing else.

He was vaguely aware of his back being pounded and his hand shaken over and over again. Cool ladies' hands. Rough, calloused farmers' hands. Sweaty store owners' hands. Tiny children's hands. There was the din of voices screaming around his ears, calling out his name. There were flashing eyes and flashing teeth and flashing smiles rolling like breakers in the darkness in front of him. There was the mayor, hugging him, and a scrawny little bug-eyed town clerk who kept stroking his arm, and then two state troopers were escorting him off the platform back over to his car.

"I'd be proud to accompany you back into town," the mayor shouted into his ear.

Connacher shook his head and continued to walk toward his car, leaving the fat mayor behind him, a little dismayed but trying to keep up the front by turning people back with vast authority.

"Leave 'im be," he heard the mayor shout. "Leave 'im be. The man is tired, by God. The man is too tired."

Then he was in his white Cad and on the road with the state trooper on the motorcycle ahead of him and the sheriff's car behind him. He looked up into the rear reflector and saw the bonfires still blazing against the sky and heard the still-continuous roar of the people. This was all his. The fire and the noise; the long line of car headlights stretched out endlessly in a line — the spotlights and the sound of the band. He had wrought all that. He had conceived of it, built it, made it exist. He felt pleasure building up inside of him, and the pleasure turned into excitement and the excitement turned into passion. There was a bar near the motel. He'd go there later. That's where the town quail hung out. They'd fall all over themselves when he walked in. Everybody'd buy him drinks — as many as he could handle. They'd pat him on the back and ask for his autograph. They'd whisper about him and throw looks at him and his name would float around the room. "Hey, man — that's King Connacher. Recognize him — that's King Connacher. King Connacher." And as he conjured up the scene in his mind, his lips moved soundlessly and repeated his own name. King Connacher. The man who built bonfires and gave birth to the roar of a crowd.

The motorcycle trooper up ahead put up his hand, indicating he was turning. Connacher slowed down automatically, his mind preoccupied with the night's pleasure just past and the night's pleasure still to come. He'd planted one kind of seed back there in the field. He'd plant yet another before the dawn came, in the mysterious forest of a woman. It was a night for passion. All kinds of passion.

The motorcycle trooper pulled to a stop near the motel and beckoned the white Cad forward and past him, then saluted it as it went by. Connacher grinned and waved his hand. He screeched into the parking lot next to the motel, got out and walked along the gravel path toward his room. A nice hot shower and a good clean shave and a couple of swigs from the flask. A change of shirt and a change of suit and then he'd drive over to the bar and get fawned on and bought for, and then he'd take his pick of the hottest dish on the li'l ole menu. They'd have a big steak and a lot of drinks and then they'd go back to his motel. But for the moment, the sweat that dampened his clothing felt good, and the expectant pressure in his loins felt good, and the sense of the night and what he had accomplished felt good. And the six thousand-odd bucks collected in hats — that felt damned good.

Oh, Connacher — you tiger sonuvabitch, you. You roaring mother's son of a white man. You've got the whole grabbing world right by the balls, right by the short hair. Swing it around, baby — swing it around. You are the number one!

He unlocked his room, went inside, flicked on a light and started to shed his sweaty clothes, dropping them in little clumps all the way over to the bathroom. Christ, it couldn't keep bein' so good — it just couldn't. One of these days he was gonna up and explode with all the joy he had. And it just kept gettin' better 'n' better — every night better, every town better, the cheers louder, the fires hotter, the quail reachin' for him, beggin' for him, pleadin' to be chosen and taken. Good God Almighty, it couldn't get any better — and yet it kept gettin' better.

He turned on the shower and stepped inside under the little hot needles of water and let it run down his head and over his face and across his body. Then he lathered himself with a sweet-smelling soap and sang at the top of his lungs. He, quite mercifully, did not know it at the time but it would be the last song he would ever sing. He was, as a matter of fact, quite correct in one observation. Things would not get better. Never again. From this one blissful moment on, King Connacher would head down into a pit. The sweet wine of his life would have the taste of ashes. This strutting little Frankenstein had created a monster more powerful than himself. Soon it would be back, pounding on his door. King Connacher had planted one seed too many.

Hours later, King Connacher sat at a booth in the little bar, filled up with rare steak and a quart of bourbon. Next to him was a honey-colored little blonde — short-legged and hippy but stacked and hard-breathing, with high breasts and a sensual mouth.

Connacher put his knee against her leg and felt the pressure returned. He leaned over, kissed her cheek, then touched her ear with his tongue. He heard her sigh and saw the naked hunger in her eyes. Her left hand touched his thigh under the table and squeezed, and for a moment they were like two panting animals.

"Mr. Connacher?" It was a vaguely familiar voice and it carried with it, to Connacher, some recollection of unpleasantness.

He looked up, unsmiling and interrupted. He'd had it with the autographs and the back slapping and the adoration. The store was closed and business was over. They could sure as hell leave him alone.

"What do you want?" he asked, not looking up but pushing the girl away. Then he saw Blake standing there.

"Sue," Blake said to the honey-colored blonde. "Run into the powder room, my dear, and busy yourself for a few minutes."

The girl rose immediately and waited for Connacher to let her out from the booth. Surprised, Connacher got up and stepped aside, wondering if at this moment he should send the man walking, or just what he should do. The whiskey had dulled him and he felt somehow indecisive.

"I'll be right back," the girl murmured, walking past him toward the bar and the ladies' room.

The old man watched her leave, then turned to face Connacher.

"I was just wondering, Mr. Connacher," Blake said, "while you were sitting here enjoying yourself — if you had any idea what was going on in the outside world."

Connacher lighted a cigarette and smiled. "Why don't you have a drink, Mr. Blake? The outside world will still be there ten minutes from now, with or without our 'ministrations.' " He stumbled on the last word and laughed at himself as he sat down.

The old man took a step toward him and Connacher noticed that his face looked very white.

"Mr. Connacher, there's a mob on its way across the tracks. A white mob. The talk is they're heading for the minister's place. They're going to fire it."

Good, Connacher thought dispassionately. So he'd connected tonight. He'd done his job. He forced himself to look somber when his eyes met the old man's. "That's too bad," he said. "God have mercy on 'em."

" 'God have mercy on them?' Mr. Connacher — you'll forgive me, but you don't have a nodding acquaintance with God and you don't know the meaning of mercy."

From the corner of his eye, Connacher saw his honey-colored blonde come out of the ladies' room and stand tentatively by the bar looking at them. He started to beckon to her when the old man leaned forward and touched his arm.

"Mr. Connacher, I think you should get in the car with me and drive over to shanty town. Get in front of that mob and turn them back."

The honey-colored blonde walked over to them, looking petulantly at Blake and toward Connacher for an explanation. Connacher smiled and rose from the table.

"Sue, honey," he said. "Mr. Blake, here, is the Paul Revere of Chaseville." He laughed drunkenly. "One if by land and two if by sea!" Again he laughed and the girl joined him. Connacher took her elbow, and led her back to her seat and sat down alongside, looking up at the old man as he did so.

"Mr. Blake," he said, "why don't you run home and write an editorial or somethin'? I'm not the mayor of this town. I'm not the sheriff. I'm not the editor of the *Chaseville Gazette*, neither."

"Then what the hell *do* you fancy yourself, Mr. Connacher?" the old man asked, his voice tremulous. "A couple of hours ago you were the town conscience, the voice of the South and the reincarnation of Robert E. Lee. After you finished your little speechin' tonight, a gang of hoodlums, some teen-agers, some fathers and some town dandies all got together and decided to take a ride across the tracks. They've got kerosene with them and shotguns. Are you sober enough to get the point, Mr. Connacher?"

The girl pushed aside her glass and rose to her feet, her face full of a drunken, frustrated petulance. This crazy old man was wrecking the evening. Or at least he was delaying the beautiful part of it.

"Mr. Blake," she whined at him, "you've got no right to be rude to King, here —"

"Gently," Blake said to her through his teeth. "I won't take up much more of his time." Then he looked at Connacher. "You've got the whole night to crawl into that little lady's pants. But you've only got a few minutes to stop a murder."

Connacher tried to look outraged, but the look simply was not available to him. The girl sat down hard — like Connacher, unable to protest. She had just finished putting on her diaphragm in the ladies' room and there was something so omniscient about this crazy old man that it was as if he knew the brand name and the size. So she just sat there and waited for Connacher to handle the whole thing.

"I'm waiting," Blake said.

"For what?" Connacher asked him. "How you people decide to spend your nights isn't my concern. If you've got a few hotheads around here whose sport is to burn crosses —" He shook his head. "— don't look to me, Mr. Blake, to start blowin' whistles and layin' down rules. That's not my style."

The girl nodded happily and Connacher winked at her.

The old man took a step closer to the table and looked from one to the other, then he closed his eyes very tightly and for a moment could not speak, then his eyes opened and he straightened up.

"Values, Mr. Connacher," he said softly. "All kinds of values. First things first — right?"

Connacher stared at him.

"You set the wheels moving tonight and you pushed the wagon. And as a result, maybe a child will die. Maybe two children. And maybe you could prevent it with some of your well-known phrase-turning. But, unfortunately, you can't spare the time. Because you've got a bottle of booze to finish with a promising roll in the hay for dessert." His lips trembled. "Well, I'll say this. You're a very good pair — the two of you. You deserve one another. A leg-spreading little bimbo and a big-mouthed stud without a heart in his body."

Connacher was on his feet. "Old man," he said, his voice tight, "if some hopped-up kids wanna go firin' on some nigger's shack — that ain't my business. And it isn't your business, neither. And you can thank God that you're just a few years younger than He is, or I'd've taken out all your teeth tonight."

He rose, holding onto the table for support, feeling suddenly sick. The food lay heavy inside of him, and a touch of nausea from all the drinking rose slowly, burning, up his chest and into his throat. There was always one, he thought — always one Goddamned nutsie who pissed all over a beautiful evening and left a stench on things that wrecked all your pleasure.

"Get the hell outa here," he said to the old man. "I'm tellin' you now — get the hell outa here!"

Blake bowed ever so slightly. "Mr. Connacher," he said in almost a whisper, "count on something, will you? Count on the fact that you'll be answering to God one of these days. The One whose name you conjure up and bandy about with such ease. Because if there is a God, He'll pay you back for what you're doing."

The old man turned very slowly, and with great dignity, and with great pain, walked toward the front door and went outside.

He paused, took out a handkerchief and wiped his brow, then looked up at the star-filled sky. To the south, and across the tracks, there was a bright orange light in the sky, and there were the sounds of distant horns honking and the throaty cries of men.

A car pulled into the bar parking lot and a man got out and walked toward the entrance. Blake looked at him in the light of the neon sign.

"Sheriff?" Blake said.

The sheriff shook his head, stopped and looked toward the orange glow in the sky. "I'm not the sheriff, Mr. Blake. That's the one happy note in an otherwise rotten evenin'."

He looked at the old man's profile, then back toward the orange glow in the sky. "They did themselves proud — those boys of ours."

"Did they, indeed?" Blake asked softly. "How proud, Jim?"

"They fired the nigger minister's shack. The minister got out ... and his wife. But a four-year-old girl got burned alive. I was over there right after it happened. She got stuck in her bedroom. She screamed for a long time. She ... she sizzled like a piece of pork." He turned to look at the grim-faced old man. "And she took much too much time dyin', Mr. Blake. Much too much time."

The old man nodded, then he turned and looked toward the door of the bar. "You going in there, Jim?"

The ex-sheriff nodded. "Yeah," he said softly. "I'm goin' in there and I'm gonna relieve 'em of all their bourbon. I'm plannin' on gettin' so Goddamned all-fired drunk that I won't remember my own name — let alone what I just seen."

He started to walk past the old man. Blake touched his arm and stopped him.

"If you should see a Mr. Connacher in there, Jim — a Mr. King Connacher — you might give him the word. And you might mention to him that he's doomed now. He's got perdition written all over him. Every ounce of blood he's caused to spill ... every fire he's lighted ... every death he's been an accessory to — that's all being added up someplace. It's all being added up. And that list is getting to be quite a tab. He's running himself up one helluva bill."

The ex-sheriff stared at the old man, only partially comprehending, then he nodded and walked inside while the old man remained there, staring at the slowly diminishing glow in the sky.

Inside the bar, Connacher pushed aside his last drink while the honey-colored blonde kept stroking his arm. Then she stopped, took out her bag and began to put fresh lipstick on her mouth.

"King, honey," she said tentatively, looking at him over the little mirror, "that old man, Blake — he's nothin' but a damned crazy old man. That's all he is Don't let nothin' he said bother you. We just laugh at him around here. We read his paper but we laugh at him. He don't mean nothin'. He's just a plain old nigger lover from way back."

Connacher nodded, barely listening to her and barely hearing her, but his stomach felt tumultuous and his mouth was sour and there was a sickness coming on him. He fought the nausea down, then turned to the girl.

"Honey baby," he said, "why don't you and me go for a ride someplace? What do you say?"

The girl smiled at him in delight. "Why, I'd love to, King. I sure could use some air."

"Me, too," Connacher grunted. "I sure could use some air."

He took the girl's arm and walked toward the front door, not noticing the tall gray-eyed man in the khaki pants and T-shirt who stared at him from the bar.

They drove just two miles up the road to a small forest of pines. There, panting into each other's ears, clawing at one another, they left the car and wound up in a sweating, wrestling jumble of ripped clothes and bare bodies — taking of each other on the moss-covered earth, screaming their passions, biting and digging with tongue and teeth and fingernails until overcome with exhaustion. Then, in the now pale moonlight, they stared at one another as strangers — satiated and bored.

Connacher drove the girl back into town and left her at her parents' home, neither of them speaking much — neither of them wanting to. Each had served his purpose to the other — a couple of sex virtuosos after a performance — each satisfied in his own way; each looking on the other as a device, but not as a partner. Connacher was content now to go back to the motel and sleep it off. Sleep off the alcohol and the musty scent of the woman's perfume and the downhill emotions of the aftermath. He wanted only sleep and a respite from thought or recollection.

He started driving down the little main street of the town, aware of a gradually building depression that kept stabbing at him. He couldn't get a clear station on the car radio — even on FM — and he didn't feel like putting in a tape cartridge for music. Yet, he hated the silence. It was the old man, he thought. That was obviously the key to this. A Goddamned fanatic with a thing for niggers. He'd do something about that old man later on, he decided. Maybe in the morning. Talk to the mayor about him, or some of the big people in town. Maybe a subtle little hint that this was a Commie. But for now, he would forget that old sonuvabitch with the big mouth. All he wanted really was to sleep. Sleep and rest.

But he kept on driving, past the main street of the town, beyond the square toward the tracks, and then he crossed them, heading toward a clump of miserable little shanties he'd seen earlier in the day and had had pointed out to him as the nigger section of the town. He didn't know exactly why he continued to drive, but he was conscious of some unexplainable compulsion.

He drove around the dark and quiet unpaved streets until he reached what he knew he would reach — a burned-out, still warm square of ashes that was on one of the corners. There were a pile of ruined timbers and smoking gray earth. A metal bedpost. An ancient washing machine stripped of its paint. And quiet. An incredible quiet. Like a grave.

Connacher got out of the car, not really wanting to get out of the car but realizing that this, too, was somehow part of the compulsion that drew him to the rim of ashes. He stared into the smoke and wondered how it must feel to have flames come up and scorch the flesh. And he wondered whether it was the minister himself who'd been burned up — or his wife — or his kids — or just who. But at the same time, he forced himself to reject any complicity in what had happened. It wasn't his doing. He had had no involvement in this. No actual involvement. He hadn't directly ordered men out with torches, and he hadn't specifically asked for a house-burning. He had simply responded to the hate that was already there — to the inclinations and the deep-rooted violence that already existed long before he arrived. He found himself shrugging as he took his strutting little walk around the periphery of the ruins. He was about to head back to the white Cad when he saw a figure come out of the shadows.

It was a small man — very small. Connacher froze and waited until whoever it was came into the light of his headlights. Then he saw the remnant of the ministerial collar and the torn black suit.

"Hey, boy," Connacher yelled at him.

The black man's head jerked up and stared across the ashes toward him.

"You got business here?" Connacher asked, putting authority into his voice.

The black man didn't look frightened, but he held his hands stiff at his sides, tentative and wary, his voice very soft. "Sir?" he asked. "I didn't hear the question."

"I asked you if you had business here."

He could barely see the colored man's face in the semi-darkness, but he thought he saw the lips relax.

"Business here," the Negro repeated. "No sir. I don't believe I have any more business here. Not any more."

Connacher walked through the ashes, skirting the little areas of red that were still hot and smoking, moving closer to the other man until the black face was more distinguishable. Flat nose, big lips, kinky hair — the usual — eyes deep and dark. Just a nigger preacher walking around in a ripped suit, that's what he was.

As Connacher approached, the colored man put his head down and stood there, silent and stoic and unmoving. Connacher stopped a foot away and looked him up and down.

"Your place, was it?" he asked.

The Negro nodded. Connacher nodded back at him. There was a way of doing this — a way of handling it, with authority and firmness but still managing to convey enough sympathy so that the nigger would know that he had carried no torch and had lighted no fires and had killed no one.

"Anyone get hurt in this?" Connacher asked.

The Negro looked up and nodded. "Yes, sir," he said softly. "My little girl. She got burned up. She was four years old."

Connacher didn't say anything for a moment and then shook his head back and forth very slowly. "That's a helluva thing. I'm sorry, Reverend."

He saw the Negro staring at him and wondered at the expressionless look in the face. You couldn't tell with niggers. You really couldn't. He found himself asking the silent question — what if it had been *his* kid? This thought, too, he pushed out of his mind, and he forced himself to look away from the colored man, toward the burned little plot of earth and then beyond to the silhouetted shacks that huddled there in the dark street so close to one another.

"Damned things are like tinderboxes. Just a spark from an exhaust is all it takes to set these things off."

He looked back to the Negro, who continued to stare at him, and wished to Christ that the black bastard would say something — stop standing there and staring at him. Stop accusing him. Because that was really what the nigger was doing. He was accusing him. You could see it in his eyes. That's where you read a nigger. You read his eyes. The eyes supplied the answer. Eyes from Africa. Eyes from centuries of chained men, torn from their own earth and shipped across endless miles, dying in their own vomit, suffocating in pigsty holds of ships. Eyes that mirrored the special anguish of men turned into animals, humans turned into studs, a race of beings predating Christ and learning of Christians through whips and branding irons. And those eyes stared at Connacher and accused him. Connacher felt hypnotized by them and could not take his own eyes away. But then, he realized, this black bastard had left his place. Too much sympathy. That's what it was. Give them their head a little and they'd try to take the whole bit and move on their own. And that you couldn't sit still for. That you couldn't take.

Connacher pointed a finger at him and made his voice cold and hard. "I'm talkin' to you, boy. You realize that, don't you? I'm sayin' words to you."

The black man looked at him. "I hear you, Mr. Connacher," he said. "And I hear your words. But I'm not a boy."

The tone, quiet.

But no more subservience set to gentle music.

No longer the habit pattern of an inflection perfected over the generations to always come out as a respectful acknowledgment of the white man's superiority and the black man's enslavement — with or without papers of bondage and with or without the burned-in brand. The brand was there — invisible under the flesh and deep, deep into the very soul of the man. But it was not in his voice at all. It was not in his look. He was talking to Connacher as an equal. And Connacher realized it.

They stood and stared at one another for a long and silent moment, the minister letting his eyes move beyond the white seersucker suit to the white Cad with its lights on. So this was King Connacher. King Connacher, who rode into town — and if your skin was black, you'd lock the doors every night for the next week; and when you walked by a white man, you kept your head down and you moved to one side. The white people let loose of their cash in a hurry when King Connacher came. But he left something behind for his services rendered. He left behind a chill that hung heavy over the streets and froze up the hottest of nights. And this was King Connacher, this bandy-legged little man with the rumpled, torn suit, talking at him. Making words. Proper and courteous words that he'd heard before. When you bought a car and signed the paper for it and the auto man shook your hand and said, "Now work real hard, boy, and stay outa trouble so's you can make the payments." The minister was black and he knew. The cloying, glutting, ball-cutting chivalry of the Southern white making "good boy" while patting the faithful retainer's woolly head. His great-grandfather had once been strung up by the thumbs for spilling water on a plantation owner's pants. And as he listened to Connacher's words, he would have preferred the clean sharp pain of dislocated fingers to the prolonged agony of standing there like an animal swallowing the grief that burst inside of him, willing — with some incredible residue of strength — that the tears not come to his eyes, that the rage not flood out his reason. Because he knew now that there was no God. God had been invented, embroidered, conjured up and passed around like a collection plate. God did not exist. The ashes existed. The heat and the residue of the flames — they were quite real. And the agony that his four-year-old baby had felt not too many hours before while she turned into a charred, unrecognizable lump of something inanimate. This was the most real of all things. Standing there, looking into Connacher's face, he began to tremble. Why didn't the white man get out of there? Why didn't he leave in the big Cad convertible? Why did he have to stand there so close to where his flesh had been murdered, and mock him. His trembling grew worse, and he was unable to keep one sob — one harsh, rasping sob — from coming through his clenched teeth.

Connacher took out a pack of cigarettes, deliberately lighted one and put the pack back into his coat. "You got other children, don't you?" he asked matter-of-factly, noticing that the nigger was shivering. Actually shivering on a hot night like that.

The Negro nodded. Connacher blew out the smoke.

"Well, it ain't like you got wiped out. It ain't as if the whole family got hit. Miserable thing, losin' a child. But at least there's others." Then he smiled. His voice was jocular. It was time to revert to type and to what was the normal and accepted relationship between a black man and a white man. He winked at him. "I never met no Negro yet that couldn't propagate." He winked and grinned again. "How 'bout that, boy? You didn't get burned in *that* place, did you?"

Connacher looked into the darkness for the flash of white, grinning teeth but saw nothing but the darkness. The black man was not smiling, and this in itself disturbed him. Hell, you could always get a nigger to laugh. You could tickle him in the middle of a funeral and he'd go into hysterics. Just get him half stewed, pat him on the head, slip him a half-dollar and send him on his way, singing and chuckling and making rhythm. That was the routine. But it was the black man's unsmiling silence that pointed out the shattering stupidity of Connacher's little speech. This was no shuffling happy-go-lucky black buck who could be turned on and off with a pint and a handout. It was Connacher who had played the clown, and the realization unnerved him and made him feel ashamed. Why, this black sonuvabitch! Here was King Connacher — the white-Cadillac-convertible King Connacher, the magnanimous, high-minded, generous, forbearing, tolerant King Connacher — driving his chariot into the zoo, trying to slip the baboon a banana and doing a little monkey dance outside of the cage. And that Goddamned chimp suddenly takes on a hard-nosed dignity. And the vastly superior and civilized King Connacher is left with egg on his face — a white Mr. Bones, a yakking idiot of an end man in a minstrel show that has somehow been turned upside down. All right, black boy — the hell with it. He'd tried. God knows, he'd tried. You show a little decency to a nigger and what the hell happens? The nigger gets uppity and sullen. It was always this way. You put a tuxedo on a gorilla and right away he thinks he's a dancing partner.

Connacher made a pretense of giving a careless, nonchalant shrug, turned and started to walk back to his car, but he heard the black man sobbing. And when he reached the car and turned back, he could see the dark-shadowed eyes glistening with tears.

The nigger was crying. That was yet another part of the night's deformities. There stood a black man shedding tears. And Connacher, because he was a shrewd man, because he could still perceive a truth amidst the murky distortions and the fables and the deceptions that were his commerce, saw in the black man's grief a very basic truth. Niggers could mourn. They could shed tears. They could be flooded and engulfed by anguish and torn by a sense of loss. All this, a passing thought told Connacher, was a clear and present danger. The savages were taking on the trappings of the white hunters and where the hell would it end. What would happen if the energies they expended on Saturday nights with their razors and their broken bottles — the collective, pent-up angers and frustrations and defeats, resulting up to now in an instinct for self-destruction — what would happen if all their grief and frustration became a force? And what if this force took on knowledge — a knowledge that white men had confiscated everything of value and left them *only* razors and broken bottles and a sick unawareness of their own value? Jesus Christ, Connacher thought, someone should have given a thought to all of this before they raised the anchor of the first slave ship; before they lighted the first fiery cross; before they added the extra plumbing for the second water fountain. You put these black children on the other side of a candy-store window for so many generations and sooner or later they're going to smash their fists through the glass and reach.

He saw the black man walk toward him and then he *felt* fear. No longer the detached apprehension — but *fear*.

"What do you want, boy?" he heard himself ask. "What the hell do you want?" He saw the large white luminous eyes blink at him.

"What do I want?" the black man repeated softly. "I don't want much. I want an answer is all. I just want to hear an answer."

"To what?" Connacher said, his voice shaking.

"To a question," the black man said softly. "Some white men come in two cars tonight makin' a lot of noise. Doused my front porch with kerosene. Lighted a match. My wife and I ... we tried to get out, but they shot at us. Kept shootin' at us. Finally *did* let us out. We got out most of the chilluns, but the littlest one ... the littlest one was scared. Hid under the bed. Wouldn't come out when we called for her. Wouldn't come out. Stayed there under the bed. I tried to get through to her. I went through the flames, tryin' to get through to her. Then I was blinded. I couldn't see through the smoke. But I could hear her screamin'. Screamin'! But then ... then it was too late. She stopped her screamin'. She was all burned up. She was like a ball of fire. Li'l thing just lyin' there on the floor, screamin', while the flames … the flames ate her away. Roasted her … fried her … burned her up."

Connacher stood there in the silence.

The black man put his head down and then said, softly, "The question, Mr. Connacher — the question is … why? What did you prove tonight? What did you gain by it? That ten white men can burn up a black baby? Was that what you were lookin' to prove?"

It would have to stop, Connacher thought. It would have to stop right now. He would have to put this nigger down on his knees either with some words or the back of his hand. But his mind had stopped functioning and could not manufacture the words. And for some reason, his hands felt like two clumps of heavy lead hanging from his sides. He couldn't raise them.

The colored minister put his head down for a moment, trying to recover himself, and Connacher used this moment to open the car door. He wanted to get out of here. He had to get out of here.

"You drivin' away now, Mr. Connacher?" The minister's voice stopped him from getting into the car. "You goin' back across the tracks?"

Connacher wanted to tell him that it was none of his black business, but still no words came to his aid. He just stood there and nodded.

"Well, I wish you'd deliver a message to my white brethren on the other side. Tell 'em it isn't no trick to burn a baby. No trick at all. And if the next time they get the hungers to light a fire, let 'em tell us about it up ahead so's we can choose and pick one of us, maybe old or sick or tired, or maybe not wantin' to live so much." He took a step over to the car. "But not a baby. Not a li'l baby."

Phrases collected inside of Connacher's mind now. The prescribed and proper retorts, tagged and filed and available; the adjectives and the metaphors and the similes that could be unfurled like flags and trumpeted like musical notes and believed like the

Scripture. But at two in the morning, standing in the moonlight by a burned-out shanty, even King Connacher, with his glibness, his shrewdness, his uncanny facility for giving eloquence to mildewed bromides, could find nothing in all that tried and true repository of demagoguery to make a black man beat on a tambourine and show his white teeth and stop mourning a dead baby. He could talk about the niggers wanting to get into the white bedrooms and chasing after white daughters and usurping all the white man's prerogatives — but at this moment the language was dead and meaningless. It was the kind of thing you said to a do-gooding minister leading a freedom march; it was a putdown to any simpering horse's ass willing to yield that inch and a half and let a nigger register to vote; it was the embroidery on the Stars and Bars that looked majestic and brave waving over the embattled redoubt of White Supremacy. But in the moonlit silence of a gutted tomb, the sepulcher of a murdered infant, all the sloganry of the South became a vast non sequitur.

Connacher deliberately turned his back and climbed in behind the driver's seat of his white Cad and closed the door. He wished, almost forlornly, that he could strike back. He wished he could find a weapon. He wanted to tell the nigger of the horror of Watts, the violence of Harlem, the anarchy of Cleveland and Atlanta, the rampant madness of his black brethren across the land. But when he looked out through the open window toward the black face, the black cheeks, wet with tears, he realized that he was the proprietor of the wrong arsenal, devoid of the proper weaponry. All of his artillery, his cannon, his grenades, his arrows were designed and calibrated for battles of hatred. They could do nothing against grief. They were impotent against a black man's sorrow. And Connacher wanted no more of this black man or his sorrow, or of the smoking remnant of the night's work — and no more of the night. He turned the key and started the engine, and then compulsively he threw another look toward the black man.

"Mr. Connacher," the minister said to him in his gentle tones, "could I ask you one more thing? Could I ask you if this is the way you wanted it?"

Connacher shook his head. "No," he said, hoarsely, "this isn't the way I wanted it. This isn't what I ordered. It isn't what I planned."

"Then why, Mr. Connacher? Why didn't you do somethin' about it? Why didn't you stop it?"

Connacher opened his mouth. His instincts, he thought, could provide the answer at this moment. But again, there was no language. He simply shook his head.

"Do you know what you killed tonight?" the black minister said to him. "Do you have any idea, Mr. Connacher?"

Connacher remained silent.

"You killed a baby, and in a funny way ... you killed God. All my life I've been preachin' about God. All my life. But tonight, Mr. Connacher, you burned down the temple. You kicked Moses off the mountain and Christ off the cross. You killed God. You burned Him up. You roasted Him to death. And you made me stop believin'. Don't it make sense, Mr. Connacher? If there was a God ... if there was some Almighty Bein' lookin' down at us, do you s'pose He'd allow an innocent li'l chile to die in the flames, screamin' like she had to do? You s'pose God would allow that?" There was a pause. "Or, Mr. Connacher, do you s'pose He'd let a man like you walk around the earth puttin' out your poison like a patent medicine. Why, God wouldn't permit anythin' like this. Not the God I been preachin' about. Not the God I believed in."

No more, Connacher thought — no more. This was all he could take. In his entire life — in his scrounging, battling, desperate life — he had never felt guilt. Pain and hunger and cold and heat — but never guilt. Hopelessness and frustration and the misery of being no one — but never guilt.

"Mr. Connacher." The minister's voice seemed to follow him. "You drive careful now. There isn't nobody to protect you. There's no God. So you're on your own. Drive careful and don't die."

Then — and only then — did Connacher see the smile.

"You die and maybe you go to hell. And you never can tell — maybe in hell they make you black."

Maybe in hell they make you black. The words echoed over the purring engine as Connacher slammed his foot on the accelerator and the big white Cad lurched away. Maybe in hell they make you black. In a lifetime of facing truths and twisting truths and turning truths aside, Connacher — as he drove back across the tracks — pondered this truth. Yea verily, brothers and sisters of the South — the rock-bottom pit of degradation, the ultimate sorrow, the maximum pain had always been to have your daughter marry a nigger. But there was one thing worse. The whites had made it so. To *be* a nigger. How about that? Try that one on for size and color. Feel that pain. And King Connacher, driving wildly through the night, felt cold and frightened. Maybe in hell they make you black. He was thinking that when the road turned sharply a mile out of town and he drove straight ahead into a concrete abutment. He was thinking that as his face smashed into the windshield and the steering wheel plowed into his stomach. Maybe in hell they make you black. That pain was much more real to him than that supplied by his torn and lacerated body.

King Connacher awoke in a world of pain. There was only pain. There were no sounds, no voices, nothing to link him to the night. There was only darkness, and with it a pain, an echo of pain, a remembrance of pain, an existence of pain. He opened his eyes and stared into the dark sky, and gradually a few stars came into focus. He realized he was lying on his back on the ground, and when he turned his head, he could see his beautiful white Cad upside down, one wheel still spinning. He tried to pinpoint the pain but was unable to. He felt infant-weak and bewildered, and then it gradually came back to him. The night, and the components to the night. The nigger minister with the dead baby. The windshield exploding against his face. His beautiful white Cad with the beige leather suddenly hurtling through the air and then exploding into the earth like some kind of missile.

But now he lay on the ground, looking into the dark sky. He reached up and touched his face. It was sticky and wet. But none of the cuts seemed very deep. He let his fingers move down his body. No ribs broken. Then down his legs. Straight, whole. He breathed deeply. His lungs were intact. He wiggled his fingers. A small ache, but they moved. Hands not broken. He very slowly and carefully arched forward, raising his upper trunk so that he was in a sitting position. Spine all right. He could move. Then gingerly he pushed himself up to a standing position. He wavered, his legs felt watery and weak. But he was standing. He walked across the ground toward the white Cad and felt sad. Rest in peace, he thought. Half the engine block was protruding, like the entrails of a giant beast. The axle was bent, the glass all smashed into sunburst patterns, the steering wheel broken in half. He saw a shimmering thing on the ground and reached down to pick it up. It was the remnant of the side mirror. He held it in his hand and shook his head. All gone. This gorgeous chariot with all its accouterments. All gone. He'd have to buy another. Then he looked down at the fragment of the mirror which seemed to shimmer and move in and out of focus, like something a half-blind man would see without his glasses. He could see himself in the mirror — or at least an outline of himself, standing there, silhouetted against the sky. A blob of nondescript color against a black velvet. Then he raised his hands and held them close to his eyes.

Then he screamed.

He kept screaming.

He stumbled against the car, fighting down the faintness that took hold of him. His legs felt like rubber bands, and he had to grab onto the wheel of the upturned Cad to keep himself upright. He held up the mirror again and stared at the apparition that was looking back at him.

His forehead was black.

His nose was black.

Cheeks black.

Chin black.

He screamed again, and the black face turned back and forth saying, "No!" One black hand in the mirror, black fingers outstretched, kept waving back and forth, also saying, "No!" "No!" King Connacher said aloud. "No, no, no!" Not the time to have a nightmare like this. Not when he was awake. Not when his eyes were open. Not when his mind was again functioning. But there in the mirror, looking up at him, stood the nightmare. A scared nigger with white, rolling eyes — black hands held up in protest, white teeth flashing in a grimace of horror. He dropped the mirror on the ground.

"Mistuh Bones?" An insane little voice tap-danced across Connacher's exploding mind.

"Yas, Mistuh Intuhlakatuh?"

"Who dat nigguh in da meeror?"

"Why, dat da King, man. Dat Mistuh Connakuh. Dat da cat wid da Caddie. Dat a tiguh, man. Dat a roarin' tiguh."

Then Connacher screamed again and blotted out the voices.

He slipped slowly down to the ground, sobbing out his bewilderment, his protest, his appeal to God to stop this monstrous thing; to give him back his white face and his white hands. He huddled there on the ground, his eyes still open, looking across at the mirror inches away from him. His hands were in front of him and he looked at them. Black fists, pink nails, tan palms — like the beige leather of a Cadillac convertible he had once owned during another lifetime, a billion years ago. He held his hands aloft and stared at them, then put them to his face and clawed, digging deep red-ribbon furrows, bloody crevices that crisscrossed his cheeks and forehead — because all that was left to him was to try to cut away his flesh with his fingernails. Then he stopped his digging and his self-torture and his pointless maiming. He closed his eyes and felt the warm loam under his cheek.

Across the field there was a continuous sobbing chant from a black man lying there. It filled the small meadow where he lay and flowed up into the night sky. It sounded like some African witch doctor stomping barefooted around a grave, wailing the primitive dirge of a black savage tribe trying to bring back the dead. That's what it sounded like. And King Connacher, lying there on the ground — King Connacher, late of the white Cadillac, and late of a festive tour of white men's fields, and late of a long line of triumphant incursions into white women's beds — opened his eyes again and looked down at his black body. The black stomach underneath the torn shirt, the black genitals, the black wholeness ... and he wished for death. There *was* something worse than having your daughter marry a nigger. There was something far worse. He knew firsthand. Which is why King Connacher wanted his breath to stop, his heart to cease, his life to end.

King Connacher, in his torn white-seersucker suit, splotched with blood and dirt, tried to run down the narrow dirt road leading to the town. But he was too weak for protracted running. He would half trot, half stumble, then fall to his knees. A moment's rest, then he would rise and try again. He saw the lights of the main street up ahead, the pallid and desultory night's illumination of a grubby town that closed up early after dark because there was so little to illuminate. But to Connacher's tortured and traumatized mind, the lights were an oasis. They carried with them reality. The thing was a dream, he decided. An incredibly, imaginatively contrived nightmare with an irony so perfect, so proper, that the whole thing must have been composed by a committee someplace. He, King Connacher, was black. The lion had changed into a hyena. The hunter had taken on the trappings of the prey. He would have to wake up, so he kept crying — stumbling, sobbing, protesting — as he headed toward the lights, trying to make the nightmare end. He was a white-suited black man, blending with the night's darkness, covered by a brand-new skin whose color was appropriate — very appropriate — to this kind of nightmare.

He reached a corner of the main street and looked down its length. He was standing in front of a drugstore and there was a picture of a white woman on the poster, drinking a bottle of Coca-Cola. A white woman. And behind her, on a beach, was a white man smiling at her. And inside the drugstore was a white man, spooning out a dish of vanilla ice cream — also white. And the walls of the drugstore were white. And the sidewalk beneath his feet was white. And two pimply teen-agers, standing there on the curb, were white, and threw him a look — a white look — of white suspicion and white animosity and white challenge. Connacher walked past them, looking at the white posters and the white moon, toward a bar where he knew they served White Label scotch to white customers, served by white waitresses. In front of the bar he looked at his reflection in the window and saw his white suit with just the dim outline of face and hands — because they were black.

The door to the bar opened and a girl came out, laughing, followed by a tall young man in blue denim. Connacher stared at her. She was a honey-colored blonde, given to biting when in passion; given to mouthing dirty profanities whenever aroused. She threw one startled look at Connacher and opened her mouth as if to say something, then instinctively shook her head and moved back a step to stand closer to her companion. Connacher continued to stare at her and then took a stumbling step toward her.

"Sue," Connacher sobbed. "Sue, honey — it's me. It's King. Sue — somethin' ... somethin' horrible has happened. But it's me. It's King."

The girl stood there transfixed, her eyes wide, as this little black man seemed about to touch her ... to grab her. The tall young man in the denim stepped in front of her and reached forward to grab Connacher as he came within arm's length. He yanked him by the lapel of the white seersucker suit, then swung him in an arc to crash against the window of the bar.

"Listen, nigger," he said in a very low voice, "you must have one helluva death wish. Or you must be from a foreign country. Just where the hell do you get off talkin' to a white woman like that? You hear the question, nigger? Where the hell you get off walkin' up to a white woman on the main street of this town like you just done?"

The tears rolled down Connacher's face as he kept shaking his head and trying to speak. Jesus Christ — didn't this kid understand? Couldn't he tell? He was King Connacher. He was *the* King Connacher. He let his eyes move past the boy to fix on the honey-colored blonde who stood there in the darkness of the doorway, scared to death.

"Sue," Connacher said. "Sue — it's me. It's King. Tell the kid who I am. Tell him about me. Tell him —"

The rest of the sentence was chopped off by the palm of the white boy's hand as it smashed against Connacher's mouth. Then his sob of pain also was cut in the middle by another blow — this time with a fist as it whistled into his face and landed just between his nose and upper lip, loosening teeth and tearing flesh. It knocked him first sideways and then down to the ground, where he remained on his hands and knees, the blood dripping onto the sidewalk, the pain and shock stultifying and confusing. He started to crawl on the same hands and knees, down the sidewalk, and then felt the agonizing shock of pointed shoes, landing on his buttocks and sending another bolt of electric agony through his spine. The kick sent him sprawling face forward, his hands stretched out in front of him.

"Nigger," the white boy said, his voice shaking with excitement and with the love of what he was doing. "Nigger, you hear me? I want you to stay right here on the sidewalk — just the way you are now — and I want you to take a long crawl across the tracks back to where you come from. You hear me, nigger? You understand? When a black animal gets fresh with a white lady — he's got to be reminded that he *is* an animal. So I want you to crawl like an animal, boy. You hear me? I want you to take a long crawl right down the street."

From somewhere there came laughter. The two teenagers from the drugstore had walked over to them and were watching — grinning and chuckling and nudging one another. Oh, God — this was good. This was a little something to break the boredom of the dying night.

"Go ahead, Sam," one of the teen-age boys said to the kid in the denim. "Let him have it again. I don't think he understands yet."

Connacher braced himself for another bolt of pain. This time it came in his rib cage, as the wing-tipped shoe plowed into flesh and bone and drove the breath out of him in an unbelievable blinding agony. He lay there, face down on the sidewalk, breathless from the kick and choking from the blood that poured from his broken-toothed mouth, and still trying to call to the girl — still trying to tell her that he was King Connacher, who had once owned a white Cadillac and moved mobs and who had taken her on a patch of moss while she screamed her pleasure.

By this time, more people had arrived. Two more from the bar, the druggist from down the street. Then a policeman, who had shouldered his way through the knot of people, hesitated for a moment, looked official and grim, and then had smiled, winked and sucked in his cheeks, deciding to let it go on for just a little bit more before he broke it up. The nigger could take at least two or three more good wallops before he passed out and before any real damage was done, so why the hell wreck the fun prematurely?

The white kid in the denim saw the wink and sent his right foot out again, missing target this time but landing just below the right thigh of Connacher at a point where there was already a giant, discolored bruise. This time the pain had no connection with any experience remotely known by Connacher. It was a special agony of a special type and it sent him into a moment's unconsciousness. When he awoke the fraction of a moment later, his instincts were only for escape. He got as far as his hands and knees and began to crawl. He saw shoes and legs and boots and women's silk stockings and the lower half of store windows and the base of a lamp post. He kept crawling, listening to the laughter and the catcalls and the hoots, but he was beyond pain now. He was beyond humiliation. He was beyond even the horror of what was happening to him. He knew he had to crawl, and continue to crawl, until he could disappear into the darkness away from these people. Away from these white people. And as he crawled through this crimson world of pain and disbelief, his yet untouched instinct for survival had already made the necessary transfiguration. He would have to crawl away from *white people*. White people were the enemy. White people were the tormentors.

So he crawled.

He crawled for what seemed like endless, pain-wracked hours.

He crawled on concrete and then on gravel and then on dirt, and finally felt steel rails underneath his tortured body. And then through the glazed eyes of his torment, he realized that he was in darkness now. There were no more lights. He could not even see the moon. Black had fused into black. Black covered him and protected him. Black had taken him into its bosom and had allowed him to survive.

How he got to his feet, how he made his legs move forward, one after the other — this he would never know. But he found himself walking toward another light — a small, square adobe-looking building with a sign that read BAR. There were black men out in front of the building and under the light. He walked toward them and then past them while they stared at him. His hand touched the door and he felt himself pushing, then he was inside — small and dark and smoky. A juke-box played. Couples were dancing and there was a murmur of voices. He stumbled forward toward a small bar with stools — past faces that stared at him. Then he saw his reflection in the bar mirror. A little colored man in a torn white seersucker suit, covered with blood and perspiration and filth. A bartender with a big moon face leaned over the bar toward him.

"What happened, buddy?" he said softly. "Who caught you?"

Just the voice reached out and touched Connacher. Just its gentleness. Just the fact that it asked him a civil question and concerned itself with him. He just stood there, shaking his head and crying, the tears rolling down his face.

The bartender reached over and touched Connacher's shoulder and stared long into the wrecked and bloody face. The whole room had turned quiet. A colored man alongside put his arm around Connacher to help him onto the stool.

"Who did it, man?" the colored man asked him. "White man do it?"

Connacher tried to respond but could get no words out. The bartender pushed a shot glass over to him and motioned for him to drink. Connacher reached out with his bleeding fingers, cupped the glass for a moment, then brought it to his lips and swallowed it down. Another colored man walked over to him, his eyes studying the wounds on Connacher's face.

"You oughta get your face cleaned, man," the other colored man said to him gently. "Some of them things are deep."

There was a murmur of assent from the group surrounding him. The voices were soft — the words were full of sympathy. They held warmth and comfort and a gentle satisfying regard for him. Connacher tried to focus on these black faces that hovered around him. He could see eyes and mouths and white teeth, but he could not distinguish looks; he could not perceive expressions. And he really wanted to know who they were. He wanted to thank them. He wanted to express his appreciation for the fact that they did not kick him or knock his teeth out, or make him crawl in agony down the concrete sidewalk. He looked from face to face, his lips trembling, and found himself unable to stop crying, because the eyes that surveyed him were sorrow-filled eyes and compassionate eyes and eyes that reached out to him with acceptance and love.

The bartender poured him another drink, and Connacher drank it down and became aware of the pain simply because he felt it lessening. He wet his lips, feeling the gap in between his teeth, then he turned on the bar stool to try once again to thank these black men and women. They were no longer looking at him. A man had just walked in and Connacher heard his voice.

"Better get on home," the man was saying urgently. "Bunch of whites in cars, collectin' on the main drag. Headin' over here. Everybody'd better get on home."

There was a stir and some murmurs and a stifled cry. There was a sense of movement, of bodies drifting past Connacher's eyes, and then a hand reached out to steady him and help him.

"What happened?" Connacher heard a voice ask.

"White lady got talked to by one of us. Called her by her first name. Tried to touch her."

There was a gasp and then Connacher felt eyes turning toward him. There was no anger. Just surprise. A shocked surprise. The fascination of looking at a deranged man and listening to what incredible thing had come from his insanity.

Connacher blinked back at those eyes, wanting to recapture the warmth of the previous moment. He wanted to explain to them about the mistake that had been made. He wanted to instruct them in the night's events and what had happened and why it had happened. The bartender's voice intruded on him.

"You got a home, buddy?" the bartender asked. "You stayin' anyplace close? You better get on back there. Earlier tonight we had a burnin'. And them white people comin' across the tracks would just love to have it happen all over again. And it's you they're lookin' for. That's true, ain't it? It's you they're lookin' for."

It's me they're looking for, Connacher thought. It's me. Mebbe in hell they make you black. It's me they're looking for. Mebbe in hell they make you black. The white lady drinking the Coca-Cola. And the white boy staring at her admiringly. And the white moon and the white sidewalk and the white walls. And vanilla was white. And Tarzan was white and Superman was white and angel food cake had white icing. And God was white. And that was certainly the God-directed order of the universe. That good things were white. And bad things were black. Good was white — black was evil. Cleanliness was white — filth was black. And so long as there were black marchers and black freedom riders and black power and black Communists, screaming for black liberty — then it followed that there would have to be a white King Connacher driving a white Cadillac convertible, collecting money from white audiences and laying white women as part of his tribute. And what had just happened? Why a Goddamned nigger ... an uppity, fresh-assed, black-cocked coon had accosted a white woman.

Connacher fell off the bar stool and laughed aloud. Why, hell, he thought, I'm drunk as a coot. I'm downright drunk. He got up and walked to the door and went out into the dirt street. People moved back and forth in front of him and he heard their voices, and again he had to laugh. He was drunk — sure — but not so drunk that he couldn't engage in whatever the sport was. And if some coon had tried to make it with a white woman, the sport would be to get that coon and string him up. And that could be one helluva lot of fun. So Connacher stepped out into the dirt street and saw the cars coming toward him. He heard them screech to a stop. He heard fenders bang. He heard the angry voices of men. He saw them running toward him. They were white men. So he grinned and waved and laughed again.

"We're gonna get a coon," he shrieked. "We're gonna get ourselves some fresh-assed little nigger who don't know his place. That's what we're gonna do tonight, boys." Then he turned like an infantry platoon leader and motioned his white Army to follow him, and he broke into a stumbling run while the footsteps and the angry voices pursued him. "We're gonna get the coon," he shouted. "Gonna get the nigger boy."

He continued to run down the dark street, hearing the voices behind him grow louder, the footsteps echoing through the night like some nightmarish herd of animals. Out of the corner of his eye he saw the dark, shuttered little shacks that flanked the streets. He was conscious of the night sky and the distant stars and very gradually, as he forced his aching legs to continue their movement, he realized he was not the hunter at all. He was the prey. It was as if he had been running all his life — a continuous process of forcing dead-tired limbs to move; a prolonged nightmare of a chase. Disjointed, unreal thoughts coursed through his brain. Stars. Find the Big Dipper. Find the North Star. He was on a black ocean being pursued by a storm.

Then he stopped dead.

There stood a short man in a black shiny suit, white skin showing through the torn trouser leg and one ripped sleeve — a clerical collar pulled out from the white neck, and the face white.

"Reverend," he said, wheezing through his torn lips and the gaps between his broken teeth, "Reverend, in the name of God — help me. Help me, please —"

He stopped and stared at the face; the familiar face. He took a stumbling step over toward him, shaking his head back and forth as he did so, because this was yet another part of the nightmare — as monstrous as all that had preceded. It was the face of the nigger preacher. But it looked like a photograph in reverse polarization — white standing out against the darkness. A black face injected with a white dye. A white face.

"I know you," Connacher whispered. "I know you. You're the nigger." He shook his head again. "You're the nigger."

The minister smiled at him. "Boy," he said, "you gotta watch your talk, you know that? You can get into some trouble. You can get into some real trouble."

Connacher slowly sank to his hands and knees, feeling the weight of the nightmare now unbearable, now crushing.

The white minister looked down at him, then walked past him toward the white mob that had suddenly stopped in its tracks. The night, Connacher realized, had turned silent.

"What's your pleasure, gentlemen?" the minister said to the mob, his voice very soft and very deliberate.

The men in the mob looked at one another nervously. One of them, younger than the rest, took a step out from the line and pointed to the figure of Connacher, still on his hands and knees.

"It's the nigger, Reverend," he said.

There was another voice from behind the younger man. "Let's forget it," the voice said. "He's half dead already. He's learned his lesson."

There was a murmur of assent. Two or three of the white men turned and started to walk back toward the cars. The younger man looked indecisive for a moment, then half turned as if to follow them.

"I reckon he's right," the younger man said. "I reckon we can forget it for the night."

Connacher lowered his head and closed his eyes. He wanted to cry with relief. He remained there on his hands and knees, then heard the minister's footsteps as they moved back over to him.

"On your feet, boy," the white minister said, the voice not rising an octave, but with a new note of authority. "On your feet now. Stand up like a man."

Connacher put his hands, palms down, on the ground and pushed as hard as he could. More pain. Fresh pain. His body was like some conduit for bolts of agony, and trying to rise was like plugging himself in for new currents to run through him, but somehow he reached his feet again and looked across at the white minister, trying to put into the look his love and his thanksgiving and his gratitude.

The white minister was very small. Eye level to Connacher. And he smiled at him. "How're you feelin', Mr. Connacher?" he asked.

Connacher blinked his eyes. How was he feeling? Why, just fine and dandy. He had turned black. And the nigger with the burned kid had turned white. And there was a mob a hundred feet away ready to lynch him. But he felt just fine. The tears rolled down his face and he began to laugh. He stood there, wavering, and then held out an arm, pointing a finger at the minister.

"Tell me, somethin', Reverend," he said, feeling his mind being squeezed and pulled and yanked at; sensing that whatever little sanity remained to him was slipping away. "Where'd you get *your* paint job? Where'd you get white?"

The younger man from the mob stopped on his way back to his car and turned, overhearing Connacher's harsh, shrill voice. He exchanged a knowing look with one of his companions, then made a gesture, and the two men began to walk back toward Connacher. After a moment, the others followed. This was quite a nigger. This one found salvation, then threw it away with his mouth. Listen at 'im. Lippin' at a white minister, makin' fresh-ass talk with a white man of God.

"Reverend," the younger man said, "what'd that nigger just say to you?"

Connacher laughed again, then turned toward the mob. "You stupid bastards," he said. He pointed toward the minister. "He's black as hell. Underneath that white skin — he's black. I know 'im."

The younger man exhaled and then whistled softly through his teeth. "Jesus," he said softly to Connacher. "You don't know when you've had enough, do you?"

"It doesn't seem so, does it?" the white minister interjected, his voice suddenly controlling the scene.

The white men, on the way back to their cars, turned, and sensing something beginning again, retraced their steps, until once again they were aligned ... and once again, a mob.

The white minister walked back and forth in front of them and then looked across at Connacher. "You're not surprised, are you, gentlemen?" he asked. "I mean, we know niggers, don't we? You lend them a few square pieces of sidewalk — and they lay claim to the whole sidewalk. That's their nature. That and tainting our blood, taking our daughters ... tryin' to 'overcome.' " He spat the last out like some sour blob that collected in his mouth. "And once this is done, gentlemen," the white minister continued, "once this is done, here comes the black mob. Here they come, my friends — get ready for the parade. The big bucks with the yellow spats and the frizzle-haired sluts with the monkey lips —"

"No!" Connacher screamed. "No, you're stealin' my words. You sonuvabitch — you stole my color and now you're stealin' my words."

The line of white men moved forward ominously.

"Which one of you," the white minister suddenly shouted, "which one of you wanted to let 'im go? I want to see that man. I want to hear 'im."

An older man in the group looked down at his feet, embarrassed. The men on either side stared at him accusingly.

"Was it you?" the minister asked him. "You, there — was it you?"

The older man nodded, shamefaced. "I just figgered ... I just figgered he had enough for one night."

"For one night," the minister repeated. "One night. For one night he's probably *had* enough. But let me tell you somethin', my friends — this ain't the last night on earth. There'll be other nights to follow. There'll be other niggers and other white women and other sidewalks. Not just sidewalks, my friends. Arenas. Fields of combat. Places where the blacks march up to meet the whites. And it becomes a question of whose sidewalk it is ... and whose world it is. Because the black man ain't content with sharin' it. He'll never be content to share it. Not this night, not tomorrow night, not the next night. The black man wants to *take* that sidewalk. Like this one here."

He pointed again toward Connacher. Connacher shook his head back and forth again. Incredulous ... incredulous. The little bastard ... the thieving little bastard. These are the things *he* would say. This is the way *he* would talk to a mob. The very words. The very inflections. He wet his lips and took a stumbling step back toward the mob.

"Now, listen ... listen to me," he said thickly, because most of his teeth were loose and his lips were swollen. "This ain't a white man talkin' to you. Believe me, now. This ain't a white man. This here's a nigger minister. I don't know what's happened. I don't know why he's become white ... I don't know why I've become black — but this one here is a nigger. This one here —"

The younger man stepped out from the line and back-handed Connacher across the face, then kneed him in the groin, toppling him backward. He lay on his back, gasping at yet another new pain that turned his stomach into ice water.

The white minister stood over him and smiled. "Hurt you, did he, Mr. Connacher," he said, "when he kicked you *there?* How about it, boy?" He winked at him grotesquely. "I never met no Negro yet that couldn't propagate." Again he winked. "How about that, boy? You didn't get permanently damaged in that place, did you?"

Connacher lay there, trying to get up. He sensed that survival was slipping away from him along with sanity, and he wanted to tell these men what kind of monstrous thing had occurred. But it was as if his mind had suddenly become glutted with broken teeth and loose, torn flesh, and the flooding, cascading waves of pain that lapped at his skull. And all that came from him were deep raspy breaths.

"Gentlemen," the white minister said, "you have to let the black man know what's what. You have to let him know with your voices ... with your right hands ... with any weapon at hand. He's inferior. Now, this ain't just a call to arms, it's a sacred duty. You have to let him know."

He suddenly bent over, grabbed Connacher's arm and pulled him to his feet — and then, in the same motion, flung him toward the mob.

"This one here," he shouted. "Let *him* know."

Connacher landed on the ground again, almost at the feet of the line of white men, but this time he did not permit himself the luxury of lying with his face in the dirt. He rolled over on the ground and then was back on his feet, running — flanking the line of white men like a football player. He ran toward the darkness at the end of the street, and he heard the sound of the shot and felt the dull, powerful thud against his back again — almost at the same moment. But this time there was no pain, and it was some moments later when he realized that he was no longer running. He was back down on the ground. And this time he could not move — arms, legs, body trunk or anything. And this time he was content to just lie there and speak to the earth underneath his face. He made a speech and he felt, then, that it was a most effective speech.

"Friends," he said to the cinders and the mud and the dust. "Friends, I weep — do you know that? I weep at what has been done to us and what is bein' done to us. I weep for the ravished ghosts of our people who were our forebears."

The cheering multitude made a deafening noise just below King Connacher's cheeks and he wanted to hold up his hands to quiet them down so he could continue. But his fractured, dismembered spine would not allow him to raise his hands. So he just smiled with his humble, righteous white smile and let them continue to applaud him. At the same time, he was conjuring up the next phrase. This would be a good one. This would be even more effective. He'd shoot the arrow — not throw the grenade. It was something about tainting our blood and wanting us to offer our daughters; something about a black mob — big bucks with yellow spats and frizzle-haired sluts with monkey lips. But the cheering persisted and drowned out even his thinking. It was so loud, Connacher thought. So very loud. God, he was good tonight. He must be better than ever. Or why would they cheer so loudly? Then he relaxed and stopped thinking. What the hell. Let 'em cheer and have fun. Let 'em roar. Let 'em clap till their hands were sore. Let 'em get the message and react to it anyway they wanted. Later on, he'd have a nice hot shower and a big steak and a coupla drinks and he'd find a honey-colored blonde. That's what he'd do. That's what King Connacher would do.

In the pale and diminishing moonlight, a man in a torn, shiny black suit stood over a mound of ashes, his head down, his eyes closed. He heard a rustle of sound behind him and then soft footsteps growing louder. He turned and looked up. A black woman was at his side.

"Josh." Her voice was very soft. "Josh, where have you been?"

The minister took his eyes from her face and looked down at his hands. They were black. Even in the washed-out, pale glow of the aging and departing moon, he could tell they were black. From far off, beyond the tracks, came the sounds of a car horn and a raced engine. The woman turned toward the sounds and her body stiffened.

"It's all right," the minister said. "They won't be back tonight. They got what they was after."

The woman turned to face him. "What about the ... the li'l feller in the white suit? People was talkin' about 'im."

The minister's face was a black mask. "Him? Why, they tied him to the back of a car. The last thing I seen, they was pullin' him across the tracks."

"Oh, my God," the woman said, shutting her eyes tight.

The little minister looked at her briefly, then down to the ashes. "It's only pain. We all know pain. That's what we're born for — that's what we live for." He stared at the ashes. "There's a quota ...

a quota of pain. That's what's ordained. Even ..." His voice choked. "... even for four-year-old chillun."

The woman stared at him, feeling his rigidness and sensing his coldness, and was frightened by his fury. "Josh," she said softly, "the chillun are all in bed. Friends took 'em. And we got a place to stay, too, now. Let's go, Josh. Let's go."

He didn't move.

"Josh," she said, in a whisper more urgent, "what's the matter? What's happened? Tell me ... tell me, and we can both pray."

The minister turned to look at her. His voice was a grating, harsh thing that she had never heard before. "No," his voice said. "I don't wanna pray no more. I can't pray no more."

"What do you mean?" his wife asked. "What do you mean by that?"

"I mean," he said, "that a man's gotta pray to somethin'. A man's gotta believe in somethin' that he can pray to. Somethin' ... somethin' superior." He looked down at the ashes again. "And the only thing bigger'n man and stronger'n man is his hate. That's what God is. God is hate."

"Oh, no," the woman said, in a hushed, shocked voice. "Oh, no, Josh — that ain't true. God help you ... that ain't true."

He pushed away a piece of charred timber with his foot and then turned away.

"We'd best get on back to where we're gonna sleep then. We gotta get some sleep." He reached out and touched his wife's face. "We gotta sleep and forget what's happened."

He took the woman's arm and the two of them walked away from the charred patch of ground.

But even with sleep the minister knew they would never forget. They could never forget. Deaths and lynchings and burnings — you never erased the memories of these violent moments. They were the indelibly engraved tombstones in the cemetery of the mind where were laid certain recollections of death. But not to rest. Never laid to rest. And as they walked, the black minister gave a thought to the miracle that had occurred; to the incredible thing that had happened when for one hour out of his eternity, he had been allowed to join the white world as a privileged member. But, he thought further — the one hour had been quite sufficient. It had been sufficient for him to renounce his God, to disqualify himself from ever again feeling a part of the race of men, and to doom himself to whatever was the afterlife debt that one paid in hell or in limbo or in whatever perdition there existed.

And down on the main street of the grubby little town, there was the other member of the two-man miracle — the bouncing body of King Connacher tied to the rear bumper of an aged Chevrolet, and leaving behind a trail of very red blood and very black patches of skin.

But King Connacher had already had his quota of pain. He was dead and did not feel a thing.

# EYES

Indian Charlie Hatcher took his once proud body down the four flights of steps one at a time, carrying his worry with him to the grubby, dirt-dark lobby of his hotel — called, with an almost comic inappropriateness, the Excelsior.

Indian Charlie was one of two dozen irregularly paying guests who hid in their decaying and depressing rooms as if they were caves. His credentials were proper for the place. He was an ex-middleweight with a hundred and eight fights — a hundred and eight grueling destructive nights carved out of his sixteen miserable years off an Arizona reservation. He had been nineteen years old, young and indestructible. Now he was no longer young and had long since been destroyed.

He walked slowly and thoughtfully down the uncarpeted rickety stairs because slowness and thoughtfulness were part of his natural condition, and because his brains had been jarred tilt by other boys off their own particular reservations. Italian boys out of Bridgeport. Colored boys from Harlem. Jewish boys off Delancey and Mott. Irish boys from southside Boston. All of them as hopeful and full of dreams as he. All of them fresh from the garbage dumps of urban America. Most of them ... almost all of them ... back now where they started from; living out their failure in dingy Excelsior Hotels across the land. Like Indian Charlie, they had graduated from poverty and had come back to poverty. There had been the brief, heady interval of glory in between — when they were sharp and fit and could hit hard and could take being hit hard. There had been now dimly remembered steak dinners and clean sheets and women full of favors. But they had discovered too late that they had followed a profession quick to discard them; quick to forget them; stoically and dispassionately unforgiving of the passage of years. Now, because they were older and beaten and no longer believed in miracles, they could accept the squalor they had run from as young men. They would never again remonstrate against whatever misery stacked and dealt them. Now they were has-beens and never-wases and never-would-bes; dancing masters of another time who walked on rubber legs to oblivion. A few kept scrapbooks. Others, punchier and farther gone, frequented certain bars where they would congregate — a fraternal gathering of thick-tongued wrecks reminiscing their poor shattered lives away. And others, like Indian Charlie, lived from gray morning to grayer morning, walking down the steps and up the steps — passing, unspeaking, the dying flotsam off the register — the winos and the grifters and the out of work pimps.

As Indian Charlie walked down the stairs he tried to remember what it was that gave him this feeling of disquiet. It eluded him as things had a habit of eluding him of late. His mind was like some cluttered attic of a condemned house in the process of being torn down; a wasting, disintegrating storehouse of worthless antiques — piled up fragments of memory and elusive ghosts of past pains and pleasures.

He did remember The Trouble. It was a memory he tried to hide in that attic of his — hide and forget. But it would come back to him on occasion — jumbled and indistinct, full of unbearable pain and unbearable longing. There had been a seventeen-year-old girl who had walked into his dressing room one night after a fight. A blonde child-woman with the sick, hungering body of a nymphomaniac. She had invited and then begged, and Indian Charlie Hatcher, full of his own sickness and his own longing, had responded. He could remember now the sweating, squirming body and the moaning voice and the searching hands. And he had responded in kind. He had felt drowned in a sensual flood that had, for one moment, totally obliterated him. But it was part of his primitiveness and simplicity, along with the damaged matter that made up his brain, that made him believe, later on, that some avenging forebear had sent down punishment from the Great Heavens in the form of the New York City Vice Squad. Handcuffed to a chair, he had been worked over worse than in any ring, but the pain had come from the loss of pride — the one thing he had managed to retain. Statutory rape was what they had called it. But after the first day of the three hundred and sixty-five he had spent in prison, he had forgotten that along with almost everything else. All he could bring to mind was the conglomerate terror of the experience, translated into a numbing fear of all women. The Trouble. He remembered it now, breathing heavily as he walked and thought. A whistle of breath came out of the gap between the white, straight teeth and wheezed through the triangularly shaped blob of a nose, splattered against his face as if thrown and stuck there like a misshapen piece of dough. The Trouble. The wisdom of five hundred years, transfused into his veins, molding his genes — the instinct that the Indian does not accept gifts from the white man, especially not his women — this he had forgotten in the moment of his passion. But he was made to remember it during the endless days and endless nights in the gray gloom of a cell, and he would remember it now as he walked down the steps to the lobby. His mind was feverish with the desperate urgency of thought. Things came back now. He could remember a phone call. Last night? The night before? One of those two nights. He'd received a phone call. It wasn't much — but at least it was a starting place for the jerking, irregular train of his thoughts. A phone call ... and from whom? Somebody. Somebody he knew. Two of the thoughts coupled together. It was from Petrozella. Petrozella — a gambler, a bunco artist, a sometime fight manager, an all-the-time con man. A manipulator. One of the peripheral sideline artists peculiar to the profession of boxing. A realist who at an early age discovered that dumb men were born to be used — and smart men used them. He had managed Indian Charlie Hatcher for over four years. And now, out of the indistinct shadows of Indian Charlie's mind, came a flitting light. It was Petrozella who had phoned him. Meet him in the lobby. That morning. That's what he had said. And that's what he, Charlie, was doing — walking down the stairs.

When he reached the bottom step he paused and thought harder and deeper. Petrozella had said it was important. Petrozella was smart. Moxie and shrewdness and savvy — that was Petrozella. He never drew to an inside straight. He never tried to bribe a cop with an unfamiliar face. And he never let loose of any one of his stable of bleeders if there was yet a pound of flesh remaining that he could job off cut-rate and in a hurry.

So Indian Charlie Hatcher stood in a dismal lobby full of aged cracked leather furniture, a phony rubber palmetto plant and a fat day clerk named Gus who signed in the Joneses and the Smiths and did a prosperous, thriving business on the side with watered whiskey, pot and diseased poontang that he would send up to respective rooms. He had talked with Petrozella on the phone before ringing Charlie Hatcher's room. He had filled the ex-manager in on the state of the Indian's affairs. The fact that he was two weeks in arrears on his room rent, had had no visitors, had spent no recent time in jail and was hungry most of the time. Gus, the day clerk, and Petrozella, the night crawler — they were partners in men's souls. Men like Indian Charlie Hatcher.

Now, Gus looked interestedly across the lobby from his catbird perch behind the registration counter and noted with some satisfaction that Charlie had come down on time. True, he looked like a motorist lost in Death Valley, but he was right there in the lobby as Petrozella had demanded. What the hell if he looked a little confused. He usually did. And what the further hell that he was a big, dumb, quiet bastard who gave nobody any trouble. The Indian was in the lobby at the prescribed time, ripe and ready for the sale of Manhattan. This was business. Strictly business. Sure, it was a rape (knowing Petrozella, it had to be), but when you were engaged in that kind of sport, you didn't start apologizing to the recipient.

"Hey, Hiawatha," Gus's voice snaked across the room, "you got a date? Little cooze this morning to start the day?" He laughed out loud. God, would you look at that Indian! Hair slicked down like with axle grease. A stained but still shrieking yellow tie, knotted in a misshapen lump off to one side from a too-tight shirt. He looked like a buck out of an Indian school on his first three-day prize weekend to the big city, sunburning his tonsils while staring up at the big buildings. This kind you had to rape. There just wasn't any alternative.

"Ask her if she's got a friend, Charlie, huh?"

Gus laughed again while Indian Charlie walked slowly across the room over to the big window fronting Eighth Avenue.

He didn't like Gus. Gus confused him. He was always talking about women and what you did to them. This, by itself, froze Charlie and made him remember The Trouble. An Irishman who used to live on the third floor, an ex-carney man, had told him that Gus had been involved in a train accident when he was a young man and had lost his manhood. That was the reason he kept talking about women so incessantly ... so continuously.

Gus's voice followed him across the room. "Hey, Charlie? If she ain't got a friend — tell her I'll stand in line after you!"

Charlie didn't turn around. He just stood there, staring out of the window, feeling uncomfortable in the tight shirt, remembering vaguely that his being down in the lobby had something to do with meeting Petrozella. But exactly when and for what particular reason he was to meet him, he wasn't sure.

"Who're yuh waitin' for, Charlie?"

Indian Charlie shrugged. "My manager," he mumbled.

"Your manager? You got a manager, Charlie? Wait a minute ... wait a minute ... don't tell me. Tonight's the night, huh?

Champeenship? Who do you go against tonight, Charlie? Carnera? Jesus, you're too young to fight Corbett." Again the laughter.

The Indian winced. He put his head down and looked at his shoes. Then he cleared his throat and shrugged again. "Mr. Petrozella," he said — so soft as almost not to be heard. "Mr. Petrozella said he was going to come here this morning. He wanted to ... he wanted to discuss something with me."

"Like what?"

"I don't know. But Mr. Petrozella called me on the telephone. He called me on the telephone and he told me to meet him. Right here. Right here in the lobby."

As Charlie spoke, pieces of the jigsaw puzzle fell into place. A memory of something whole and consistent. Mr. Petrozella had phoned him, he remembered, and he was to meet him here in the lobby at ten in the morning. He remembered that, too. He turned, smiling, toward Gus. "That's why I got dressed up," he said simply. "Because Mr. Petrozella told me to."

Gus smiled back at him from behind the desk. Oh, Jesus — he wished there were more like this one around. And if only this Indian owned an oil well, he could sell him one half the hotel, the Triboro Bridge and all the concessions at Shea Stadium. And while he was sticking it into him, the Indian would probably cry with gratitude! A pity. A real pity. Humpty Dumptys like this Sitting Bull were almost extinct. But what the hell. He felt suddenly bored and no longer up to baiting. The Indian was too frigging dumb to respond to a rib anyway. To hell with it. He'd let Petrozella take him for the day's ride and he'd lick what was left on the spoon later on. He sat down behind the registration counter and picked up a newspaper.

Indian Charlie left the window. He felt better now. He had remembered something. That softened his apprehensions. To be able to remember — that was something. Even Gus didn't unnerve him any more. He went over to one of the cracked leather chairs, simonized by a million pant seats, and sat down. He didn't quite know what to do with his big hands. He looked at them for a moment, then interlocked the fingers and kept them on his lap. Once or twice he tried to loosen his collar, but did so gingerly for fear of wrecking a button. After a moment he began to hum — more a single-note nervous chant than any kind of music.

Gus dropped his newspaper and glared across at him. "You workin' up a war dance?"

Charlie blinked a him.

"If I wanna hear Indian music, I'll order it from Muzak." He jerked the paper up in front of him again. "Jesus, why the hell do the freaks check in here! What the hell's wrong with the YMCA!"

As usual, Charlie didn't understand. Not the words anyway. But the tone — even his damaged brain could perceive the dislike and the derision. He stared, fascinated, across the room over to Gus and wondered about him. He had met many men like Gus. They made fun of him and laughed, but there was no humor in the way they spoke. They were angry men and dissatisfied men, and laughter was a weapon with them. It was odd, too. He, himself, felt no such anger. Even in the ring, he did not strike out to hurt. This he could never do. He had taken no pleasure in rendering pain to other men. And on the occasions when his opponents were either too young or too old, and he could hit them at will, he did not, like some men, play with them round after round, cutting them up, slicing them, prolonging their night's pain. He did not like Gus but he could never return the little man's peculiar hatred in kind. Then his mind tired from thinking. He relaxed in the chair and looked at his hands and waited for Mr. Petrozella. It was good that he remembered. Ten o'clock in the lobby. And there he sat, just as he was told to. And that was good. After a moment his mind journeyed away from him as it so often did. It went back to Arizona and to purple mountains and the warmth of the sun. Moments of his boyhood came back to him, and he could remember fishing and running and his father's voice and his mother's smile. Then he dozed and remembered nothing. He floated in a canoe on a starless ocean. He had never heard of the Excelsior Hotel or The Trouble or Mr. Petrozella. There was no relentless desert sun, nor was there the equally relentless white klieg that turned him into a dark silhouette against the white canvas of the ring. None of these things existed.

This but for a moment. Short night and brief crossing. He awoke and Mr. Petrozella was looking at him from across the room, talking in whispers to Gus. Mr. Petrozella had graying, wavy hair and a little mustache, and his suit, unpressed and shiny, had been expensive and it fitted him well.

He smiled as he turned from the desk and started over to Charlie. The smile never quite reached his eyes. "Charlie, kid," he said, as he approached him. Mr. Petrozella always called him "kid." It made Charlie feel good.

He rose from the chair, smiling and warm. It was good that Mr. Petrozella was here. It was good that there was someone he could depend on ... someone to tell him what to do and what to think.

Mr. Petrozella pumped his hand and continued to smile at him. "You look good, kid. You look real great."

Charlie nodded happily, not releasing the hand. Mr. Petrozella had to do that. After a moment he pulled his away and slapped Charlie's back.

"I've missed you, kid. I've been wondering what's been goin' on with you." He gently prodded Charlie toward the door.

Charlie moved with the pressure of Petrozella's hand, unquestioning and contented. When Mr. Petrozella was around, he no longer *had* to think. That dead-weight sack of cement he carried on his back like a hump when he was alone — he dropped it off to one side and let Mr. Petrozella guide him. This was good. This was very good. Mr. Petrozella would tell him what to do and where to go.

But even as they went out the door into a gray October morning, Charlie felt some little stab of something cross his mind. The warning light that flitted in the shadows of the attic that made him look at Mr. Petrozella again through the corner of his eyes and remember some other times. Someplace, a long time ago. Someplace. A locker room. After a fight. Not sure when. But sometime. And Mr. Petrozella had done something to him. Slapped him across the face. Called him a tanker. And spit on the floor and told him to get out. And Mr. Petrozella wore no smile that night.

Charlie shook his head back and forth, feeling an ache when he tried to think back to all of it. He had lost a fight. He could remember that. He had lost a fight — a long one. And his knuckles had been broken. But Mr. Petrozella had slapped him — and he could remember that much. He turned to look at the face alongside. It was smiling at him. He could feel the arm thrown over his shoulder as they walked down the street. Charlie stopped thinking and stopped wondering. It was better this way. Mr. Petrozella would tell him where to go and what to do. It was better and it was easier. So Charlie just let his feet move and he let himself breathe some of the good fresh morning air. He had a friend again. A guide. Someone to look after him. Like a father. Not the tall man with the white hair and the deep-set eyes and the gentle voice. This one had a little mustache and red-rimmed eyes that looked at him furtively and never held a look. But it was all right. It was good. Now he didn't have to try to think any more.

Madison Square Garden had once been the Mecca for all the fighters on earth. Now shabby, colorless, it squatted on Eighth Avenue like a decaying dowager. And on either side were small, dark bars, grimly and tenaciously struggling for survival, just as the Garden was … and just as the whole institution of boxing was. They were like dirty little scows attached to a leaky mother ship and sinking along with her. It was to one of these that Petrozella took Indian Charlie. He ushered him grandly through the front door, across the nearly empty room, past the pictures of fighters and famous fights spread around the walls — and the championship belts hung over the bar. He patted his arm and massaged his back and subtly led him to a corner booth, where he seated him on one side of the table and then quickly sat down across from him. He winked at Charlie, then looked briefly up toward a picture of Rocky Graziano kicking the hell out of Tony Zale, then he smiled.

"Good boys," Petrozella said, motioning toward the picture, but with two fingers of the other hand held out to a sleepy-eyed bartender across the room. Petrozella always called prize fighters boys. So long as they wore trunks and gloves, they were boys. But down deep, of course, because he was one shrewd and perceptive cookie, he knew that they were old men. They were the oldest. They forfeited youth one minute into the first round of their first fight. But Petrozella's perception was on more than one level. He read people like clear smoke signals. He knew the broads that would allow themselves to be boffed, the rumdums who could be shaken down, or any loser on his way down who crossed his path who had a weakness that Petrozella could find, recognize and exploit. And the weakness of Indian Charlie was worn like a war bonnet. He was a bewildered and lonely man, lost in a perpetual storm, threading his way through fog, desperate for a hand to lead him and to hold onto.

Years before, when Petrozella had first met him, when Charlie could still distinguish between the past and the present and the reality of each, he had talked of his father. There had been both love and longing in his reminiscing. It was Petrozella's nature not to understand such sentiment. He was bemused first by the fact that an Indian could even have a father. Petrozella put all minorities into very specific categories. Indians were like niggers. They were animals. Sometimes valuable animals, like race horses. But that they should weep for their boyhood was inexplicable to him. And Charlie's boyhood, by Petrozella's lights, rated no nostalgia and, Christ knows, no tears. It was a brief history of grubbing in a hard and unfriendly earth, eking out a mean little living with no pay-off nor even a hope. But a man with the longings of Hatcher was an especially vulnerable item to someone like Petrozella. To con him, to back him against a wall, to twist him up — this was child's play. It was like mugging a basket case. Indian Charlie wanted a father figure. Check! Mr. Petrozella softened his eyes and looked concerned. One father figure coming up!

He deftly whisked the drinks out of the bartender's hands as he approached the table and plopped one shot glass down in front of Charlie. Then he held out his own glass and clinked it against the Indian's.

"Geronimo, baby."

Indian Charlie, as if in a trance, downed his drink in one swallow and sat there, numb and stoic and waiting, while Petrozella went through the motions of surveying him.

Finally Petrozella shook his head back and forth with apparent deep concern. "I'll tell you something, Charlie," he said. "I'll give you the goods, baby. You don't look good to me. You look raunchy as hell. When was the last time you had a square meal?"

Charlie blinked at him. As always, Petrozella's words zoomed in at him from different directions — always fast, always staccato, always difficult to understand.

"Meal?" Charlie mumbled.

Petrozella tapped the glass on the table. "A good square meal of beeksteak or roast chicken. What the hell — ham and eggs ... anything. When did you last sit down to something that would put flesh on your bones?"

Indian Charlie crisscrossed a fingertip around and around the wet circle on the table left by the shot glass. "I've been looking for work," he said in his slow, deliberate voice. "There was a fellah ..." He stopped, knitting his brows, desperately trying to remember something that had again eluded him. It was something about a man he'd met in a bar a few nights ago, or maybe a few weeks ago. Someone who had an idea for a job for him. He shook his head, capitulating to that impossibly scrambled brain of his. He simply could not remember. He looked up at Petrozella.

"Some guy ... some guy said he might have a job for me."

Petrozella smiled again and shook his head. "Some guy," he mimicked. "Some guy. Some frigging ghost. Somebody you dreamed about." He shook his head again. "That's one of your problems, Charlie, baby. That's always been one of your problems." He tapped his head. "You've got a garbage dump in there. You can't think past your frigging first name." He shook his head unhappily and motioned to the bartender to bring more drinks.

The bartender glided across the room, silent and omniscient, with two more shot glasses.

Charlie downed the second drink and then nodded. Mr. Petrozella was right. He could *not* think beyond his first name. He sat back in the booth, feeling the whiskey warming him. "I ... I've been looking around quite a lot. I've been to employment agencies — places where they give you work."

Petrozella's smile was an editorial comment on the absurdity of Indian Charlie looking for and finding a job. He leaned across the table and briefly put his hand over Charlie's big mallet fist. "Charlie, baby, are you serious? Do you think a bunch of underpaid social workers are gonna get your groceries?" He shook his head and puckered up his lips in a little disdainful look. "Charlie — the only help you're gonna get is from friends. Buddies." He tapped his chest expansively. "Like me. Petrozella never let you down, did he? Did I ever let you down?" He shook his head again. "Baby, when it gets down to the fine strokes — when it gets down to the performance — don't go to strangers. Don't go to City Hall. You come to the people who give a damn about you!" Then he looked away as if a little embarrassed at the depth of his emotions. "People who ... who love you, kid."

Charlie's eyes drifted up to the picture of Graziano knocking the mouthpiece out of Zale's mouth. He could not meet Petrozella's eyes. When the man talked of love and friendship, he somehow felt guilty. As if he'd let this fine man down somehow. That was why Petrozella had slapped him across the face that night. That must have been the reason. He wasn't sure, of course. He wasn't even sure what they were doing here now or what had prefaced the meeting, but he did have this vague sense of guilt that Mr. Petrozella was offering him affection and he had nothing to reciprocate with.

His voice, thick and sluggish, blurted out, "I'm sorry about that fight. I really am, Mr. Petrozella."

Petrozella looked at him through squinted eyes. What the hell fight was he talking about? Jesus God, it was a chore trying to have any kind of a dialogue with a punchy. "What fight?" he said a little impatiently, but maintaining his smile. "What fight are you talking about, Charlie?"

"The last one. The one where I got licked. I really done my best that night. I really tried. The kid was much too fast for me. Much too young."

Petrozella half closed his eyes. The things these punchies dredged up. Inconsequential, meaningless, disconnected. Indian Charlie Hatcher had lost twelve of his last eighteen fights. The last five had each been stopped before the fifth round while Charlie hung on the ropes, arms down at his sides, as stronger and younger men targeted his head and face and were beating him to a pulp. But here he was, bringing one out — like a dented trophy from a hock shop — as if it had some special meaning. To Petrozella, a fighter's life was divided into the aggregate totals of his wins and losses. Nothing else meant a damn. He looked past Charlie's shoulder to a clock on the wall. He'd have to button this thing down in a hurry. Time was running out.

"Charlie, baby," he said softly. "Don't worry about the last fight. Don't worry about any of the fights. You were a good boy. You were a good, fast boy. You made us both a lot of money."

Charlie nodded happily. Again, a flitting ghost moved across his mind at the mention of "money." He wondered where it was. He felt a little spasm of regret that somehow he had let loose of it. He had *had* money. He just couldn't remember what had happened to it.

"I'll tell you what —" Petrozella's voice was smooth and syrupy and very friendly. "I'll tell you what, Charlie. Since I don't forget my friends, I've done some looking for you." He held up his hand as if protesting Charlie's remonstrance.

Charlie, of course, did nothing but sit there.

"Don't thank me, Charlie," Petrozella said. "It's what a friend does for another friend. You can believe me." "You know, Charlie," Petrozella continued, "how many times ... I put this to you, kid ... how many times you see some hustling bastard pick up a good, fast boy — overmatch him, overfight him ... let him get the shit kicked out of him to stick on some other guy's record — some guy on the way up? How many times you see this, Charlie?"

Charlie nodded eagerly. Mr. Petrozella was talking to him in confidence. He was talking to him man to man. Just as if they stood eye level — friends ... confidants. He waited expectantly.

"Well, Charlie," Petrozella continued, "you know it. I know it. Most of the time, in this racket, one guy walks away with a roll. The other guy lies facedown, shoved up the keister — and he ain't got six friends to carry the casket."

Charlie nodded eagerly again. As usual, when Mr. Petrozella talked fast like this, he could only understand every fifth or sixth word. And there was no central thought that he could pounce upon and follow. But he was not alone in his dirty little room now. Nor was he stifled in a barred cell overlooking the Hudson River. And there was no Gus around to make him feel dirty and cheap. He was having a drink with his friend, Mr. Petrozella. Just two guys having a drink together. And that was good.

"Do you understand me, Charlie?" Mr. Petrozella asked.

Charlie nodded with delight.

Mr. Petrozella leaned back against the booth, his furtive, red-rimmed little eyes like fiery oysters. "So it comes to me, Charlie. I'm doin' okay, myself. I mean ... I got my eyes on a few good boys. And I gotta roll to tide me over till I make a proper connection. So

I make out okay. But then I think to myself — what about Charlie? What's happenin' to my buddy?"

Indian Charlie felt a warmth surge through him.

Petrozella leaned forward again across the table. "Well, you know me, Charlie. Right?"

Charlie nodded, smiling broadly. He was enraptured.

"A sucker, Charlie, right? Always a sucker. I can be layin' the greatest broad on earth, but if my buddy's by himself — it turns out to be a lousy lay. Anyway, the point is, Charlie, that I been doin' some lookin' around. A little huntin', a little peckin', and I come up with somethin' for you." He sucked in his cheeks and looked like he'd just parked one over the left field fence to win the Series.

Charlie stared at him expectantly, his smile still broad — waiting.

A small, flickering impatience crossed Petrozella's eyes. It was a measure of his own desperation that he had to sit there with this punchy, this tanker, this garbage-brained, half-assed Indian, and go through the extravagant and flamboyant pretense of a friend cutting off his right arm. There had been a time, not so long ago, when he had owned this dumb bastard lock, stock and body. And if there had been some urgent need to shove it into him, he had only to tell him to lie down and prepare. But this one he had to play on tiptoes and he knew it. He wasn't certain how deep the hooks were in. And he couldn't blow it. Christ knows, he couldn't blow it.

He smoothed down his mustache and kept his voice low and comforting. "You wanna know what it is, Charlie?" he almost whispered. "You wanna know what I got for you?"

Charlie held his breath and moved his head up and down. Maybe now, Mr. Petrozella would say something he could understand. It seemed so, anyway. So he remained motionless and tried to clear his brain to let some clarity seep in.

"There's this ... this woman, Charlie," Petrozella said.

Charlie froze. The Trouble. Not this time. Not again.

Petrozella saw the look across Charlie's face and he felt relief. It was important in his plans that this big, dumb slob remembered the nympho kid and the rap he had taken because of her. And obviously, Charlie did remember. Petrozella forced a smile and patted the big fist clenched on the table top. "Don't panic, kid. For Christ's sake, don't panic. This is on the up and up. She's a rich, blind lady, and she needs a bodyguard. No strings. No hanky-panky. Just a bodyguard.

"A bodyguard?" Charlie mumbled, as if repeating a foreign phrase.

Petrozella removed his hand from the big fist because he felt an overpowering urge to sink his nails into it. "Charlie," he continued softly, wishing he could grind a jagged bottle into the broken-nosed face in front of him, "you just have to talk to the lady. Answer some questions. If you want the job — fine. If not, take a walk. Understand?"

Charlie shook his head. He didn't understand. Didn't Mr. Petrozella understand? This was a woman. A woman. Jeopardy and danger. Vice Squad and Hudson River. And the sick and shattering humiliation of it. He wet his lips and tried to speak. It was a moment before words came out. "Mr. Petrozella," he stumbled, "remember? Remember what happened?"

Petrozella looked blank, as if trying to remember, and then made an extravagant face of sudden recollection. "You mean the nympho, kid?" he asked. "You mean her?" He laughed aloud, noting the bewilderment on Charlie's face. "Charlie," he said. "Charlie, kid, you got burned by some crazy little broad. But that was nothing like this. This is a legitimate job. This is bonafide. What you got cookin' here is three squares a day, a nice place to sleep, and nobody on your back. You just open the door when the bell rings. It's five days a week and maybe a C-note." He leaned back, tapping his fingers on the table, then he smiled. "I tell you what, Charlie. I don't wanna push this, kid. I'll come pick you up this afternoon about three. We'll go over and talk to the lady. And we'll see what cooks. You don't like it — you don't take it. Simple? Simple, Charlie?"

There was silence.

Petrozella felt a little knot of cold ice deep inside his gut. If this Indian didn't perform, there was a certain resident of Las Vegas, Nevada, who had connections and who would take a shabby little man named Mr. Petrozella and fix it so they could scrape what was left of him off a wall and spoon him into a cup. Mr. Petrozella had welshed on a bet and had forty-eight hours to come up with exactly nine hundred and eighty dollars. Mr. Petrozella didn't have nine hundred and eighty dollars. Mr. Petrozella didn't have the price of a cheap meal. And sitting in front of him, in stoic frightened silence, was all that stood between him and a brief visit to an alley where he would get his skin stripped off.

"So, Charlie," he said, as he rose, "I'll pick you up at three. Right?"

Charlie waited a moment before nodding, but then he did nod. "Three," he said thickly.

"That's right," Petrozella said. "Three o'clock. We'll talk to the lady. We'll run it around the block a coupla times and we'll see how she rides." He grafted a smile onto his face and forced himself to take a sauntering walk over to the bar. With a look toward Charlie to make sure he was being watched, he threw a bill on the bar and waggled his fingers as if assuring the bartender that he could keep the sizable tip. Then he went out the door.

The bartender looked down at the two-dollar bill, threw an acid look toward the disappearing man, then rang the money up on the cash register. He turned to stare across the room at the big Indian, wondering how long he'd stay there and if he had any money, just in case he would ask for another drink. But Charlie was like a statue. He remained in the booth, staring down at his hands, while in his poor and befuddled brain little impulses of fear crisscrossed, taunted and haunted him.

Petrozella crossed the street, went into a tobacco shop and used the pay phone. He dialed the Excelsior Hotel and got Gus on the other end.

"Excelsior Hotel." Gus's voice was like a tinny-sounding old record.

"Gus," Petrozella said into the half-covered mouthpiece. "Petrozella."

"How's the Indian?"

"Screw 'im, but don't worry about 'im. He's all right. But when he gets back there — you tell 'im you're gonna take his room key."

"Why?"

"Because I want 'im spare and lean for the afternoon's event. You dig, Gus, or do I have to come over there and diagram it for you?"

"What if he gets sore?"

"If he gets sore, you tell 'im you'll send in the cavalry." His voice took on a warning note. "But listen, Gus — I want him to think he don't have a place to sleep tonight. That's the condition I want him in. Now do it right."

There was a silence for a moment at the other end. "What d'you got goin', Petrozella?"

Petrozella almost snarled into the mouthpiece. "You just sign 'im in and sign 'im out. Don't worry about what I got goin'. If the thing works out, there's a hundred bucks in it for you. Now just do what I told you."

He hung up the phone without waiting for any further response, then he lighted a cigarette and looked through the open window of the tobacco store toward the bar across the street. He saw Indian Charlie walk out onto the sidewalk, look briefly around as if trying to find him, then take his usual slow, shambling, unsure walk back in the direction of the hotel.

For just one little fragment of a moment, Petrozella felt sad. He felt sorry that he had to do this to Indian Charlie. In some deep and little-used portion of his makeup, there was a tiny nugget of decency buried under the layers of his desperation. What a Goddamned and miserable shame it was that God said to some men the moment they were born — "You lose." He had said it to Indian Charlie Hatcher. And Indian Charlie Hatcher *had* lost. He had lost by embracing something men called a sport, which was no sport at all. If there was head room, boxing matches would be held in sewers. This sport had robbed him of most of his brains, much of his body and all of his youth. And now, Petrozella mused, this very afternoon, it would extract another payment. For value received, and precious little value at that, Indian Charlie Hatcher would forfeit his view of Eighth Avenue and his view of everything else. Through the good offices of Mr. Petrozella and some other unknown parties ... Indian Charlie Hatcher was about to lose his eyes.

Twenty-four hours before Petrozella had started working on Indian Charlie Hatcher, a woman named Miss Claudia Menlo stroked the satin indentations on the arms of her Louis XIVth chair with a lingering, sensual pleasure while she listened to Dr. Heatherton's soft-stern voice. From outside she could hear the sounds of cars pulling to a stop at the light on the corner of Fifth Avenue and 83rd Street — and then, exactly fifty seconds later, start up again. This, as a matter of fact, was the way she had followed the transition from gear shifts to automatic transmission twenty-odd years before — by sound. Miss Menlo's world was one of sounds — footsteps, car engines, voice inflections. A rustle of wind was the autumn; tiny b-b shots of rainfall was the spring; Christmas was bells and distant laughter; Easter was the chimes of St. Patrick's. And on the second level of her existence were scent and feel. The fragile lavender of her handkerchief — or the satin smoothness of the furniture — or the cold alabaster of one of her many pieces of statuary — or the rough, flowing grain of an oil on the wall.

She was blind. She had been since birth. She had left a womb at midnight and the clock had never changed. The first fifteen years of her life had been spent stifled by the over-protective grief of two much older parents. Orphaned before she was twenty, she then suffered the dotage of other mothers and fathers, like trustees, bank presidents, several brokerage firms and a phalanx of lawyers — dedicated, consecrated and in the service of seeing that the heir to the Menlo estate would live in luxury the rest of her days. She studied no Braille because there were hired women to read to her. She learned no hobbies because there was nothing left for her needful of creation — it was all supplied. What her fingers and nose and ears learned to perceive was an unconscious adaptation and gave her no pleasure beyond a small sense of satisfaction that in some areas she was better than the men and women who waited on her.

Now on the downhill side of fifty, she was molded into a tiny, delicate, luxuriously dressed, regal figure, sitting amidst the splendor of a Fifth Avenue apartment overlooking the Park; a changeless queen of darkness who acquired paintings and statues and first editions and everything else, including maids, butlers and footmen. She felt no passions, enjoyed no laughter, and had no capacities for either love, attachment or tenderness. It was as if the blackness that curtained her functionless eyes had permeated into all the other human sensitivities. She was neutral to others' pain; unforgiving of others' mistakes; oblivious to anything and everything that did not directly concern her own comfort and welfare. And gradually, with the passage of dark and dreamless years, she became what she was — a reigning monarch whose kingdom was a thick-carpeted, expensively appointed four thousand square feet of darkness. Whose subjects gave her loyalty but never love, and for this reason were unconcerned that this woman — with the vapid face, the big but emotionless eyes, the mouth turned downward by the lines in the corners, etched deep from years of petulance and silent bitterness — that this loveless creature of comfort was being warped and shriveled and mummified.

"Miss Menlo?" Dr. Heatherton's voice was soft. "Did you hear what I said?"

Miss Menlo turned toward the sound of the doctor's voice. Her eyes grew wide, as they always did when she was being spoken to. Her voice was modulated and full of a faint hauteur.

"I heard you quite clearly, Doctor. My hearing is unimpaired. Please continue."

Dr. Heatherton took a deep breath and continued. How like a corpse this woman was, he thought. So totally devoid of any kind of warmth. "I was saying, Miss Menlo, that the surgical procedure which you mentioned to me has been tried only on animals. One of the subjects was a dog — the other anthropoidal."

"Go on."

The doctor settled his short, squat body back against the desperately expensive and equally desperately uncomfortable settee.

"The point is," he continued, "that since it has only been tried on animal subjects, it is premature to discuss this in terms of how it would work on humans."

"The point is, Dr. Heatherton," Miss Menlo said, "that it has been successful when tried on animals. Now, this is so, isn't it?"

The doctor nodded, but then — as always — remembered that the wide eyes were sightless and made his response vocal. "It has been successful, in a manner of speaking, Miss Menlo. On two occasions — one with a chimpanzee and the other time with a dog. Both subjects had optic nerves regrafted from donors whose visual organs were unimpaired. In both cases the subjects were able to see. One for a few moments, the other for a period of hours. The donors, of course, were rendered permanently sightless. You see, Miss Menlo, this can hardly be considered anything more than a beginning — just a ... a preliminary breakthrough."

Miss Menlo's thin, bloodless, unadorned lips twisted slightly upward. Her voice was on the same neutral pitch that never seemed to ask, but simply demanded verification. "Dr. Heatherton," she said, "if it has worked on animals, it is altogether possible that it might work on human beings. Even a layman can project to this extent."

"I'm afraid not," the doctor said. "There is no assurance whatsoever that the process would work on human beings. There is a suggestion, of course, that this might be the case. But at this stage of the game, Miss Menlo, there isn't a surgeon on earth who would make anything like a guarantee to this effect."

Miss Menlo remained perched on the edge of her Louis XIVth chair like some kind of wan little bird. "I am not asking for guarantees, Doctor," she said, as if quietly reprimanding him for an unpardonable stupidity. "I am simply saying that I should be delighted to take any and all risks for the privilege of sight. I am therefore requesting of you that you set up the necessary arrangements for me to undergo the surgery."

Dr. Heatherton stared at the woman. It never ceased to surprise him — the imperious quality of command that came from this sparkless, satin-draped skeleton who dabbed at her slightly perspiring, almost-pretty face, and delivered orders for sight as King Canute had once, with similar impotency, ordered the tide to stop coming in. He forced his tone to be gentle. "Miss Menlo, I'm not sure you understand. There are rather pressing and urgent reasons why such surgery would be impossible."

"Name them," the cold little voice ordered.

The doctor shrugged. "First of all, the very best you could expect is that assuming the transplanting of the central optic nerve were successful, you would still have only ten to twelve hours of sight. As I explained to you, this is very much like the transplantation of kidneys, liver, heart. The body gives battle to the transplant and ultimately rejects it. This would apply in the case of optic nerves, as well. The transplanted optic nerve would function only until the body defeated it." He spread his hands out. "Then you'd be blind again."

The women nodded but responded in no other way.

"So you see, you would undergo what is an excruciatingly painful operation for the privilege of roughly ten to twelve hours of sight." He paused for a moment. "And then, of course, there is the other insurmountable obstacle —"

Again, the thin, colorless lips curved upward. "And what is that 'insurmountable obstacle,' Doctor?" This time her voice was a jeer.

The doctor looked at her steadily. "Simply the fact, Miss Menlo, that you need a donor. Someone who would be willing to part with his sight for the rest of his life — to give you twelve hours of it." He shook his head. "And I seriously doubt that there is such a person around."

He leaned back, his last statement unequivocally the nail on the coffin of this woman's wishes.

Miss Menlo stared back at the sound of his voice and seemed to almost physically wipe away the conviction. "That, Dr. Heatherton, is nonsense. There is always someone who has a price. Always a price."

The moment's silence that hung between them was the brief recess before the final round. Her conviction against his.

"That, of course, Miss Menlo," the doctor finally said, "is highly conjectural. I frankly wouldn't know where to go or whom to turn to."

"Wouldn't you?" she asked, again challenging.

"No," he said. "I don't believe that there is anyone walking the earth who would put a price tag on his sight."

"May I assure you, Doctor, that within a period of a few hours, I can find said person — and I can deliver him to you. This, as a matter of fact, is the least of my concerns. Be good enough, if you will, Doctor, to phone my lawyer for me and tell him I wish to speak to him."

Dr. Heatherton, accustomed to her whims, shrugged and picked up the telephone on a table near the settee. He dialed the lawyer's number. After some twenty-odd years of catering to Miss Menlo and keeping the fragile little body alive, he was quite accustomed to answering orders.

"Parker, Hanley and Jordan," the metallic voice of the secretary at the other end answered.

"I'd like to speak to Mr. Parker," Dr. Heatherton said. "Tell him it's a call from Miss Menlo."

"Immediately, sir," the secretary said.

There was a click and a pause and then Parker's voice. "Yes, Miss Menlo?"

"It's George Heatherton, Frank," the doctor said. "Miss Menlo would like to speak to you."

"What the hell kind of cob has she got up her ass *this* afternoon?" Parker said. Like the doctor, he had been exposed to Miss Menlo over a period of years — and while he was unerring in his selection of the buttered side of the bread, he was sufficiently human to dislike the hell out of the rich but repugnant recluse in the Fifth Avenue apartment.

The doctor forced a smile. "She'll tell you all about it, Frank."

"I can't wait," Parker said.

The doctor put the receiver into Miss Menlo's hands.

"Mr. Parker," Miss Menlo said, "your law office handles criminal cases, does it not?"

"Yes, Miss Menlo." Parker's voice was tentative. There were times when he wasn't sure how sane this woman was. Once, when a maid had slighted her, she had insisted that Parker find some New York State statute whereby a maid could be imprisoned for breaking private property. This as a result of a shattered vase that Miss Menlo had been fingering and had left, precariously, on the edge of a table. The maid had knocked it over. Miss Menlo had been as disappointed as she was shocked that a human being could not be ordered into prison as she was ordered to open the drapes on a given morning.

Again, Parker's voice was tentative. "We handle some criminal cases, yes, Miss Menlo. Why do you ask?"

"I'm looking for a man or woman, Mr. Parker, who, because of special circumstances, would be amenable to having his sight taken from him and given to me."

There was a long silence at the other end.

"I'm not sure I understand —"

"I'm not asking you to understand, Mr. Parker. I am requesting of you a certain type of person who will be susceptible and amenable to a direct order that he undego surgery and lose his sight. I presume that with any criminal element, there are men who would find a loss of freedom even less desirable than a loss of eyesight."

Dr. Heatherton found himself staring at the grimly determined little white face and marveling at the almost incredible will of the woman. The incredible will combined with a total disregard of anyone else. It was a combination of strength that was Miss Menlo's religion.

Parker's voice ceased to be tentative. "I'm not at all sure I get what you're driving at, Miss Menlo. Am I to understand that you're asking me to find someone who can be blackmailed into doing anything you want?"

"That is essentially the case," Miss Menlo said. "The term is a bit harsh — but the principle is quite accurate. Can you find such a person?"

"I cannot, Miss Menlo," Parker said. It was both a period and an exclamation point.

Miss Menlo's voice was an imperative. "You're quite wrong, Mr. Parker. You *will* find such a person and you will do so by tomorrow afternoon. May I offer you, now, the alternatives? If you are not successful, I will do the following. First, I will remove my business from your office. I will then publicly make mention of the fact that twelve years ago you were involved in some stock market chicanery for a friend of my late father's — and while only an accessory, you would find yourself in the questionable position of explaining away what was a most unethical transaction. I rather imagine, Mr. Parker, that disbarment would be the first of the indignities you'd have to suffer. I know enough of law to make that prediction. And since you no doubt are aware of the transaction I have in mind, I think you'll agree that you would find yourself without a law office, without a profession and without your good name."

There was a silence at the other end while Parker stared into the mouthpiece. He knew some of the things Miss Menlo did to while away the time. She collected data. She hired private detectives to search out old newspaper clippings. She compiled a list of men and activities, unearthing hundreds of skeletons from hundreds of closets and then keeping the destructive data, like little time bombs, in her dresser drawer.

The idle rich, Parker thought, bitterly. A little something to ease the boredom. Such as scrounging around in the dirt like a dog looking for a bone and finally unearthing whatever it was that a man had to keep secret to guarantee his survival. Like Heatherton, Parker felt an ice-cold surprise that so much power could emanate from this wispy blind freak who had trouble lifting a fork and spoon. The stock market transaction had been a bald and naked power play that he could never excuse or even justify. It had come during a hungry moment and he had succumbed to that hunger. Miss Menlo had him. She had him by the ears and the short hair. She had him by a ring in his nose. There was no question about it. She could destroy him at will.

"I'll tell you what I'll do, Miss Menlo," Parker said, his voice shaking ever so slightly. "Let me check this out. I know a few people," he said vaguely, desperately wishing he had time to compile some answers.

"Mr. Parker." Miss Menlo's voice was firm. "Don't 'check this out.' Just give me your assurance this moment that by three o'clock tomorrow afternoon you will have someone here at my apartment who will readily and understandingly forfeit his eyesight for a few thousand dollars and a few assurances."

"Yes, Miss Menlo," Parker capitulated, wishing to God that if, indeed, he could find so abject a human being, that person could be perverted and made to put his hands around that scrawny bitch's neck and stop her breath, along with her sight.

Miss Menlo returned the receiver to its cradle, feeling ahead with her left hand to find it. Then she turned with those wide, sightless eyes and fixed them on the doctor, waiting expectantly for him to say something.

Heatherton rose from his chair, staring at her. A quiet-voiced little mummy — yes. A blind and helpless creature without strength — most assuredly. But also a monstrous vessel of acid that could spill over and burn and scar anyone around.

He took a deep breath. "Miss Menlo," he said, "before you go any further, I think I'd best let you know the lay of the land."

Miss Menlo blinked her big useless eyes. "Please do, Doctor," she said softly. "I'd like to know what *is* the lay of the land."

"There are four men who could conceivably perform the operation that you're talking of. I am one of the four. I have tended to you over the years from a sense of loyalty. I knew both your parents very well. As you know, however, I'm not a general practitioner. I'm also not a friendly family physician. I'm an eye surgeon. That's my job. That's my profession. It's really all I care about. But in that capacity, let me assure you that I would no more remove the eyesight of another human being so that you might enjoy a few hours of sight than I would deliberately kill a child. That's clear to you, isn't it?"

Miss Menlo's petulant twisted little mouth arched upward in what appeared to be a smile. She nodded her head. "Of course — it's quite clear. It is also clear to me, Doctor, how much I owe you for your constant attentions. I realize, of course, that holding the hand of a rich old blind woman is neither an avocation with you nor a source of much pleasure to you, either."

There was a pause as she leaned forward, her fragile blue-veined white fingers fluttering around her lap like sick little birds.

"I realize, Doctor, that you're a man of great compassion. You care about other human beings. If anyone were to sum you up, I believe you'd come out as a man of substance — an essentially decent individual. You'd say this of yourself, wouldn't you?"

Heatherton just stared at her.

"And yet," Miss Menlo said, her voice very soft, "we are not always what we think we are — or what we pretend to be, are we, Doctor?"

He continued to stare at her.

Her nervous little fingers reached into the pocket of her dress and extracted a piece of folded paper. She thrust it out toward Heatherton. "Read this, if you will, Doctor," she ordered. "You'll find it interesting. It's a minor piece of historical data regarding yourself and this deep-rooted commitment you make to the human race. It also proves a point," she added, as Dr. Heatherton took the paper from her. "It proves that not only do men have a price — but the corollary to *that* eternal truth is that all men have something to hide."

Dr. Heatherton felt his heart skip several beats and then suddenly seemed to pound all the way up to his throat. She couldn't know. She couldn't possibly know of the thing that had happened so long ago. But when he unfolded the paper with his unwilling hands and looked at it with his unwilling eyes, he knew that she did know. She had found out, It was all down there, typed on the paper. The case history of the one tragic mistake in his otherwise impeccable life.

Miss Menlo felt him reading it and her mouth turned into almost a smile. "The essentials are all down there, aren't they, Doctor? How the rigidly moral, antiseptically pure good doctor was involved in a particularly gamy little item having to do with an abortion. I think the correct date's on the paper there, is it not? And the woman's name? And your involvement?"

Dr. Heatherton's voice was a whisper. "How did you find out?" he asked. "How could you possibly find out?"

There was triumph in Miss Menlo's voice. "The art of track-covering has never attained really a perfection, Doctor. There are traces always left behind. In this case, there was someone who knew of the incident. The fact that a married man made a young woman pregnant and had not the modicum of courage it would take to see her through. She died on an abortionist's table, did she not? Isn't that what it says on the paper?"

It came back to Heatherton. The name, the face, the incident he thought he had buried deep and unexhumable. But how quickly it came back. How shallow it had been buried after all. A chance meeting. An assignation. A love affair, doomed from its beginning, And then the nightmarish threat of exposure. He had sent the young woman to an abortionist. Someone he had heard of. He hadn't dared go to any one of the circle of his medical friends. And the young woman had died on a kitchen table because the abortionist had the hygienic habits of a pig and the surgical deftness of a paper hanger. But it had happened ten years before. Ten years — and yet it came back to him now with a startling clarity ... and a feeling of almost nausea. That girl. That poor unsuspecting, desperately innocent girl ...

"Rierden was her name, wasn't it?" Miss Menlo asked. "Grace Rierden? She died on an abortionist's table?"

"She did," Heatherton admitted. "But I thought the man was reputable. I really thought he was —"

Miss Menlo sighed. "I think you miss the point, Doctor," she said righteously. "I really don't think that even after all these years, you perceive what was the issue. The moral issue."

He stared at her. "And you, Miss Menlo ... you are sufficiently perceptive, aren't you, to recognize the morality or the lack of it. Tell me, Miss Menlo —" He stared into her white, pasty-looking face. "Who in the hell gave you the right to make any judgment as to what is moral and what isn't? What the hell kind of woman are you, anyway?"

Miss Menlo's tone was bland. "A simple kind of woman," she answered. "A woman with a point of view — and perceptive, as you've already noted. But the story is essentially correct, isn't it, Doctor?" She pointed to the paper. "Just as it's written down there? And it goes without saying that you're an accessory in a murder. Your sense of medical ethics alone should point that up to you."

Heatherton nodded. There was no sense in fighting this woman. "What I did was indefensible and without a vestige of honor." He looked up at her again. "How *did* you find out, Miss Menlo?"

She smiled at him. "Why, the abortionist, Doctor. He's still around. He's still working both sides of the street, performing cut-rate little butcheries. The kind you're familiar with. He has considerable to hide, Doctor — as does everyone. Do you understand, Dr. Heatherton? Everyone. No one is immune. There isn't a creature on this earth who hasn't something to hide!"

Indeed, thought Heatherton — everyone. He lowered his head, his shoulders sagged in defeat. These were the sort of wheels Miss Menlo was accustomed to putting into motion. A threat to destroy passed down through channels. Do it to him or I'll do it to you — until it reached the very bottom echelon and there would emerge one poor bastard who could find no one lower or more vulnerable than he. And this was the one you destroyed. He looked up at her.

"And what is your price to me, Miss Menlo?" he asked. "What do I have to pay to keep what I want hidden?"

"Simply to perform the operation, Doctor. First on the person they find and then on me."

"When?" he asked.

"As soon as possible. Just as soon as possible."

She turned away from him toward the sounds of Fifth Avenue. "Ten hours or eleven or twelve. Fewer or more — it makes no difference. I want to see this world. Just once before I die. I want to look at things. Trees and buildings, statues and pictures, grass and concrete. I want to see the sun and the moon, stars and sky, flowers and leaves, faces, airplanes, color." She turned to face him again — the little white face usually so without emotion, now twisted into a kind of mask that suggested all the hunger that there was on earth. "I want to crawl out of this darkness just once. *Just once!*" There was a pause. "Do you really believe, Doctor ... that I give a good Goddamn *how?*"

Dr. Heatherton got his hat and walked quietly from the room. He felt stifled and ill, and he felt beaten.

After Frank Parker had hung up the phone on his client, Miss Menlo, he stared at the top of his desk. Who in the hell could he speak to and where in the hell could he go? A few names crossed his mind. A few recollections of some criminal cases. And then he remembered one particular name. A scroungy bastard who had once managed prize fighters. He had represented him once on a fight-fixing charge. If there was anyone in the city of New York dirty enough to be qualified for this kind of thing, it would have to be one Anthony Petrozella — dirty enough and desperate enough, as well. No longer than a week ago Petrozella had tried to reach him on the phone and Parker had refused to talk to him. His secretary had said that the man had told her that it was "life and death."

Parker buzzed for his secretary. She walked into the room.

"Shut the door," he said to her.

A little surprised, she closed the door behind her and stood there with her pad and pencil poised.

"A week ago," Parker said, "we got a call from a guy named Petrozella. I want you to find him and then tell him to get his ass up to my office before suppertime today. And tell him if he doesn't, I'll reopen that rap of his and get him burned, like he should've been burned when I so ably represented him. Do you understand that?"

The secretary nodded, then turned and left the room.

Parker remained at his desk staring at the picture of his teenage son now attending Exeter. He wondered vaguely if they gave a course at a good private school in how human beings could cut out the hearts of other human beings and then bury their consciences on the eighteenth hole of a country club green or in the wake of an expensive yacht — or over the fantail of the *Queen Elizabeth* on a holiday trip to England ... or in the deep dark dungeon of a man's soul where he administered the final rites to his conscience and lowered it down into the guilty ground and hoped and prayed that there was no eternal hell where a man had to pay for this kind of funeral service.

It took the better part of the afternoon and a dozen phone calls for Parker to get a line on Petrozella. But once accomplished, it took only a three-minute meeting to get a hook into him.

Petrozella arrived at Parker's office, cracked down the middle — one half of him panicky as to why a lawyer would call him into an office, the other half hopeful — because a hope was all he had left now.

The two men talked. Parker laid it out; Petrozella ran a mental check through the index of his mind — thumbing through the patsies and the rumdums. What was it Parker wanted? Somebody vulnerable and dumb; somebody pliable and hurtable; somebody who would sit still, get violated, then move off the premises without making any waves. And who else but Charlie Hatcher, who was so born, built and bred to the assignment? A hundred and sixty pounds of scrambled eggs — once hard steel, now soft lead — and so punished beyond any kind of logic, the loss of a couple of eyes would seem part of a natural progression to him. Yes, it would be Charlie Hatcher. It would have to be Charlie Hatcher.

When Petrozella left Parker's office he was a man with a mission. He chuckled when he got on the elevator. When the elevator reached the lobby, he was laughing out loud.

"Charlie, old warrior," Petrozella said to himself in the midst of his laughter. "Charlie, old warrior, I'm gonna pay you back for what you did to Custer."

He hailed a cab out in front of the building — a flamboyant and cheerful salute to his soon-to-be-solvency — and blew two bucks of his last four-eighty on a ride back to his ratty apartment, where he would start the wheels rolling.

An hour later he put the call in to Indian Charlie Hatcher and told him that he would be at his hotel at ten the following morning.

And that night, both Petrozella and Indian Charlie Hatcher spent sleepless nights — Charlie, because of his old torments; Petrozella, because he was planning the new ones.

It came to Petrozella during his all-night wakefulness, what was Indian Charlie's particular Achilles heel and what particular tendon he could cut. He suddenly remembered the statutory rape, and Petrozella's jack rabbit instincts came up with the formula. Whoever the old lady was who needed Charlie's eyes, she would have to play it by Petrozella's rules. And since Petrozella had larceny in him all the way from his crotch to where he parted his hair, it would mean conning the Indian with subtlety and flair — and the old lady would have to be part of the act.

The next day, shortly after Petrozella's first meeting with Charlie, and a few hours before the three o'clock appointment that was to follow, he phoned Parker in his office.

"Mr. Parker," he said, when he'd been put through to him.

"Go ahead, Petrozella."

"I got us a boy. An Indian. His name is Charlie Hatcher."

"Go on."

"This is an ex-fighter who'll do everything but lie down and die for you just so long as I tell him to."

"Keep talking."

"This one's got a big fear. He got hung up on a rape charge once. This is how you reach him — right between his legs. Right where he lives."

Parker's stomach felt queasy. The whole thing was getting monstrous now. "Get to the point, Petrozella," he forced himself to say.

Petrozella smiled into the phone. "I'll take him up to meet the old lady. I'll leave him alone with her. Five minutes later this old lady should yell 'rape,' then that Indian'll do everything but offer her his scalp."

Parker gripped the receiver tighter. His voice didn't sound like his own, and what he said, he didn't want to say. "She doesn't want his scalp, Petrozella. It's his eyes. Will he be scared enough to give up his eyes?"

"I guarantee it," Petrozella said. "I give you my personal guarantee. The price is ten thousand — payable to me. I'll split with the Indian later."

Sure he would, Parker thought. He'd split with the Indian later. He'd give him the time of day, a tin cup with a couple of pencils, and then boot his ass down a flight of stairs.

"All right, Petrozella," he said, wishing that the whole Goddamned thing was just a dream, but knowing that he had never been more awake in his life. "You have him at Miss Menlo's apartment at three o'clock. You know the address."

He put down the phone and laughed. Get ready, Miss Menlo. No more the regal Egyptian mummy with the overstuffed carpeted crypt overlooking Central Park. Now, little woman, you have to play it like any five and dime broad on the make. You have to close your legs and yell "rape" and play a scene too tawdry and too shoddy for even a fraternity film.

He picked up the phone again and dialed Miss Menlo's number. Maybe God would be kind. Maybe she'd fallen out of the window or maybe some glimmer of sanity had returned to her and she'd call off the whole thing. But when he got her on the other end of the line and told her what Petrozella had laid out as the ground rules, he knew that Miss Menlo's sanity had left the premises along with her eyesight.

"I see," the little voice answered him back. "I see what Mr. Petrozella has in mind. You tell him that I'll play my part quite effectively. I'll do just as he suggests."

Parker sat in the silence. The office was empty. It was Saturday and he was alone. He sat there, staring at the receiver as if it were some floating blob in a septic tank. Then, without saying good-bye, he hung up. He wanted to wash his hands and gargle. He didn't know who Charlie Hatcher was. He'd never heard of him before. He was just some faceless, brainless slob that Petrozella had dug out of the woodwork — a hit-and-run victim with no next-of-kin. But Parker wondered, as he locked his desk and prepared to leave for the day — he wondered at how deep in the pit men would go for the luxury of survival. He knew that Miss Menlo's pit was bottomless. And Dr. Heatherton's. And certainly, his own. And as low as these levels were, Petrozella's was even more subterranean. But what about this … this Indian? This Charlie Hatcher. What kind of a tag did he put on survival?

As he walked through the empty outer office, past the shrouded typewriters and the closed venetian blinds, it occurred to him that Mr. Petrozella's protégé would have to be far more desperate than any of them. He had a further thought as he went into the lobby toward the bank of elevators. What would make a man — any man — so full of fear, so wretched and despairing as to willingly turn off the lights for the rest of his life?

The elevator doors slid open and Parker entered the empty car. He had one more perverse thought as the doors closed and he started downward; one forlorn echo of guilt. He hoped he would never meet Indian Charlie Hatcher. He hoped to God he would never have to look at his eyes. That would be too much. That would send him under the wheels of a train or into the medicine chest for a bottle of pills. And as the echo died away, it asked the final question. Were those eyes black or blue or brown? And had they filled this anonymous man's brain with enough beauty to compensate for the blindness that would follow; had they given him sufficient memories of things good to behold — to dwell on in the coming darkness? He hoped so. He hoped to God they had.

As he walked through the marble pillared lobby, his footsteps echoed through the emptiness and supplied a funereal drumbeat to accompany the tears that came out of his own eyes. He was crying for a stranger. But he was crying more for himself. Be satisfied, Miss Menlo, he thought to himself. Be satisfied. For a whim, for a fancy, for a few sweeps of the clock hands, while you indulge yourself — a man will deliver up his eyes. And he was the middleman in the transaction. Oh, Christ, he thought as he walked out into the October afternoon — would this poor, martyred bastard ever realize how much he had sold for so little?

The second stage in the violation of Indian Charlie Hatcher began at a quarter to three that afternoon. Petrozella picked him up once again at his hotel and hustled him out of the lobby into the back seat of a waiting cab.

The cab started up Eighth Avenue, continued around Columbus Circle, down Central Park South over to Fifth, and then uptown toward Miss Menlo's apartment.

Petrozella never stopped talking. The words were thick with cajolery or sweet with flattery or pointless with small talk — but the words came, and kept coming. Like a flurry of rights and lefts, feinting, hooking, crisscrossing, uppercutting pounding against Indian Charlie's muddled brain. Momentum! That was the thing. Keep the dumb slob moving, and give him no chance to think. He was like a sweating statue, sitting bolt upright in the seat, and Petrozella knew that if that momentum were stopped, it would be like trying to pull an oak tree out of concrete.

The cab pulled in front of a big white stone building and a doorman opened the door. His right hand was enroute to the peak of his braided cap for a salute; his left was discreetly down at his side, fingers stretched forward revealing the fast palm — ready to share the secret of whatever honorarium was to be paid him for the monumental task of opening a door. But when he looked at Petrozella and then at the scarred, broken-nosed man who followed him out, the right hand stopped as if someone had removed the flag. The unctuous servility on the face gave way to a naked suspicion.

"You gentlemen have business here in the building?" he asked.

Petrozella surveyed him up and down as if passing muster on his uniform, ready to slap him with a demerit. "The question is, Jack — do *you* have business here?" He nodded toward the front door. "You're supposed to open that for us, aren't you?"

The doorman hesitated, noting that the big man had already backed away to the curb, looking as if he were about to run — but the sharpie with the mustache seemed to know his way around.

"I'm supposed to announce you," he mumbled, his voice half cautious, half superior.

"So announce us," Petrozella said. "Tell Miss Menlo that Mr. Petrozella and Mr. Hatcher are here." He turned toward the curb. "Let's go, Charlie."

The Indian left the curb and took slow, reluctant steps toward the front door. He walked as if an invisible ball and chain were pulling him down to the sidewalk, but he walked because Mr. Petrozella was beckoning him.

After they had disappeared into the lobby, the doorman phoned the Menlo apartment and got confirmation from a maid that, indeed, they were expected. He put the phone down, looking through the glass of the foyer toward the elevator as Petrozella and Hatcher got on. He shook his head. Screw it, he thought. If those are the kind of creeps the old blind broad wanted to entertain — that was her business. Then he went back outside, hoping for better things.

When Petrozella and Indian Charlie had finished walking down the carpeted corridor toward Miss Menlo's door, Petrozella patted the Indian's shoulder and smiled at him.

Charlie stared back at him numbly, his face blank.

"Now, kid," Petrozella said softly, "there ain't a thing in the world to worry about. You just answer the questions that she asks and you just sit there and you breathe through your nose. Do you get it?"

Charlie felt his teeth chattering. "What if she ..." he mumbled. "What if she —"

"What if she what?" Petrozella asked him sharply.

"What if she asks me about ... my record?"

"What the hell do you mean, 'your record'? This dame doesn't dig boxing. You can forget that."

"I mean, my ... my prison record."

Petrozella shook his head. Oh, God — they built some of them like bulls and stuck in pigeon brains. "You bury that one, Charlie," he said impatiently. "You just forget it. Now go on in there and grab a little icing off the cake."

Charlie's eyes went wide. He suddenly felt panicky. "You mean ... you mean me go in there ... alone?"

"Well, am *I* lookin' for the job? I'll wait out here for you."

He turned to walk away. Indian Charlie grabbed his arm, and Petrozella felt the pain of the fighter's strength. He grabbed at Indian Charlie's hand, pulling the fingers off his arm. It was like unbending little coils of steel. He felt anger, hot and instant.

"Will you keep your frigging hands off of me?" he shouted at him. And then seeing a look of shock on the fighter's face, he sucked in his breath and tried to force a smile.

"Charlie," he said, with gentle firmness. "No more Mr. Nice Guy now, right? I've done all I could. I set it up. I come over here with you. I even walked you to the door. Now we'll just ring the doorbell real easy —"

Petrozella pushed the buzzer near the door. Charlie's whole body jerked spasmodically as if an electric current had suddenly hit him.

There were muffled footsteps on the other side of the door, then it opened. A maid stood there in black and white. She held the door open wider and stepped aside.

Petrozella gave Indian Charlie the elbow and the big man walked stiff-legged through the door, taking one last forlorn look at Petrozella. The maid looked expectantly at Petrozella, who shook his head and motioned for her to close the door. The last look he got of Indian Charlie Hatcher was of the scarred face full of panic and incredulous fear. Then the door closed and he saw nothing more. He'd delivered the meat and there was nothing left to do now but wait. It depended on Charlie's panic — which was the known quantity. And the old lady — whoever she was; it depended on whether or not she could play the scene properly.

He walked down the carpeted corridor over to a window at the far end near the elevator bank and looked out at a view of Fifth Avenue and Central Park beyond. Autumn had stayed around late and there were still colored leaves. Of course, Mr. Petrozella didn't notice the trees or the leaves or anything else. The once dapper little man, going to seed around the edges, couldn't care less about nature — unless it had to do with the physiology of a female sharing his mattress and warming his bed. A basic man was Mr. Petrozella. He thought of a warm topcoat or of at least two weeks at Miami Beach and the giggling quail he could hunt, using his new bankroll as a trap. Things were looking up for Tony Petrozella. It would be first class from this point on. No more crummy spaghetti joints. Uo more watered wine. No more the ratty little room. And no more busting his nuts patching up the wreckage of an overmatched three-rounder at St. Nick's so he could get "the boy" ready for another slaughter three weeks hence. No, from now on it was to be gravy and cheer and comfort.

Mr. Petrozella took out three-quarters of an already smoked cigarette, carefully smoothed out its pleats, stuck it in his mouth and lighted a match to it. The basic man thought of his gut and his groin and the future pleasures of both. He did not think of Indian Charlie Hatcher in the apartment down the hall. The few drops of errant compassion eked out on the previous afternoon were all he had to give up. Poor Charlie. Poor beat-up Indian Charlie. But there was a tall, rangy redhead dancing at the Copacabana who had once complained about winter in New York. He was going to warm that broad in the sun of Miami Beach. And he would warm her further at night with the frantic thrust of his middle-aged body and his scrawny little arms and hands. It never occurred to Tony Petrozella that the best part — the most merciful part — of his condition was his stupidity. He could never — and would never — distinguish between lechery and love. And in that hungering little brain of his, he would never know that at this stage of the game, it was his last dance — and the music was a litany to the floating crap game that had been his life. He would be buried — still kicking in time to the music — with fading visions of broads and "good, fast boys" and a cashmere topcoat. And he would never know that in all his second-rate, cheap grubbing years, he had never drawn a really happy breath or felt any kind of contentment. The shrewdness it took to pick out a particular patsy who would uncomplainingly put himself on a rack did not extend to an aware-ness of himself. He lived and he would die with his own ignorance. And as he walked down the corridor, flipping the cigarette into the deep-piled rug, grinding it out with his heel, he thought only about a fifty-cent cigar that he would buy before the week was up. He never thought of Charlie Hatcher, soon to be sightless — and he never real-ized that of all the poor, blind sons of bitches walking the earth — he himself was probably the blindest of all.

He was halfway to the apartment door when it burst open and Indian Charlie ran out. Underneath the perpetual copper tan of his face was the mottled gray look of a corpse.

"Mr. Petrozella!" he screamed. "Mr. Petrozella!"

He ran to Petrozella, grabbing him by his coat front, his lips moving, his mouth opening and closing but no longer producing words. The sounds were those of a grunting, frightened animal. And Mr. Petrozella slapped him hard, twice — first with a right and then with a left.

"Charlie," he said, through his teeth. "Charlie, get the hell with it. Just tell me what happened."

The tears flowed down the scarred face. "The old lady ... the old lady ... she screamed. She said —"

The big-boned body jerked spasmodically. Petrozella had to grab him, fingernails furrowing deep into the already scarred face.

"Charlie," he shouted at him. "Charlie — for Christ's sake, talk sense now, will you? Get hold and talk sense!"

"She said ... she said I done bad things. Mr. Petrozella — I didn't do nothin'. I swear to Christ — I didn't do nothin'. I was just sittin' there ... just sittin' there ... and she started to scream ... and then the maid come in and some other guy. Mr. Petrozella —" He cried harder. "Mr. Petrozella, I didn't do nothin' —"

The big head went down, the sobs were rumbling harsh spasms.

Petrozella pulled the Indian down to him, cradling his head against his chest. "Charlie," he said soothingly. "Charlie, kid ... relax, baby — relax. I'll get it straightened out for you. I'll go back in there and I'll get it straightened out for you."

He looked past Charlie to the open door and saw Miss Menlo standing there with a half-smile on the blind white face.

"Hear me, Charlie?" Petrozella said loudly so Miss Menlo could hear. "Do you hear me? I'm gonna go in and fix it all up for you. I'll make a deal with her somehow. I'll see to it that she don't blow any whistle. I'll fix it up, Charlie. I'll fix it up, kid."

He left Charlie standing there in the middle of the corridor and walked toward the door.

"Miss Menlo," he said — with a look toward Charlie to make sure he was being listened to. "Miss Menlo, there's been some real bad mistake here. Charlie didn't mean no harm — no matter what he did. He didn't mean no harm at all. Now, is there any way we can straighten this out? I mean," he said, smiling, "isn't there somethin' I could do — or maybe Charlie could do — that could square this with you?"

The reedy little voice of Miss Menlo had great composure. "Are you Mr. Petrozella?" she asked.

"That's right, lady. I'm Petrozella."

"Perhaps, then, you'll explain to Mr. Hatcher that I'm willing to forgive an attempted rape if *he* would be willing to perform a small service on my behalf."

She stepped aside and beckoned toward the interior of the apartment. Petrozella took a step inside.

"There are certain papers," Miss Menlo said, "on a table in the living room. They will require Mr. Hatcher's signature."

"His signature?" Petrozella asked, playing it dumb.

"That's correct. His signature. It's in the form of an agreement. There is ... a small operation involved having to do with his eyes. And having to do with *my* eyes."

Petrozella nodded happily. He turned. Framed in the doorway, standing out in the corridor, was Indian Charlie Hatcher, head down — arms, shoulders slumped — big hands now still and lifeless at his sides.

"Charlie," Petrozella called softly. "Charlie, kid. Miss Menlo's takin' this real good. There's been a misunderstanding — but she's willin' to square it with you. You just gotta walk in here once ... and sign somethin'!"

Indian Charlie turned very slowly and walked back into the apartment. Petrozella led him into the living room, pleasant thoughts in his mind rubbing against other pleasant thoughts — like warm, moist palms — thoughts of redheads, fifty-cent cigars, Miami Beach and the other good things in life.

At ten o'clock that night, Indian Charlie Hatcher sat on the sagging mattress in his little cubicle of a room in the aftermath of the day's nightmare. The tired body, the distended nerves, the demolished and scuttled brain had all passed the point of maximum suffering. Body, nerves and mind now were in a state of repose. Indian Charlie had taken pretty much all the unfriendly elements could throw at him. There was only so much pain and so much panic and then a man's being had to shrug and walk away. The night had turned cool and Charlie sat there, no longer afraid — feeling an eddying breeze come through the window from the alley outside. His mind was clear and his thoughts were orderly and his recall dispassionate and logical.

He looked up and spoke to the ghost of his dead father who had entered the room an hour before. "My father," Indian Charlie said to the shimmering thing that stood in the center of the room. "My father, I did no wrong."

"I know," his father answered him, inside his brain.

"The woman without the eyes said I had assaulted her — but I did not. I sat there in a pool of my own fear, being drowned. The thing the sightless one accused me of is the thing I was most fearful of."

"I know that, too," the ghost responded.

"Then what shall I do, father? I have signed some piece of paper. I am told that I am to forfeit my eyes or else I shall be dishonored. What shall I do?"

The ghost shadowboxed across the room and drank a bottle of beer — and suddenly looked like Mr. Petrozella. Indian Charlie was bemused, but not frightened at all.

"Kid," the ghost said, "I could be layin' the most gorgeous broad on earth but if my buddy, Charlie, was in trouble, it'd be a lousy lay."

Charlie nodded, just to keep the ghost quiet and satisfied. It was odd, he thought, how clear his mind was — how rational. How he understood everything, past and present. And the most incredible thing of all was that for the first time in so many years, he could make a decision.

"I am a proud man," he said to the ghost who was now a big fat man eating popcorn. "I am a proud man from a proud tribe. I will never be the middleweight champion of the world. I had my mind destroyed trying to be."

"It's what's up front that counts," said the ghost who looked like Miss Menlo.

Charlie smiled and his voice was very gentle. The breeze massaged his naked shoulders and made him feel invigorated and comforted. He rose from the bed and with a wave of his hand dismissed the ghost. And then he was alone. He looked up toward the ceiling where the old cracked gas fixture emerged out of the yellowed plaster. He looked beyond it to the starry Arizona sky and felt a warm Mexican wind mix with the alley breeze. How strange it was, he thought, how he had chased a spirit for all those years and suffered all that pain and watched as his pride was chiseled off in little flakes without ever realizing the truth. The real insanity was when he had left his own people. He need never have fought a single fight. He had lost on the day he had moved away from them.

Indian Charlie went through his battered dresser and removed a rope from a bottom drawer. He very carefully took his one belt from the top drawer and tied the two pieces together. One end of the rope he tied around his neck. He pulled the lone chair of the room to a point directly beneath the fixture hanging from the ceiling, then climbed onto the chair and attached the belt buckle to the fixture. He looked around the room. There was a dresser, a table, one lamp, the sagging dirty mattress and a yellow tie. This was the fortune he had amassed over the past sixteen years. Those items and the scars that puffed up his eyes and flattened his ears and smashed in his nose.

"My father," he said to the beckoning figure that floated outside the window, "I will go home now. I will leave this place. I will stand naked in the sun and feel the hot sand under my feet and rest my body when it is tired."

The voice of his father floated through the window. "And what will you leave behind, my son?" it asked him.

Indian Charlie smiled and felt a serenity he had never felt before. "Only pain, father — only pain."

Then Indian Charlie walked off the chair and in his last conscious moment felt a mild surprise that the breaking of a man's neck in a fragment of an instant was not nearly as excruciating as what he had suffered over the past sixteen years.

The thin man who waited for Mr. Petrozella in the shadows of his darkened room looked like a tie salesman or a Red Cross collector or anything but what he was. When the door opened and Petrozella entered, the thin man said — "Tony? Don't turn on the lights, Tony."

Petrozella whirled around, flattening himself against the door. He felt his heart stop and his skin grow cold and clammy.

"Who is it?" he whispered.

"Don't give me that shit," said the voice from the shadows. "A certain party has asked me to come over here and collect a bill. Nine hundred and eighty dollars past due. Now, Tony, don't run around the barn with me. You hand it over or you pay the interest. Now which is it?"

Petrozella stood there in the dark, wanting to scream out a protest; wanting to make an announcement to the entire city of New York and all its boroughs that God had gone sour on him. God had stacked the deck and dealt off the bottom. God had handed him loaded dice and drugged the wrong horse and put a fix on the main event. God had kicked his ass right out of the arena and right out of the world.

"Look," Petrozella said in a hoarse voice, shaking and quivering. "I had it all fixed up. I had Indian Charlie Hatcher goin' for me."

The voice at the other end of the darkness chuckled. "Honest to God, Tony? You had Indian Charlie Hatcher. Goin' for you where? Goin' for you how? That guy took dives like it was a federal law to get down on his hands and knees. You think we've been in Alaska someplace, Tony? You don't think we know who's up and who's down? C'mon, Tony — you gotta do a little bit better. That don't grab at all."

"You don't understand. I don't mean he was fightin' for me. I had somethin' else lined up. I had a deal workin'. I was gonna have the money for you tomorrow. Honest to God — tomorrow. But you know what the Goddamned Indian went and done? You won't believe this — I swear to God, you won't believe it. He goes and he hangs himself. That's where I've been. I just come from his hotel. I got a call this morning. Buddy of mine runs the desk over there. Guy named Gus." Petrozella's words fell on top of one another. "Gus calls me. He says, 'You better get your ass over here in a hurry. That dumb Indian hanged himself right in his room.' " There was a sob in Petrozella's voice. "He hanged himself. I left him at five o'clock yesterday afternoon. Everything was all set. He'd signed the papers. He was gonna show tomorrow mornin', then by tomorrow night I was gonna get the payoff. But he hanged himself. That dirty, rotten, frigging Indian. *He hanged himself!*"

Petrozella stood there amidst his sweat and tears and shaking body, heaving crying sighs of desperation and disappointment and nightmarish fear.

"Tony," the voice in the shadows said very softly. "You are one slippery, slimy sonuvabitch. I don't know what kinda deal you had goin'. I don't know what kinda payoff you expected. But my orders were to collect nine hundred and eighty bucks before the moon comes up. And Tony, if I don't get that nine hundred and eighty bucks, I'm gonna make you look like you belong in a freak show."

In the ensuring dark quiet. Petrozella heard the sound of a switchblade clicking into place. He slowly sank to the floor, feeling its hardness digging at his bony knees.

"Please," he said, "please. Just till tomorrow. I swear to God — give me till tomorrow. I'll make it an even grand. One thousand bucks guarantee — in cash on the line. Just till tomorrow."

There was the sound of the switchblade clicked back into place and a pause.

"All right," the voice said. "Tomorrow afternoon. Four o'clock. I'll be here. And Tony — you be here, too. And you have a thousand dollars with you. I don't care if it's in nickels — but it better add up to a thousand."

"You'll have it," Petrozella said, gasping. "I swear to God, you'll have it. Tomorrow afternoon — right here. And I won't take no runout either. You can count on that. That's my personal guarantee. I won't take no runout."

The voice in the darkness chuckled again. "Runout? You. Tony? Tony, don't even give that a thought. Because you couldn't get as far as the delicatessen on the corner. And if you tried, Tony ..." The voice took on a different tone. It was flatter and had a funny inflection. "If you tried something like that," the voice repeated, "we wouldn't just carve you up. We'd go the route, Tony — and we'd take three days doin' it. Toenails, ears, tongue, eyes — the route!"

Petrozella shut his eyes and heard the footsteps draw closer to him, then go past him. There was the sound of the door creaking open and then closing shut. He remained there on his knees, listening to his heart beat, wishing it could end right there and right then. A fast coronary like you read in the paper. But life — perversely and unbidden — stayed with him. He lay, facedown, on the floor.

And then he knew.

All his life he had dished out. He had been an operator — a wheeler and dealer, a fixer, a pusher. He had sat on top of an ant hill thinking it was Mount Olympus and had manipulated men — poor, bleeding men — into doing his bidding. But on this night all the worms had turned. This was the elusive truth that suddenly hit him while he lay on the floor.

He rose slowly, feeling the dampness around the front of his trousers, and then smelling it. For the first time, Petrozella knew what he was, and hated what he was — hated what he had become, and hated what he was forced to do. He took a stumbling step toward the telephone, felt for it, then lifted up the receiver.

"I want Trafalgar 6-7832."

A few moments later, Frank Parker was on the telephone.

"Mr. Parker," Petrozella said in a whisper, "we got crossed. Charlie killed himself."

There was a silence at the other end. It was a waiting silence. It was an asking silence. It put the question back into Petrozella's mouth. If not Charlie Hatcher's eyes — then whose?

Petrozella felt the inside of his thighs hot and wet and itching — and it occurred to him, just before he spoke that he was a stinking and dirty old man who'd fouled himself — an Eighth Avenue breed who went cheap and wholesale at any public market. Why, in God's name, should he even care what was done to him. But his voice said — "Mr. Parker, tell Miss Menlo and the doctor that I'll take Charlie's place. I'll be at the hospital tomorrow morning, just like we planned. But make sure she has the cash with her. I gotta have the cash." Then he hung up the phone and stood in the darkness and in the middle of his own stench.

"Charlie, kid," he said aloud to the night. "Charlie, kid — how could you do this to me? How the hell could you do this to me?"

He looked around the darkness. He would have to get used to the darkness. He knew that now. He sure as Christ would have to get used to it!

Nine A.M. the following morning — and Tony Petrozella was being wheeled down the corridor of the hospital. He saw the ceiling pass above him and the white walls and an occasional blurred blue smock of an intern. Some snot-nosed kid playing doctor had shoved a needle in his arm and his eyes felt heavy now. A not unpleasant lethargy was seeping through his body, bringing with it an irresistible urge to sleep.

The cart was wheeled to an elevator door, where the nurse pushing him stopped and pressed the buzzer. She looked down at the gaunt, mustached face. Petrozella stared up at her. His lips trembled.

The nurse leaned over him. "What, Mr. Petrozella?" she asked softly. "Did you want to say something?"

Petrozella looked into the nurse's face and felt some aged passion. A broad. A cooze. Great face. Great body. And young. He wanted to reach up and touch the face and caress the brown curls and feel of her lips. But he saw the displeasure on her face. He saw himself mirrored in her eyes. The hell with it, he thought. Screw it. There'd be plenty of time to touch things later on. He would spend his life touching things, feeling for things, groping through darkened rooms with hands outstretched. There would be ample time, indeed.

He reached down into the cracked and rotting receptacle where he stored his anger and let the last bit dribble out.

"Did I want to say something?" Petrozella asked. "Yeah, baby — I want to say something. I want to say this. Frig Indian Charlie. How about that? Write that down. Frig Indian Charlie. That comes from me to him. Frig him! And I hope that red-skinned sonuvabitch rots in hell for what he's done to me!"

The nurse raised an eyebrow, then put a finger to her lips.

Petrozella continued to stare up at her, still wanting to reach out to touch the starched white collar of her uniform, rip off the pert little cap. He felt words coming out — words that were the captions of the dirty pictures in his mind. "Hey," he said. "Hey, baby — would you do me a favor? Would you take off that Goddamned uniform and let me look at your knockers and everything else? Would you do that for me? It'll be the last thing I see. How about it? How about it, baby?"

The nurse looked into those red-rimmed little eyes that stared back at her unblinking and unwavering as if trying to probe under her dress ... as if trying to burn her image indelibly and lasting into his mind. She was silent because she could see that Petrozella was about to go to sleep and probably wouldn't hear her, no matter what she said. This was an odd one — this one here. Typical, in a way, of some of the sexy cowboys hopped up briefly on pain killer and amorous as hell. But he was donating his sight to some unknown old woman. And this took something. She looked at the still open eyes — those wolfish, hungry fiery little eyes that were now closing. And she wondered on what impulse he had agreed to do what he was doing. Those eyes when next opened — would be useless, functionless, glassy adjuncts to the sagging face of an old man. She didn't know — but Petrozella did — that the old man from then on would have to seek his solace in one of the bars — one of the dying rooms — on Eighth Avenue, listening to the sounds of a fight on television and clutching at the arm of whatever punchy was alongside and saying — pleadingly — "What did he do? Who hit who? Who went down? Who won?"

Petrozella felt the shadows collecting and his awareness ebbing away. He heard the elevator doors open and he felt the movement of the cart as he was wheeled inside. He opened his eyes again for the last time and saw the indistinct face of the nurse hovering over him, and in the small gap between consciousness and the encroaching shadows — he forced his eyes to remain open for a moment longer. And then he laughed aloud.

"I'll be a sonuvabitch," he said. "The last thing I see is what? A frigging elevator!" Then he turned his head to one side and the eyes slowly closed. "Charlie," he whispered. "Charlie, kid — how *about* that? You finally won one!" And then the movement of the elevator was like a cradle rocking — the low hum of its ascent, a lullaby. And Petrozella slept.

There were dreams for Miss Menlo on this particular morning as she lay on a hospital bed, her flat-chested, childlike body curled up against the white sheets, the dead blue eyes fixed on the ceiling. The dreams were rich and expansive and imaginative. She dreamed in colors, though she had no idea what colors were. She dreamed of faces, though she had never seen a face. She dreamed of myriad and diverse things — of automobiles and horses and theater marquees and television. The drugs administered her as a preliminary to the anesthesia she would receive in surgery a few minutes later soothed her mind and relaxed that grim ferocity of will that hovered always just under the surface of the bland little face. Her dream was a fantasy of sights attached to sounds; hues and tones and tints attached to physical things — things she had only known through her fingertips or her nose. She dreamed of seeing them.

In her apartment — on her desk — was a five-page list of the places she would go and the things she planned to see. There was the Museum of Modern Art, the Metropolitan Opera, The Empire State Building and the Hudson River; the United Nations, the Bowery, Greenwich Village, Fifth Avenue; the Staten Island Ferry — then Broadway. The objets d'art acquired by her over the years had been rearranged so that at the moment of her eyes' awakening, she could see them all in a prearranged chronology. There was the multicolored Picasso that had felt so rough and grainy to the touch. There was the brilliant Bernini statue whose rippling contours made hard marble seem like living flesh; it had been so provocative to her fingertips, and now would be seen. There was an Epstein statue full of grandeur that had teased her with its elusiveness and its mystery. Now she could decipher it with her sight. And there were dozens of other things duly notated and categorized and put into this culminative moment of her entire existence. They would be packed and sandwiched in this brief twelve-hour period, but she had written them all down.

She smiled in her sleep — and to the nurse, watching her from across the room, she seemed to blend with the room — the white hospital smock, the almost dead-white flesh which showed tiny little blue veins — like a slightly imperfect ivory.

The door opened. An intern and another nurse entered with a wheeled cart. They lifted the slight, almost weightless body onto the cart and took her out of the room toward surgery, where waiting for her in a bowl of blood and alcohol were the optic nerves of one Tony Petrozella. Twelve hours of sight was all she'd have. Twelve hours out of the eternity that Mr. Petrozella had donated to her.

Eight days and an odd number of hours had passed, and outside Miss Menlo's apartment it was a November midafternoon. She sat in her living room, stiff and rigid in her chair, facing the window — her fingers twitching, her whole body poised like a quivering arrow pulled back in its bow — taut and a moment away from flight. This was the day — and when she heard the tiny bells of the clock on the mantle announcing five o'clock, she realized that there were but three hours left. At eight P.M. it would happen. The fluttery little hands went up to touch the bandages, and it took all the will, all the resolve, all the remaining strength of her fragile and atrophied being to keep from tearing them off. No longer was her blindness dark and unassailable. Now it was wrapped around her eyes. So much gauze and bandage there to touch and feel and know that the chasm that had stretched across her life had now shrunk to just a two-inch cloth.

She rose and walked slowly and carefully to the window, reaching out to touch the cool pane. Then the silk drapes. Then the windowsill. Then those hands turned on herself to touch her cheeks, the tip of her nose, her thin lips — and then crisscrossing her body, to feel her slender shoulders. The silence was more than usual. Two blocks of city street outside had been blocked off against traffic. They were putting in sewer pipes, or some such thing. Earlier she had heard the machine gun blasting of a pneumatic drill and the rumbling roar of trucks — but now they had left.

It was the door chimes that intruded on the silence. It was her nature to whirl around, ready to scream for somebody to answer it, but as soon as she started to do so, she remembered that she had dismissed the maid and the butler. The cook had been discharged. She was quite alone.

Feeling her way across the familiar route of the room, touching a chair here and a table there, she stopped near the door.

"Yes?" she said. "Who is it?"

"Dr. Heatherton." The voice was muffled.

She felt her way through the small foyer to the door, unlatched it and pulled it open. She felt Heatherton's presence and heard his footsteps as he entered.

"How nice of you to drop by," she said, stifling the instinct that made her want to tell the man to leave her alone. He'd served his purpose and was superfluous now and unneeded. She felt his hand at her elbow and allowed herself to be led back into the room. She sat down in her chair and heard him move closer to her, his voice from up above. He was standing, looking down at her.

"Won't you sit down, Doctor?" she said tersely. "You're here so you might as well sit down."

"Your message said that you were not to be disturbed. I won't stay but a moment. I'd like to remove the bandages myself, Miss Menlo."

"You told me you thought it was an unqualified success."

"I told you that that was a reasonable surmise. The appearance of the pupils, the reaction to light — I'm quite certain that when you take off those bandages you will have sight." His voice sounded tight.

"Then what are you doing here, Doctor?"

He smiled but the voice was not really his own. "To enjoy the fruits of my labor, Miss Menlo."

The bandaged little head tilted up. "You've already enjoyed the fruits of your labor, Doctor. You've retained your good name. Undeserved, of course. But you may go home to wife and family without fear of exposure. That, my dear Doctor, is your payoff. What happens when these bandages come off will be *my* enjoyment. You'll forgive me, of course, if I choose not to share it with anyone."

The doctor studied her. There were little dots of color on her cheeks like those on a painted doll. He comprehended, while staring at her, the volcano that must be bubbling underneath the little frame. God, what a moment. He could understand her, even while standing there disliking every inch of her — her petulance, her will, her uncaring selfishness. He took a deep breath.

"All right, Miss Menlo," he said. "I'll leave you now. I hope — for both our sakes — that when you remove those bandages it will be all as you expected."

"For both our sakes," she said, "I hope this is the case."

He had to marvel at her. There she sat just moments away from an incredible adventure — but with her guard still up. The fortress intact. The brittle, unyielding walls of her personality that shut out things far deeper than just sight standing unbreached. She must be ready to explode, he thought. To detonate. But there she sat, frigid and dispensing orders.

He turned and walked across the room toward the door, half stumbling over a large vase that had been placed on the floor. The days were much shorter and already the gloom of early winter was filling the room. He reached down and steadied the vase, then he noticed the other vases all in a row — and the oil paintings spread around the room — and the statuary. He looked across at the little figure in the chair and realized, as much as anyone *could* realize, how carefully wrought was this twelve-hour blueprint for the observation of a world she had never seen and would never see again.

"Good afternoon, Miss Menlo," he said softly. But in his mind he thought, "I hope to God it was worth it to you. Whatever the twelve hours bring." He thought of the wreckage left behind to pay for those twelve hours. "I hope to God it was worth it to you."

Miss Menlo turned her bandaged profile to him. "Good afternoon to you, Doctor."

She heard the door close, listened for a few moments, then put her head back, closed her eyes under the bandages and let her mind swim in the silence. She dozed intermittently, marveling at her own control as the moments raced on and soon it would be eight o'clock.

She had been dreaming of color when the sound of the clock chimes woke her. The little tinkling bells had rung eight times. For a moment she was unaware of where she was and then everything flooded back. And she knew.

She rose from the chair and walked over to the window. Her thin lips were a tight line that gave in to a tremble and then rearranged themselves. It's now, she thought. It's that moment. What does a saxophone look like? What *is* color? What is concrete and grass? What are ears and a nose? Now I will know. Now I will see. All the billions of things commonplace to those uninspired ants who walked the streets — those miserable advantaged and self-satisfied insects who never even thought of their eyes — while she had spent her entire life knowing all things only as abstractions.

She reached up to the little metal clip on the part of the bandage covering her left temple and pulled it off. Now she would know. She began to slowly unwrap the bandage, then she smiled and then laughed. It suddenly occurred to her — what did *she* look like? The oft-felt familiar flesh — the nose, the lips — that abstract mystery as unknown to her as everything else on earth. She continued to unwind the bandage almost in unison with the growing darkness of the coming night. She caught her breath as after five unwindings the light changed in front of her eyes. She could perceive shadows and moving things. Her hands trembled, her breath was short. Another length unwound — and then another — and there were more shadows and more moving things — and then her eyes were free. The bandage dropped to the floor. She very slowly opened the glassy blue things that had failed her so long.

She let out a little cry.

She saw nothing.

She was staring into the all-too-familiar darkness.

There were murmured voices, a clock ticking, the sound of distant traffic. There was the smell of freshly cut long-stemmed roses in a vase.

She flung herself against a wall, where she knew the light switch was, scrabbled for it, found it, switched it on. Nothing. No shaft of light. Just the darkness.

She clawed at her eyes and cried out and stumbled back toward the window, smashing at the pane with a tiny, powerless fist. Her flailing arms touched a table lamp and knocked it over. She picked it up and flung it against the glass of the window, hearing the smash but seeing nothing.

Her voice was like a thin little siren wailing in the darkness as she stumbled across the room — upsetting another lamp, overturning a table, knocking over a picture that had been laid against a chair. She wound up on her knees near the door, scrabbling with her nails, banging her wrist against the door jamb, pulling herself up — hanging onto the knob, flopping there like an injured bird, then pulling against the night latch — pulling, straining, then realizing that the door was locked — fumbling with the latch, then opening the door. She fell into the corridor outside. Still darkness. Still total darkness. She crawled down the corridor, crying — feeling of the walls, feeling a receptacle for cigarettes, then feeling the elevator doors.

"Heatherton!" she screamed aloud. "Heatherton! You quack! You miserable, filthy quack! You charlatan! You four-flushing fraud! You medicine man!"

She pounded on the elevator doors. "You filth — Heatherton! You rotten sham!"

Her fingers found a button and she pushed it, then waited for the sound of the elevator. But there was no sound. Again she pushed, then pounded against it with her fist — and still no sound. The stairs, she thought. Go down the stairs.

Again, bouncing off a wall, then down on one knee, then back up again, she headed down the corridor toward where she knew the stairs were. One foot suddenly hovered in mid air and she felt herself falling forward. She grabbed ahead, first at nothing then at the railing that suddenly loomed up and cracked against her wrist. Her fingers grabbed for it and held on. She pitched forward down the steps, but the railing had stopped her forward momentum and she wound up motionless just three stairs down. She began to crawl down the stairs, one at a time — feeling her way ahead of her. She was sobbing and crying and shouting — a tiny bundle of noise moving through the darkness. Flight after flight until she felt the marble of the lobby floor. She hung onto the railing and pulled herself to her feet. She stopped and stared across at what appeared to be some kind of light. Straining her eyes through the gloom she recognized the outline of a door. A swift lightning bolt of hope. Maybe sight was coming. She moved toward the light, reached it, felt the glass of the door, pushed forward and felt the door move behind her weight. She was then outside. The cold air enveloped her, but so did the darkness. She moved forward, feeling the sidewalk beneath her feet. There were many noises now. She could hear them. There seemed to be a wail of voices. Frightened voices. Questioning voices. She raised her eyes toward an unseen horizon. Buildings, she thought. The buildings would have lights. But there were no lights. There was nothing but the darkness.

Then her foot went off the curb and she sprawled onto the street. Feeling in front of her, she touched a pipe, then a clump of mud, then the wheel of some kind of vehicle. She was right by a ditch. One hand brushed the empty air and she hurriedly inched her way backward to the curb and then back onto the sidewalk. The quick, buoyant surge of hope dulled and then disappeared. There was no more light. There were no more outlines of things. It was the darkness again — just as it always had been.

A cold November wind whipped across the Park and pinioned her there, plastering her thin muddy dress against her body and cutting at her thin flesh with a thousand biting needles. She half crawled back over to the building, reaching out in front of her until the massive hard surface met her groping fingers. She put her body against it — her poor, cold, frigid little body — and realized then that she could not cry. The disappointment was bile that choked her, and the cold wind left her breathless and speechless. She let herself sink back down to the concrete, thinking to herself that the whole thing was impossible. She could not be that cold and survive. She could not be so torn and misery-laden and retain rationality or even sanity. But she continued to live, her head moving back and forth, scanning the icy darkness — all her aborted tears welling up deep inside of her, leaving her body full of pockets of sadness and grief and anger. It wasn't fair. Oh, God — it wasn't fair. That she should come so close to be turned away; that she should undergo such agony only to have it end on yet another level of agony. Why didn't someone come to her? Why didn't someone offer her warmth and help? Why didn't someone comfort her?

Wet, filthy and cold, she huddled on the sidewalk — this silk-draped little skeleton with the blue flesh who had spent her life being tucked in, her lap covered with blankets, her room temperature tested, her shoulders massaged, her hair combed for her.

It isn't fair! she screamed again — inside of her mind — not fair at all!

She beat at the sidewalk with her frail and transparent little hands, leaving patches of her flesh and her pale blood — and then she crawled back toward the door of the building, always feeling ahead, always groping — half wishing for warmth and half wishing for death — yoked and anchored, as always, by a persistent and perpetual night. It was instinct, and only instinct, that got her through the lobby. Reflexes took her up the stairs. A hidden well of strength got her back into her apartment, where she crawled to her chair, pulled herself up and let herself fall into it. A blue little corpse returning to the mausoleum; a bleeding and mud-splattered mummy moving back into the crypt after a brief moment of horror among the living. And there she sat — and there she remained

— tears frozen against her cheeks, her grief conquering her anger, because she was no longer strong enough for both.

And the hours crawled by. A semblance of warmth returned to her. She could breathe again. She found her voice and she could cry, but her mind remained cold — frozen little recollections of her trip outside stuck together; all the hopes and expectations and dreams aspired to over the years to culminate in that given moment — floating away from her to the other end of limbo, untouchable and unreachable. And before she dozed off, before her feeble and put-upon splintery little body could surrender to its desperate need for sleep, one thought hit her — like an icicle imbedding itself into the back of her brain. This chair in the middle of darkness, surveying darkness — this was the way it had been. And this was the way it would continue to be. This was the future — all of it. She would sit there, brewing venom and hatching hatred — anything as a remonstrance against her blindness. She would shout for a blanket or a cup of tea or her slippers. But never — never to see any of these things until on the last dark day, marking the end of a long and almost endless procession of dark days, her poisoned body would stop functioning and they would commit her to a grave. An eternity of darkness would culminate in yet another eternity of darkness.

She was crying when she finally went to sleep. It just wasn't fair. It wasn't fair at all.

Down below, on this November 9 of 1965, on the corner of Fifth Avenue and Central Park South, a harried cop answered a question of an equally harried motorist — and he answered it for the hundredth time in the past four hours.

"What the hell's going on?" the motorist asked, leaning out of his window.

The cop walked up to him. "Blackout, Mister. The city's having a blackout! No lights, no phones, no nothing. You live in town, do you?"

"Westport."

"Take a left here," the cop directed, "on Fifth — and go down to Seventy-ninth — then go west and get home. This town'll be buttoned up tight inside of an hour. No place to eat ... no place to stay. You better get on home, Mister."

The motorist thanked him, rolled up his window and sent his car ahead — and the cop went back to his beat, explaining to frightened people who congregated around him that yes, there was a blackout and no, he didn't know how long it would last. They should get on home. That was the battle cry of the night's republic. Get on home.

Miss Claudia Menlo awoke from a shallow and troubled sleep, but kept her eyes closed. Her memory of the night was unbearable and she sought out darkness to superimpose over all the other darknesses. She reached up to touch her face. She felt the dried tears and stiff mud. She had never even seen herself and she would never see herself. The servants were due back soon. She didn't know what time it was but she gathered she had slept for a number of hours. She must wash herself. It would never do to be disheveled and dirty when the help came.

She forced herself to her feet. Her legs felt weak and rubbery. And then very suddenly a warmth spread over her face. A warmth that was enveloping and persistent. It was the sun. She reached forward as if to touch it — as if to clutch at it. Here was the elusive light. Here was the ultimate destroyer of darkness — the sun.

She moved her spindly little legs forward, her hands undulating through the space in front of her. When she reached the windowsill, she opened her eyes. There was one flash of fiery light bombarding her retinas. It blinded her with its suddenness and its ferocity as it poured its fire into her eyes.

My God, Miss Menlo thought. It's the sun. I am seeing the sun.

Her amazement stayed with her even as she felt the windowsill hitting her legs. The momentum of her body kept her moving forward. Her upper trunk bent forward, and she went through the broken window and out into the empty space beyond.

Unlike Indian Charlie, she did not welcome the death that waited for her below. The thing had happened too quickly for protest. But in the short moment that she flew, spread-eagle, through the air down toward the sidewalk, her eyes kept looking up at the sun and she saw it. Why, it's red, she thought. The sun *is* red.

Before she had hit the concrete, there was darkness again. Her twelve hours were up. Her eyes had stopped functioning. But a second later the rest of her broken little body had no need of them.

# ABOUT THE AUTHOR

ROD SERLING was born in Syracuse, New York, in 1924. He served with the paratroopers in World War II after he had already begun a successful career as a radio writer. After the war, he began to write for television. His plays have appeared on Kraft Theater, Studio One, U.S. Steel Hour, Playhouse 90 and many others. Mr. Serling is well known for being the writer-producer of the well-loved "Twilight Zone," a weekly television program featuring stories of the supernatural. He is the recipient of numerous awards for his script writing (notably seven Emmy awards). He is married, has two children and resides in Pacific Palisades, California.

Made in the USA
San Bernardino, CA
07 December 2016